Paris in May

D. A. Grey

Fulton Books, Inc.
Meadville, PA

Published by Fulton Books 2020

ISBN 978-1-64654-049-5 (paperback)
ISBN 978-1-64654-979-5 (hardcover)
ISBN 978-1-64654-050-1 (digital)

Printed in the United States of America

To my grandchildren
Nia
Nile
Daine 3rd
Shelby
Daniel
Sasha

1

Looking out of his expansive office window on a bright September afternoon, Dr. Philip Hickman, the son of German immigrants, and recently appointed CEO, was determined to succeed. His drive was no different than it had always been. As early as junior high school, it was clear to all that he was a motivated achiever. Even then, he always tried to put himself in leadership positions. Always impeccably dressed and conscious of how he was perceived socially, Philip wanted to lead and make money. Not only did he sell candy and cigarettes out of his locker, he also held down an after-school job and participated in student government, all the while concentrating in the sciences. In high school and college, his primary focus was course work with an extracurricular involvement in choir. With that laser focus, he ultimately graduated near the top of his class. There was hardly any time to socialize with girls. One of the few exceptions was his junior and senior prom where he took very attractive dates. At his senior prom, he and his date were voted King and Queen of the affair. He was too smart to be needled or harassed by the guys because he always found a way to turn their wisecracks back on them. He knew how to play their macho games without spending too much time with them or becoming one of them. A few suspected his sexuality, but if he got wind of the talk, he would always show up with a girl on his arm to defuse the suspicions. At five feet, nine inches tall with a muscular build, black semi-curly hair, and a face like a model, he seemed to control every aspect of his life's trajectory into his career. Now he was in control of the Tremont Pharmaceutical Company and determined to help make it grow.

How to best approach new offshore business potential was much on his mind. South America, the Pacific Rim, and a few countries in the Middle East were all moving toward allowing the Tremont Pharmaceutical Company to sell its products in markets that had previously shut them out. However, building a viable business in every location simultaneously was not possible. A limited number of markets had to be chosen so products could be successfully matched to the demographics of each region and the countries within it. At 9:00 a.m. on Wednesday, Hickman, as chairman, called the executive committee together to hear the present state of the pharmaceutical markets within a given global region. Every member was present and ready to hear what had been uncovered since the last monthly meeting. Dr. Hickman called the meeting to order at 9:30 a.m., which gave the membership a few minutes to greet each other and chat a little.

"Jeff, what do you have on the Pacific Rim?" Jeff was Jeffery Huggins, a hyperarticulate wordsmith with a seamless delivery and an aptitude for language. A natty dresser with a head full of unruly brown hair, he was a model of corporate elegance. Managing and representing competent people was his strength. Jeff and Philip Hickman were both food and wine connoisseurs who like to ply high-level government officials and leading-edge research scientists. Jeff had been with the company ten years and developed the reputation as a no-nonsense politico who, during years of government service, had learned to speak four Asian languages and cultivate lasting relationships among the powerful players, and even some shady characters in and out of public service around the world. Even though he had been asked numerous times to run for public office, he disliked being restricted by regulations and he liked the flow of money he always had access to.

"As you all are aware, China has the largest market, but that market is saturated. Spending time and money there might be a waste of time. I think we will find our greatest success in a stable, unsaturated location. Of the four next most populous countries, the Philippines, Thailand, and Indonesia have or might have political difficulties that could significantly change the ease of doing business. Each has potential and needs to be watched. My people will keep me informed of any and all changes. Of the four, only Vietnam is worth serious attention at the moment and for the foreseeable future. So why should Vietnam be considered the best place to do business in the region? First, it has a stable government and wants business growth. Second, it has a governmental goal for universal healthcare. Healthcare rolls will explode shortly, and so will the need for pharma. Third, forty percent of the population still has no form of public health care. So even if the goal of universal health care doesn't happen, the market will remain large. Fourth, because the sanitation infrastructure has greatly improved in the last twenty years, there has been a significant increase in life expectancy. Fifth and last is the very low corporate tax rate of nine percent. Taken together, it's my considered opinion that Vietnam is the place for us."

"Thank you, Jeff. You've given us much to consider. We hope to receive your formal report soon. Well, Jeff has set the bar fairly high," Philip said jokingly. "What do we have from South America?"

"Those government types always seem to talk a lot, and if you let them impress you, they will. I come from the world of science, and most often we tend to get it right. A bar should be set by the accuracy of the data and not by political intrigue," said

Wayne Moore with a smile, aiming his comment toward the chairman and his good friend and colleague, Jeffery Huggins.

"So let's see what we have from South America?" Dr. Moore continued. Wayne Moore was unusual for a corporate executive committee. His physical carriage did not fit the corporate boardroom stereotype. Tall with unusually long arms and legs, Dr. Moore ambulated like the joints that held him together were all moving in different directions, causing onlookers to think that at any moment, he might collapse into a heap on the floor. He smiled all the time. Some suggested he even smiled in his sleep. He had a pleasant word for everyone, and staff throughout his building loved his temperament. Though he never appeared serious or intense, he had an unusually sharp mind and held PhDs in Biochemistry and Pharmacology from Princeton and Harvard. A research record that would make most scientists blush brought him profound respect and praise. There was never a question of whether or not he should hold his position on the executive committee. Wayne was first a scientist who always followed the data and second an administrator whose job it was to help make things better.

"Of the most populous South American countries, including Argentina, Brazil, Colombia, Peru, and Venezuela, the largest economy by far is Brazil. Its population is about half that of the United States. I think it is extremely attractive for a number of reasons, the first being intellectual property rights, which happen to be very weak. Some active pharmacological compounds could be rebranded and marketed on our terms. Conceivably, we could become competitive in numerous niches without a new product. Second is the fact that Brazil is an attractive country for research and development. Quality studies can be done because of the high enrollment rates in drug trials. Labor costs are low, allowing for much larger sample sizes and less dependency on statistical manipulation, giving us a much clearer picture of what effect a product is really having, and even though participation rates in product studies are much higher, clinical trials can be carried out with fewer regulations. All of this would make the time between development, efficacy studies, and manufacture much shorter. Additionally, because labor costs and corporate taxes are much lower, manufacturing costs would be cut in half. Everything about Brazil is attractive. And that, Mr. Chairman, is all I have, but more details will be forthcoming."

"What is the current status of the antidepressant Lopresid?" asked Philip Hickman.

"The case of Lopresid is a difficult one. It has been on the market four years, and in that short time, we have recouped our costs. All sales after February will be profit. In its remaining years as a proprietary drug, we will make significant profits. On the other hand, we continue to get credible warnings that the drug has been associated with unacceptable numbers of suicides and unexplained deaths more often than chance would predict. I predict the warnings will soon turn into bad press. That we don't want. Some data suggest the people adversely affected were not taking the prescribed dosages of Lopresid or were taking the medication inappropriately. I think we need to get ahead of this now. We need better research from the field, including reevaluating dosages and patient protocols to understand variables that affect its efficacy. Or we can take it off the market until we get a better handle on what's going on. My tentative recommendation would be to take it off the market temporarily and rebrand it after we get the pharmacology worked out. Either way, I could use some help with the blowback. We need communications to start work on effectively interfacing with the public and the media now."

"I trust that we will all receive a written report soon," said Philip Hickman.

"And now, what's happening in the Middle East, Dr. Abadi?" Amal Abadi was the only female and the only medical doctor on the executive committee. With black hair and average height, she never covered herself as she would in Iran. Her father had cornered the bicycle market during the Shah's regime in Iran, and she had attended elite English-speaking schools in Britain and the United States. When she spoke, elements of her various cultural experiences were clear. Growing up in a male-dominated Iran, she took on the tone of her male relatives, who told her what to do and when to do it. Consequently her speech was clipped and directive with a slight air of certainty. Additionally, the few formative years spent in English boarding schools left her with a multitude of British idioms listeners often thought cute or exotic. Her American experience pushed her in the direction of practicality, efficiency, and a barely detectable self-serving arrogance. The uninformed listener almost always intuited that she was a person of some influence or importance. When the revolution came, she was enrolled at Radcliffe and later attended Emory University for medical school before a three-year postdoctoral fellowship at the National Institute of Health. Recruited from the NIH, Dr. Abadi had risen through the Tremont Pharmaceutical ranks and for the last two years served on its executive committee.

"We all know, of course, that the watchword in the Middle East is *stability*, and to that extent, the most stable, most populous, and most promising country for Tremont is Saudi Arabia. It has the largest pharma market in the region and a growing population. In the last twenty years, the Saudis have experienced tremendous economic and industrial growth spurts. Simultaneous with that growth has been a dramatic increase in incidences of obesity, diabetes, high blood pressure, cardiovascular disease, and a host of ancillary medical problems. The government has made health care a high priority. I think Tremont could provide solutions for these burgeoning disorders."

"Thank you, Dr. Amal. I'm sure the Saudis will be happy to meet with us to discuss how we might be of some help."

"Is there new business that needs to be discussed at this meeting?" Philip paused and looked around the table. "If not, those of you who have updates on existing markets and need to meet with me should schedule meetings with my secretary, Rosemary. Those with emerging market concerns should ready reports for the entire executive committee as soon as possible. Thank you for your time. I know you're all terribly busy." And with that, the meeting was concluded. Philip Hickman went back to his office and filled the rest of the morning making calls to various strategic decision makers. The negotiations for potential partnerships were soon to begin. Three countries would be approached to see how the relationships could be mutually beneficial to the company and to the people of the host countries. He was about to embark on the most intense and demanding expansion effort of his already successful career in business. It would also cause hardship for his wife and children, as he would need to travel the world regularly. Nonetheless, the lure of establishing himself as a world-class business magnate was irresistible. His family would have to sacrifice in the short term for long-term security and comfort.

"Pardon me, boss," said his secretary as she opened his office door. "Your two o'clock has arrived."

Philip straightened his tie, put on his "captain of industry" face, and invited representatives from the National Security Apparatus into his office.

"This is Special Agent McKay, and I am Special Agent Sanchez." The agents each shook Philip's hand.

Philip immediately noticed little things about the two men that sent his mind racing. There was no time to dwell on the differences, but his eyes landed on the surface attributes like the surface tension of water causes a drop to rest on an absorbent material before it is drawn in. Sanchez had thick black stylishly cut hair on a frame of maybe five feet and ten inches. An average build with a dark suit tailored large enough to conceal a pistol made him look like a white-collar professional. When he spoke, he sounded as if he had spent time at boarding school and with deliberate, controlled decision makers. He was clearly not a field operative.

McKay struck a different impression. A ruddy Irish redhead with an athletic build and a suit that looked slightly rumpled, like he had worn it several times since the last cleaning, McKay had hands like a blue-collar hard hat. He clearly had not spent much time honing a polished look and was quite comfortable being who he was—a tough guy who was no stranger to using intimidation.

Phillip thought, *The two were there to send a signal. Good cop-bad cop. 'We can do it easy or we can do it the hard way' was the message.*

"Thank you for meeting with us," said Sanchez. There was a short-lived attempt at small talk to establish camaraderie, but they soon got down to the purpose of their visit.

"It's no secret to us that you are planning to extend your business into other parts of the world," said Sanchez.

Philip nodded.

"We think we can help in ways that you might appreciate," continued Sanchez. "We have assets in places that could help business negotiations move more smoothly than they otherwise might. I'm sure we could help you save considerable time and money."

McKay leaned almost imperceptibly toward Phillip and said in a slightly hushed but assuring tone, as if he wanted to say something that he wanted to keep secret. "We know people in a number of countries who can ease the cost and difficulty of doing business." He then gave Phillip a knowing wink and smile.

Sanchez picked up the thread. "You will be going places and talking to people that we might not have access to. Some are actors who want to talk to us but can't for fear of reprisal. Others are people willing to work for our security efforts but who need a communications conduit."

"This would be a quid pro quo, Mr. Hickman. And it would be more than beneficial for you, with very little effort required on your part. It would also give you the opportunity to talk to important business operatives working on the world stage whose interests are similar to ours," said McKay.

Agent McKay then made a quick search of his pockets, eventually reaching into his sagging jacket pocket, and retrieved a plain white business card with only a phone number. "If you are interested in talking further, call this number and someone will be in touch with you. Interested or not, this meeting did not happen, and no part of what has been said should be shared with a single person. The NSA will completely disavow ever talking to you. Do you understand, Mr. Hickman?"

Although Philip Hickman had never been approached by the Feds in the past, he knew intuitively that what was being offered was a chance at success that might allow him to avoid the time-consuming drudgery of normal business negotiations. All he had to do was carry information back to his government from areas of the world where he was doing business. It seemed to him to be quite patriotic, and it also played into the fantasy that most men have: that of being a spy. How could he refuse the offer? It could possibly put him and the company on the front page of *Business Week*.

"I have one question," said Philip, "Would my family ever need to be protected?"

Sanchez looked at him as if surprised and said, "Yes, but I can't imagine the need would ever arise. What we are asking you is not a page torn from a John Le Carré novel. This is not the movies, Mr. Hickman. It's more like sharing gossip before the newspapers get it. Some of that gossip could bolster the strength and stability of our government. However, if there is even the smallest possibility of a threat to you or your family during or after an association with us, your family will be protected at all costs. The NSA always stands ready to protect real patriots."

"Thank you for your time, Mr. Hickman," McKay said. "Good luck with your company."

"I hope we will be hearing from you," Sanchez said.

As the men left, Philip leaned back in his chair in disbelief and contemplated the number on the white card. Having the government function as a shadow partner during negotiations with the target markets would be a great asset. It might even open interesting cultural doors that would allow him to play in the same places as international political and financial elites.

2

Are you beyond Influence?

1980s

D r. David Walton stood in front of his class at Flemington University trying to illuminate the relative difference between free will and determinism. Looking around the audience, he noticed Jason Wynn seemed to be deep in thought and might be a reasonable candidate to engage.

"Jason," he asked, "Do you think the decisions you make are free from outside influence?"

"Yes, I do!" Jason answered emphatically.

"Well, in that case," retorted Dr. Walton, "could you give us an example of a choice or decision you've made in the last week that was made independently of anything else in your experience?"

With some hesitation, Jason answered, "I decided to get up this morning and come to this eight o'clock class, even though I was tired and hungry and still am. That is an example of exercising my free will."

"You might have been tired and hungry, Jason, but your history with this class significantly influenced your coming here today. Yes, you might have willed yourself to overcome your being tired and hungry, but coming here was controlled, if you will, by your experience. So your choice to come to class was not entirely free," answered Dr. Walton.

With that, the small class burst into an animated analysis of the issue that ended with Dr. Walton working out an argument using a biblical analysis.

"Thou shall not kill, steal, commit adultery, or covet thy neighbor's stuff, etcetera. These commandments are the bedrock of every civilized code, and if each of us violated them, anarchy would ensue. Under these conditions, civilization could not persist. So we live with the commandments, internalize them, and when we do, they become our conscience. We live with them and they become our moral law. We live with them and they become our civil law, and we even hire men and women with guns to make sure we follow them. We must have a regulating force or…"

"Do we have free will?" he tentatively concluded. "Heavens no!"

And with that, the class ended and filed out in lively conversation. Gathering his papers and with briefcase in hand, Dr. Walton left the building and headed toward the student center, where he briefly chatted with students and bought his morning coffee and *The New York Times*. Back in his book-lined office, he organized his day, which included some time spent in his laboratory and some time to peruse the travel section of the newspaper. This day, the spotlight story, "Paris in the Spring," was just what he needed to break up the humdrum of a relatively successful life that had emerged from an unlikely beginning.

The Professor's Story

Early 50s

As a child, David Walton was not so different from other black boys his age. His circumstances would not surprise anyone in his community. Almost all of them carried the same weight and had the same narrow future. There were dreams about the future, but those dreams were muffled by the long insidious shadow of slavery and the lingering oppression of reconstruction that pervaded almost every aspect of the African American experience. In general, black people were invisible throughout America and were persona non grata outside their communities. For most young people coming of age, the future was limited. What did pervade the community was the knowledge that their blackness was hated and reviled.

Generational hardship and pain were ever present and came in many forms. Never getting the value or products of their labor, as if both were a gift to humanity, offered as a thank-you for manumission. Stay where you are, where you belong, among other souls as black as yours. Don't ask for more, else your memory of the lash will be made a reality. The reality of racism, of forced segregation and ownership of almost nothing, poisoned aspects of everyone's life. A psychology of worthlessness was deeply ingrained and hidden from view but invaded every corpuscle of black private lives. Frustration and anger often exploded into aggression, and its pervasiveness offered a model of behavior for the impressionable. These things were so pervasive that proclamations, political action, and economic growth could only chip away at the hard crust of oppression. It would take time. It would take generations to outgrow. In the meantime, widespread impotence caused by social and economic injustices formed the cognitive maps that delineated and limited physical and aspirational boundaries beyond which one simply did not go.

Yet all around them was a world of plenty. No one had to look far to find it. Those with radios or televisions had it streamed into their understanding of what the world was really like outside of their narrow slice of reality. There were the laws that stopped blacks from participating in the so-called American dream. There were the false beliefs held by whites, insisting that blacks did not have the brain power or work ethic to do the jobs necessary to transform their lives. People felt trapped but continued to work hard to provide for their families. Many looked for help from above and found relief in the church, even though a worldly change in circumstances was not offered by the church. Some in the throes of this degrading reality vented the constantly accumulating frustration by not wanting to be black. Mimicking the poison that whites had injected into their veins by treating other blacks as the white man treated them was pervasive. It made them feel better calling another black a nigger or by copying the white man's assessment of blacks by parroting that attitude in sayings like, "If you're black, stay back; if you're brown, stick around; if you're light, you're all right."

David's father, John Walton, was a man born of this history. A man who dragged it into his understanding of the world, and even though time might have given him a multitude of possible destinies, he died with a single identity carved from a past that, from his understanding, had not and would not change. The unconscious need to hide from life was his everyday reality. The mundane habits of a subsistence life melded into a long junk heap of days indistinguishable from one another. It did not have to be that way. He was aware of paths other than the one he was forced to take. But given his personal experience, he was not among the few who could avail themselves of opportunities that would make him slightly acceptable beyond the boundaries of blackness. Those doors were never open to him. The path he took required little, only a bit of luck. Unfortunately, he was not gifted with the kind of knowledge that would transform him into a person who might change the outcome of his life. After his move from the south, he tried. As a young man, he tried.

For a few years, he was a fix-it man for a bus company. At his wife's behest, whenever he was paid, he would always stop by a used bookstore, but he only bought picture books so he might see how the world looked. Unfortunately, the job only lasted a few years before the company went out of business. After that, his only hope was standing on the corner with other men, praying that someone needing a day laborer or semiskilled person would give them work. A person who couldn't or wouldn't pay the rates being charged by white tradesmen could get the same work done for less than half the cost. Since blacks were not allowed in any of the trade unions, men with real skills could be hired as a helper by a plumber or carpenter. The tradesmen would pay his helper much less than the boss was paid but the help would never be allowed into the union or get union wages. The helper could make enough to pay rent and feed and clothe a few mouths. Both women and men had people they worked for on a regular basis. Cleaning house, cooking, taking care of kids, or handling the physical upkeep of the house and garden were some of the jobs that kept the black community going. In any household, you might hear, "I got Miss Jane on Tuesday and Miss Talbert on Thursday," or "On Monday and Wednesday, I got to oil the floor and clean the shelves at Mr. Mac's grocery store," and most of it was paid under the table. These hardworking men and women became grateful to Miss Ann or Mr. Charley for allowing them the opportunity to help feed their families. These attachments became so strong they often felt familial.

For David's father, John Walton, luck did not come easily. For him, like others, it was a day-to-day effort. Getting up and searching for a job that might never come, and when it came, it was always something like sweeping the streets or sweeping out stores or digging ditches or doing a multitude of menial jobs that he knew were far below his mental ability. As time passed, nothing much changed. He had to grovel and often demean himself for the same menial jobs. When his wife died in childbirth and he decided to raise his only son, he tried, but nothing changed. Through all of his unsuccessful trials, he had become helpless. He believed nothing he could do would make a difference. In a word, John Walton became pathologically and chronically depressed. For him, the future was fixed by the past, and his behavior would not make any appreciable difference in his tomorrow. So he chose a behavioral repertoire that set him on the road to smallness and perdition, one that constricted life and made it anything but bearable. The darkness of his myopic character was set early, and it never changed. All that he could depend on was a monthly check from the welfare department, periodic visits from a social worker, and despite everything he wasn't, a son who loved him.

It was a social worker who first suggested to John Walton that he might need a medical and psychological evaluation. If it was determined that he was a candidate for medication, he might be eligible for a free monthly supply. Trusting in the education and knowledge base of his caseworker, he agreed to the evaluation. Given his gloomy outlook and dispirited behavior, it was not surprising he was diagnosed and labeled with high blood pressure and clinical depression. He was told that taking the pills would make him do better, or at least feel better. So through state approved channels, the caseworker was able to get a pharmaceutical manufacturer to supply John Walton and others in need with medication for hypertension and depression.

For the first few months, John Walton felt better. There was a noticeable change in the atmosphere of the household. However, before long, he slipped back into a quiet lethargy that seemed to get worse.

In time, his son, David Walton, came to think that maybe his father's medication might be doing more harm than good.

Serendipitously, while reading a magazine in the school library, he read a brief article on the drug Lopresid and its efficacy. It said that the drug may work in the short term, but over time, it might do more harm than good. Upon checking what his father was taking, his worst fears were confirmed: his father was taking Lopresid. When checking with the social worker and with his father's doctor, neither showed much concern and reassured David the drug was what his father needed. When he sent a letter to the manufacturer, he got nothing back but boilerplate touting the effectiveness of the drug. When he tried to get his father to stop taking the drug, he was unsuccessful. His father believed those in authority were much better able to know what was best for him. After all, the pharmaceutical company had smart people making medicine. His doctor was a smart man who knew about medicine and how it helped people feel better, and the social worker had his best interest in mind. There was no reason not to trust their judgment. However, this did not sit well with David, and his anger was ignited. But in short order, he realized that there was nothing he could do. Eventually the anger subsided, and David came to think maybe his own concern was exaggerated and all he was doing was making a bad situation worse. But even though his concern waned over time, he was nagged by a lingering suspicion.

David understood his father's psychology but did not accept it as his own. He knew he would not allow himself to be seduced by the demons of the past. Even without assets or support, he had an inchoate optimism driven largely by his sports-oriented community that allowed a way out of the dreary box-like existence that offered little more than a driving need to escape. He had known only the hot, dank, heavy musk of a tiny apartment filled with the smells of fried pork and chicken parts and reused bacon grease that permeated almost everything but made him simpatico with his equally poor friends and playmates. Because of school, he saw the look of neatly frocked, well-groomed classmates and smelled the sweetness of their presentation, so he knew something of another path and wanted it for himself. To discharge himself from the legacy foisted on him by a history of societal sin, few doors were left open except those that led to sports or entertainment. He was aware these were the only gold rings he could grab. Luckily, David was the proverbial jock. He played every sport with grace and high intensity. Football, baseball, and basketball were the sports in which he excelled, and even though he was considered a gifted athlete, his aspirations were unknown, to himself or to his boosters. Years later, he confessed to a friend that he often played sports so he would not have to face going home to his father and the legacy of the oppression that had spawned him. Nonetheless, it was clear to all that his physical gifts were considerable and could take him far.

While taking the bus to the next town in search of a cobbler to repair his worn shoes, David happened upon a window sign advertising something he could not pronounce and knew nothing of. The sign read "Aikido," a strange word that he could not place. He looked in the window with both hands cupped around his face to block glare, and a man wearing odd white clothes saw him at the window and waved him into the space with mats on the floor. Except for some black and red calligraphy that lined the walls and looked to be painted with a broad brush, all there was to see was a small Asian man and three others not much older than him throwing each other around on heavy mats with an ease and smoothness of motion that David had never seen—bodies thrown and hands pressed in prayer-like formations followed by a respectful bow. David did not know what to make of it. He could see, however, that whatever it was required skill. He was immediately drawn to it and wanted to learn to do what he saw them doing.

"Please come in," said the man cloaked in white with an accent David guessed was Asian in origin. "I'm Sensei Kim."

"What does Sensei mean?" asked David, a little unsure about whether or not he was welcome. Feeling uncomfortable being in a strange place was not a foreign feeling for a black kid away from home. There was always the likelihood that he would not be treated well. But even with that potential threat, David was not able to withdraw himself.

The man smiled, extended a welcoming hand, and said, "Sensei means teacher."

"From the way things look, you teach wrestling."

"No," the man said softly. "I do not teach wrestling. I teach aikido," he said with a sense of pride. "It is a Japanese form of self-defense and martial art that uses locks, holds, throws, and the opponent's own movements to subdue him. Would you like to try?"

"Sure. What do I have to do?"

"Nothing," said the man, who held out a hand to meet David's in friendship, but in a blink, David was on his knees in pain, begging to be let go. It happened so fast that he found himself in disbelief, wondering how such a little man could so quickly subdue a six-foot-tall athlete in prime condition. When Sensei Kim released him, he stepped back and bowed. In the time it took to recover his lost sense of pride and appreciate his sense of amazement, David thought of a hundred questions.

"How did you do that? Will you teach me how to do that?"

"What you have just seen was a tiny demonstration of the science of aikido. It takes time, patience, concentration, and self-control. If you have respect for others and aikido as your friend, you will be able to walk through the world unafraid and unmolested. If you are willing to join the dojo and take the practice of aikido seriously, be here next Tuesday at three o'clock and we will discuss fees and appropriate dress and begin your instruction. So goodbye until then."

David said goodbye to Sensei Kim. He waved to the students and turned and walked toward the street, so excited he could hardly contain himself. Except for baseball, some small jobs and the light demands of school, he would spend most of his time studying and practicing with Sensei Kim. Through it all, he never told anyone of his involvement.

In a high school counseling class designed to help students think strategically about their futures, students were asked what professions they would like to pursue. As in all his classes, David found himself one of the very few black students. Students would have to present their aspirations in a report before the class. Influenced by their professional parents, other students wanted to be doctors, lawyers, engineers, or other professions they thought would be interesting or exciting. One by one, they stood up to share their hopes and dreams. Then David was asked to stand.

"David, what would you like to be?" the teacher asked. David stood, nervous, not knowing what to say but knowing that a few things were true. He had not done his homework and he was willing to admit it. That was not the question before him. Also, he knew what he did not want to be. He did not want to be a day laborer; he did not want to be invisible or treated with disrespect. He finally answered.

"I don't know what I want to be."

"You must have some idea. Everybody wants to be something. Everybody has a dream."

He tried to think, but nothing came. Time seemed to move slowly as he was caught up in a vortex of embarrassed confusion and the expectations of the class waiting for him to speak. The warm day and the closed windows heated the room, and David pulled at his collar.

"I don't know what I want to be. I just don't know."

He could feel the unsympathetic eyes judging his irresponsibility in not having done the homework or his stupidity for not having an aspiration. Or the sometimes spoken accusation that he was just another shiftless "coon" from the projects going nowhere. Either way, as the room got hotter, he was frozen with feelings of inadequacy, and the only way out was hostility toward the teacher.

"You must participate like everybody else, David," she said insistently. "So say something, even if you have to make it up. I want you to stand there until you do."

"I don't know what I want to be. Please stop asking me." All David had left was anger. All he wanted to do was fight.

Uncharacteristically, David gathered his nerve and defied her.

"I won't stand here and be embarrassed and belittled by your insistence. Leave me alone." He walked out of the classroom and out of the school. The students and the teacher were surprised. Some were dumbfounded, others laughed, and still others said they would have expected nothing more given who he was and where he came from. The next day, upon returning to school, he was suspended for a week for leaving school without permission.

David's experience in the counseling class cut him so deeply that he never spoke of it. To be put on display and humiliated was beyond anything he would ever allow again. His remaining time in high school was affected because of it. He did little and spent no time doing the things that would put him in good standing for graduation. He seldom carried books, he played hooky often, and he depended on friends to tell him when tests were scheduled. He always perused his books just before an exam but always did well enough to get a passing grade. He also wrote a term paper for a history class but did little more.

3

Piano Lessons

The 50's

Ken Carle sat straddling the piano bench, looking through the large living room windows that exposed Chesapeake Harbor. *Nice view*, he thought as he watched small tourist boats ply the circular harbor and pedestrians dart in and out of the small shops and eateries that lined the dock. This was his first visit to his parents' expansive new apartment after they sold the family estate on the eastern shore of Maryland and moved to town. Now in their seventies, they no longer wanted the burden of house and property.

Ken, or Kenneth, as his parents called him, had grown up as a member of the landed gentry and, like others of his ilk, took on the affectations common of those who attend private schools and have vacations in Europe and trips to New York City to wallow in the culture and rest at the St. Regis.

"What would you like to do today?" Mr. Jason Carle would ask of Ken and his older brother William on such trips.

William was now fifteen, and his body had turned his mind to something that his family had no ability to understand. When he wasn't hiding in his room picking at his face and doing heaven only knows what else, he was talking about girls and trying to emulate his father.

"Bob Munzer is in town with his parents, and we plan to meet at the Museum of Natural History and then spend some time with other friends in Central Park. If that's all right with you, Dad?"

"It's fine with me, and I think it's fine with your mother."

A few years younger than his brother and not yet able to explore on his own, Ken added, "I'd like to go for a ride on the carousel in Central Park. I like the carousel music and painted horses. And then Mom and I can take a walk through the mall in Central Park, and maybe we can hear some other kind of music."

It had been clear for some time now that William and Ken had vastly different sensibilities. William, who was very much like his father, had eclectic tastes and, like his father, was a thoughtful reader with an academic bent. Ken, also like his father, was an analytical person but demonstrated a clear preference for the arts, especially music. When the boys had different preferences, Mrs. Carle was always there to make sure they each had the opportunity to exercise those preferences. "Okay boys, to keep each of you happy, let's split up. William, you and your father may go do the things you like, and Kenneth and I will make a separate agenda. That should make everyone happy. Do you agree, Jason?"

So Ken and his mother would have musical adventures built mostly around Carnegie Hall, Lincoln Center (especially the opera and the symphony), and Broadway. When it came to theater, their taste ran toward musicals. Mother always met friends when they went out, and they always had great seats and dined well. Like his mother, Ken had a love affair with New York, and the two returned as often as they could. In time, Ken could not hide the fact he one day wanted to be a great New York musician.

Now, as evening approached and shadows from the buildings surrounding the harbor moved across the water, light reflecting from nearby commercial establishments danced and glistened like the western sky at night. Watching the harbor lights change from the heights of his parents' penthouse apartment, Ken was inspired, so he turned to face the eighty-eight keys of the Steinway grand and laid his hands on the keys, first a single finger and then a chord, as the music that defined his adult life broke through. In his hands, the melodies of Berlin, Rogers, Carmichael, Mercer, Ellington, and others filtered through a jazz idiom that spilled out onto the keyboard effortlessly and transformed Ken's early evening through the magic of the Great American Songbook.

This piano is a wonderful instrument, he thought, and with that, his musing changed to a different scene. A distant and cherished memory from long ago.

A flashback, the early '50s

"What kind of music are you whistling?" An eleven-year-old Ken asked the man repairing the bit and replacing the reins used to guide a favored pony. The man, Bootsy, was concentrating on his work and failed to process this question from a boy he saw only once in a while. Apparently the boy had no affection for horses and did not like to ride. The stableman rarely saw him and consequently felt no affection for him. The man saw the boy asking questions as just another silver-spooned ofay kid annoying him. The kid was the younger brother of William, who he liked, and the second son belonging to his cracker boss, who underpaid him and assumed the only reason he existed was to serve the boss' needs. He also knew only some of that was true. It was just a reflexive response to the poison he'd been injected with throughout most of his life, poison brewed by pervasive racial discrimination that broke his heart and shattered his dreams. The boy had done nothing to him and did not deserve his gruffness. At his job on the Carle farm, he was treated almost like a person worthy of at least a little passing respect. Even so, he was like an invisible cog in the machinery that supported Mr. Carle's belief that wealth justified fealty, even if you don't show it.

Mr. Jason Carle, purchased the land in the late 1930's from William Ogden, whose family had owned the land since the 1860s, and in the spirit of the times and the politics of the south, treated people of color as things to be lauded over and handled. On the other hand, Mr. Carle did not sympathize with Southern politics, but neither did he stand against them in reaching the heights of society's privileged few. The only time he interacted with the help was to have a worker satisfy a want he thought he needed. Otherwise, he knew nothing of people dissimilar from him. Regardless, most of the time, he had the humanity and good judgment to treat them fairly.

As Ken passed the dimly lit stables on this day, he noticed not much had changed since last he'd passed. Some stalls were clean; others needed attention. The sound of horses bumping against stall walls and the smell of urine-soaked hay and manure filled the air, mixed with periodic neighing. Past the stalls, through to the other end of the stable, the afternoon sun illuminated a great willow oak tree under which the stableman sat at his work.

"What kind of music were you whistling?" Ken asked again.

"It's just a tune. What difference does it make? Right now, I've got to fix this rig."

"I would really like to know," Ken replied. "I liked it."

Impatiently, the stableman said, "It's 'Honeysuckle Rose.'" He looked up at this lanky kid standing rigidly upright, with penetrating eyes and long fingers, and said "You like music kid?"

"I like all kinds of music," said Ken. "Classical music and American show music are my favorites."

"Is that all you like?" the man asked.

"I do enjoy other things, like puzzles and mysteries. I like math and I'm way ahead of my class and I've read almost all of Agatha Christie."

"You good at those things?"

"Yes, but what I like the best is music."

"Why?" the man asked.

"Because I've always liked it. I can remember it, and it stays with me. I love to listen, and when I play, I lose track of time and I can concentrate. Most of all, it makes me feel good."

"That's good. Can you play an instrument?" asked the stableman.

"I've been taking piano lessons since I was seven years old, and I'm eleven now," answered Ken with some pride.

"Can you play European classical music? You know, people like Chopin, Stravinsky, and Debussy."

"I've played those and others," answered Ken. "You're just a stableman. How do you know those composers, and why do you ask me if I can play their music?"

"You ever heard of Art Tatum, Oscar Peterson, Fats Waller, Nat Cole, or Bud Powell?"

"I never heard of those. You made them up, didn't you?"

"You ever heard of jazz? If not, boy, you've missed the great American piano players. If you want, someday I'll show you what they can do and how they sound."

At that moment, another worker came calling for Kenneth to tell him he was wanted at home. The boy picked up the stick he was carrying and, without another word, ran across the meadow through the knee-high grasses and wildflowers in the direction of the Carle family house.

One afternoon, while Bootsy was currycombing one of the horses, which had been ridden pretty hard by a visitor, Mr. Carle stopped the stableman to ask him about the conversation he had with his son Kenneth.

"Kenneth tells me you and he were having a talk about music."

"Yeah, the boy told me he was good at math and liked puzzles. Those two things will carry him far," said Bootsy in an effort to tilt the conversation in a direction away from music.

"He is good at those things," said Mr. Carle, "but he was very interested in why you'd asked him about music."

"I didn't ask him. He asked me about a tune I was humming." Jason Carle was an astute reader of men, and he knew instantly that Bootsy had tightened and become defensive.

"Maybe. But there was something in the conversation about music that caught his attention. Something about American piano players. He's asked me three times to find out what you were talking about. I know little about music except what my wife and son tell me. The only people he has to talk to are his teacher and his mother, who doesn't play an instrument. So I'm here to find out about what you said to him and why he found it so interesting."

"Mr. Carle, I had no intention of getting into your family's business and disturbing that boy of yours. I only wanted to talk to the boy. The last thing I wanted to do was upset him. I like my job working for you and I don't want to lose it."

"I think you misunderstand, Bootsy. Talking about my son and his love of music is all I wanted. Are you willing to sit and have a chat with me?"

Bootsy hung the curry brush back on the nail inside the barn and walked the horse back to its stall, all the while trying

31

to still his thumping heart and relax and ready himself for a talk with the boss. He had been here before. Most black men worried about their jobs because of a minor infraction they didn't know was an infraction. At the hardware store, he was let go by the owner who wanted to have a casual talk because he didn't charge enough for a bag of feed when the price he charged was written on the bag, then again by a landscaper on account of not cutting down a tree he was told to cut down but the homeowner wanted to save. He never received payment for the work he had done. This kind of treatment was fairly common, but still he would have to go, hat in hand, looking for another job that would sustain him. He steeled himself as he returned from the barn, stood by the rail fence next to Mr. Carle, and waited for the hammer to fall.

Mr. Carle looked at Bootsy and asked, "So what do you mean when you refer to an American piano player?"

Bootsy thought for a moment that the question might have a double edge. Mr. Carle might be looking for a reason to assume that he was an uppity black man. In the political history of the area, that alone would have been justification enough to terminate Bootsy. Or it may be a real question in search of a genuine answer. So with some nervous hesitation, he chose the latter and answered honestly.

"Okay, so an American piano player is an American who can play the piano, but that is not what I meant when I was talking to the boy. What I was talking about was a jazz piano player. A player who knows the music of America and can play it with a jazz feel. It is not European music played in that style. It is one hundred percent American. It is what some musicians call American classical music. It springs from the American experience and sounds like the American experience. How the music sounds is different. The scales are often different. In one common blues scale, for example, the third, fifth, and seventh are flat."

"You mean it's played differently than serious music?" asked Mr. Carle.

"First of all, people make a big mistake when they talk like that. Jazz is as serious and as complex as any other music. I think the only way you would understand is for you to listen and try to appreciate it."

Even though he had no real way of judging, what the boss heard first was his stableman talking intelligently about something that he, Mr. Carle, knew little about. It both surprised him and made him more curious about what else he didn't know. It seemed that the essence of this man went beyond caring for horses and cleaning stables.

"Do you play an instrument Bootsy?"

"Yes. I started out playing guitar when I was a kid, and then I switched to the piano. I just play for myself now. I used to play for a living, but that was a long time ago."

"Did you play jazz?"

"Yes. I played jazz and everything else."

"What do you mean by 'everything else,' Bootsy?"

"Just that. After years of studying European classical music, I switched to jazz. So yes, I can play anything."

"That's very interesting," said Mr. Carle. "Who taught you to play the piano? What I mean is, where did you get the exposure?"

"Mr. Joe Alfred lived down the road from me and gave me lessons. He was a great teacher and an expert musician. When I was in New York, I met a few people who remembered him."

Bootsy could tell that Mr. Carle did not believe a word he was saying. Mr. Carle himself began to think his stableman was outright lying and had a vague notion that the whole episode was somehow comic, maybe even sad. What it said about a man who could create such a fantasy out of thin air was beyond his ability to grasp. Nevertheless, he kept his conversational composure and continued to be polite to his stableman.

"That's great, Bootsy. It was nice talking to you. We like the job you're doing out here. Keep up the excellent work."

"Maybe I'll see you tomorrow, boss."

Bootsy turned and walked into the barn past the horse stalls. He showered, changed his clothes, and prepared to leave for home, where, at the end of this day, he would make himself dinner and, like every other day, would watch the news on TV. He would then sit at his beloved piano and work his talent on the things he could not yet play, always searching for the pieces that could help him maintain his technique and inspire his imagination.

For reasons that eluded him, Mr. Carle was haunted by his conversation with Bootsy. It played in his mind repeatedly as he looked for the key that would open the door of truth. How could his stableman have achieved what he professes? The years of study it would take to develop the required knowledge and skill would not land him in a place like the stable. On the other hand, at no time in the years that Bootsy worked for him had he been disingenuous or a teller of tall tales. Other men who worked on the farm had tried to bullshit him and were noted storytellers, but he never had reason to suspect Bootsy was one of them. Until today, he saw him as a good, trustworthy employee. Was he telling the truth, or was he just another prevaricator?

When he arrived the next day, Bootsy saw the boss' truck parked near the barn under the umbrella of the willow oak. Mr. Carle leaned out of the window of the truck and waved Bootsy over. The sun had not yet warmed the atmosphere, nor had the stableman gotten warm enough to want to talk. At this time of day, Bootsy saw talking as an annoyance.

"Is all that stuff you said yesterday true, Bootsy?"

"What stuff, Mr. Carle?"

"Can you really play anything on the piano?"

"Well, I might have stretched the truth a bit, but to the unschooled ear, the answer is yes," Bootsy answered.

"Okay then. Jump into the truck and come with me to the house."

The man wants to test me," Bootsy said to himself. *"I'm not up to this shit this early in the morning. Why can't this mother-fucker leave me alone?"*

They drove the short distance to the house, and Bootsy followed behind Mr. Carle through the back door and into the kind of wealth he had not seen since he played for the private parties of the well heeled on Fifth Avenue and Central Park West. He shook off the morning slows and, out of necessity, cleared his head. He instinctively knew where he was being taken. So wide-eyed and slightly nervous, he readied himself for the challenge. Bootsy followed his boss into a well-lit room with sunlight streaming in through the floor to ceiling windows on the east and south side of the house. There, in the middle of the room, stood a 1916 ebony Steinway Grand, model A3, that Mr. Carle introduced with pride, even though he knew nothing about pianos. This was the quality instrument that a talent like Bootsy should be playing, but he rarely got the opportunity.

"Here is our piano, Bootsy. The one Kenneth plays."

"This is a beautiful instrument, boss. Your son is an incredibly lucky boy to have the opportunity to play it."

Bootsy walked over to the piano and smiled as he stroked it like one would touch a lover or beloved child. He turned to the boss. "Is there something you're in the mood to hear, Mr. Carle?"

The evening before, Mr. Carle called Kenneth's piano teacher and asked her about difficult pieces. "If one were to ask a piano playing braggart to play a piece of music that would expose his or her limited knowledge and talent, what piece would that be?" Then armed with a request that a man like Bootsy could not possibly know, Mr. Carle asked for Rachmaninov's Piano Concerto No. 2. They were now at the Rubicon—the moment when Bootsy would be slapped down by his own exaggeration. The moment when his stableman would be publicly humiliated and marked as a liar. Mr. Carle had practiced the speech he would give if this whole thing was a mistake. He would pile the stableman back into the truck and dump him into a pile of horseshit where he belonged.

There was no sheet music to read, so the stableman sat quietly for a minute with his head bowed as if in thought and his hands in his lap. For Mr. Carle, time seemed to have stopped. All his questioning, all his need for truth, and the consequences he had imagined if Bootsy was not genuine hung in balance in a ball of anticipation. Then Bootsy raised his arms, and his fingers lay softly on the keys without making a sound. First, a two-hand chord followed by a bass note and then another followed by a bass note, and then the sound of the concerto filled the room produced by fingers so swift and smooth that they could not be seen. Mr. Carle could not believe what he was hearing and seeing. Mrs. Carle appeared with the household staff and gathered around the entrance to the piano room to hear music as they had never heard it before in the house. He played for five minutes to demonstrate his ability, and after the point was made, he stopped. The maid and cook clapped and cheered without inhibition, and Mr. and Mrs. Carle stood speechless, knowing that they had just witnessed something special. Something out of the ordinary had been loosed in their music room that was worthy of being heard in a grand concert hall. Then the room fell silent, in part because of the unforgettable sound they had just heard. The incongruity between what they knew of their stableman—the almost ragged work clothes he was wearing versus his display of pianistic ability—made the scene almost bizarre. The myths of magical transformations take place in literature when frogs become princes and farm girls lead armies. But here in front of them, a similar emergence had taken place. Hidden in their stables was something beautiful, something that no one would have ever suspected. It left them agape with surprise, speechless, and palpably excited. In a word, they were all stunned.

"Would you like to hear something else?" asked Bootsy, who watched the whole scene with a touch of "Gotcha" and an internal glee that only he could appreciate.

"By all means," answered Mrs. Carle at a volume louder than her speaking voice, which was both a sign of approval and a prod meant to accelerate the process.

"What about some jazz?" asked Bootsy. "That's what I like best."

The Carles, the cook, and the cleaning lady all found comfortable seats, and for the next hour, they listened to a master play melodies they all knew. He knew what he was doing. The intention was not just to play the piano well but also to seduce their sensibilities, so they wanted more. The rhythms may have been a little different and the melodies embellished, but they knew what was being played, and they all hummed the melodies and mouthed the lyrics to many of the songs that were played. They lost track of time and space, totally consumed by the music. After the shock and awe had worn off, Mr. Carle approached his stableman. Still sitting at the piano bench with a respectful nobility that Mr. Carle could now see, he asked the question.

"Would you like a change in your job description?" Bootsy was not expecting this, but he did know his employers had been jerked out of their business heads and into a place that allowed purely emotional decisions. "Would you like to teach my son Kenneth?"

Bootsy knew he had to strike while the iron was hot, and he did.

"Would this be a complete change in job description, Mr. Carle?" This might be a chance for him to make a living doing what he was born to do. Even though he did not consider himself a teacher, he could certainly do it, and maybe he could wind up doing something that he loved and could finally leave the filth of the stable. Finally, he might be able to get back to the thing he loved most in the world.

"Yes," said Mr. Carle. "The only thing you would be responsible for is teaching Kenneth."

Then he hesitated and added, "You might also be periodically asked to play for the family's entertainment and parties. If you agree, I think it only fair that your pay would be what any pro would make putting in the same hours. I'll check into that. I could see you becoming the boy's musical mentor."

"This might be too much to ask, Mr. Carle, but could you help me set up a retirement account? Right now, I have nothing to take me into old age," said Bootsy.

"Don't push it, Mr. Johnson. But I think we can do that."

"Then I say yes to your offer and look forward to teaching your son. By the way, it's been a long time since I've been called Mr. Johnson, and I thank you for that."

Mrs. Carle approached and stood by her husband, trying unsuccessfully to contain her excitement. She grasped Mr. Carle's hand and said with a slightly exaggerated sense of dignity, "Mr. Johnson, dirty work clothes are not to be worn in the house."

The Carle family soon discovered what and who Mr. Daniel "Bootsy" Johnson really was. He was the grandson of slaves and not just an old stableman but an influential, genius-level piano player who had taken the New York jazz scene by storm in the late 30s to early 40s but did not like the lifestyle and the way he was treated, so he came home to rural Maryland and stayed.

Mr. Johnson took Ken under his wing. They spent hours walking around the farm talking about music. In the music room, sitting at the piano and on a removable blackboard that was brought in, Ken was taught theory, harmony, and composition. They practiced fingering and technique. They listened to all the great jazz piano players—Cole, Tatum, Peterson, and Garner—and with Mr. Johnson's help, Ken had the opportunity to play with some of the quality bands in the area. He learned to play different styles of music and to do so with competence. Bootsy helped him extract from all of it a style that was uniquely Ken's. And by the time he was eighteen years old, he was more than ready to call himself a piano player who could play with anybody in any style.

Bootsy had done his job, and when Ken left for college to study mathematics, the old man knew he had been responsible for doing something special. Before he left, Ken promised him he would take everything he learned to his beloved New York and make him proud.

*****

Evening had now settled over the harbor, and for the first time, Ken appreciated the expansive elegance of his parents' new apartment. He knew the chances of ever approaching a comparable lifestyle in New York was impossible for him. After years of trying to make enough money to support a truly middle-class lifestyle, he was no closer than he was when he first arrived. Yes, there were memorable jobs and plenty of high times. Some people knew his name, and a few times, he recorded with known artists, but with the flood of competition and changing musical styles and taste, the opportunities diminished over time. He'd get gigs at cocktail parties and house parties and the few remaining jazz clubs, but it was not enough to sustain what he considered a respectable lifestyle. Like his teacher, Bootsy Johnson, Ken had come back home. It was not a triumphant return, and as he waited for his parents with his head resting on his hand and his elbow leaning on the piano, he wondered what tomorrow would bring.

4

New York

Early 1960s

After entering Yale University and except for his room and board, Ken no longer needed the support of his parents. He was a diligent, responsible student, and although not a standout in the mathematics department, was thought of as a good student. By the end of his first semester, when his versatile piano talent was recognized, Ken Carle was sought after for a variety of student activities requiring a piano. Before long, other student musicians began to call, and soon the Ken Carle Trio was born. Music students and faculty alike often brought instruments to Ken's monthly jam sessions in the student center, where the level of musicianship was high, and an enjoyable time was had by all. Toward the end of his first year, club, bar, and restaurant owners in Hartford and beyond began to visit the campus to hear what the buzz was about. It was not long before playing in the local clubs provided him resources enough to explore the music scene in Boston and New York. Yale had been the perfect choice to nurture his analytical and musical skills. While there, he worked with many kinds of music and played with musicians of all types. He was known and he was requested. By the end of his fourth year, he thought he might be ready for the real challenge: New York City. Ken was prepared to fulfill the promise he made to the man whose essence was with him daily—his teacher, guru, and inspiration, Bootsy Johnson.

It wasn't much, just what he could afford—a two-room basement apartment on Norfolk Street just off Houston and relatively close to bus routes and train lines. In one room, his bed was flanked on one side by a stove, sink, and refrigerator, and on the other side, by the toilet and washbasin. Maneuvering in the room was difficult, but it was separated from the living room by a wall with a window. The place was different than anything he had experienced, but for what he intended to do in the city, it was adequate and affordable without having to appeal to his parents. With enough room to watch TV or invite a few friends, it wasn't what he was used to, but it was all Ken needed.

"*When I start making money, I'll move to a better place,*" he would say to himself with absolute certainty.

The Lower East Side was inhabited by second and third-generation immigrant families and young people who worked or aspired to work in the arts. Musicians, craftspeople, performance artists, painters, and visual artists of all types trolled the streets, eating establishments, and bars. Creative people were everywhere, and Ken inhaled the atmosphere and wallowed in the possibilities for artistic collaboration. For Ken and other young talented people, the atmosphere on the Lower East Side and every other place in Manhattan crackled with opportunities and hopes for a future in their chosen art. But most of all, the Lower East Side was affordable, and struggling youths could follow their inclinations.

A few days after settling into his new digs, Ken found a restaurant and a bar close to his apartment that would soon become his hangout and practice venue. The place had a small stage and an acceptable piano. If no one was scheduled to play at the bar, Fat John, the owner, would let Ken play. John was the grandson of Ukrainian immigrants who came to the neighborhood and never left. Over the course of three generations, they bought property and opened businesses, legal or otherwise.

"John!" Ken would say. "You've got eight tables and a thirteen-stool bar. I see five people. One sleeping and the other four have been nursing a beer for the past hour. You should let me liven the place up."

"You can play kid, but don't expect to be paid. I'm not making any money tonight. At this rate, I'll start losing weight."

Ken walked to the piano and began experimenting with musical styles that would work in Fat John's dull, undecorated, stale-beer-smelling joint. After a few minutes, two people came through the door.

"John," said Ken, "do you mind if I place a tip glass on the piano?"

"If you can get tips, you can keep them," said Fat John.

Ken walked into the small kitchen and took a large pickle jar from under the counter.

"If you want your money to smell like pickles, sure, you can use it," John joked.

Ken settled down and began to play a wide range of jazz-inflected songs. In the next half hour, four more people wandered in. But unlike the usual customers, they came because they heard the music.

"I do take requests," announced Ken. "But it has to be music played in America."

The few people in the bar began to make requests, and when a piece finished, a dollar or two was placed in the pickle jar. Wisely, Ken continued to take requests, and as more people entered the bar, more bills appeared in the jar. People were sitting at the bar, and the waitress was serving Fat John's limited finger food and drinks at the tables. Conversations at the bar and at the tables were animated, and the usually laid-back, advice-dispensing bartender was working at close to full capacity. The place was abuzz, and much of the conversation, which was not often heard in the bar, was about music or popular piano players and their styles. Ken and Fat John listened carefully to conversations and noted the tunes being played. Looking around the room, it was clear the patrons were as young as the piano player, and what they liked, he played. Ken had been in the city less than a month and found an audience he could play to.

As a tune ended, an attractive lady approached the piano and asked if she might sing a song.

"I would love it," answered Ken. "But you have to get permission from the boss." Ken waved John over and communicated the lady's request.

"Can she sing?" queried John.

"I don't know," answered Ken. "Give the girl a chance. Tonight you can be generous. Both of us are having a good night." He glanced at the pickle jar as proof that the night had been a good one.

Fat John smiled and said, "Let her rip."

After a brief break to answer the biological imperative, Ken returned to the piano and motioned to the hopeful singer to sit with him on the bench. As she moved toward him, he could see she was a lady having a slightly understated sense of style with a graceful flow that suggested an updated Katharine Hepburn. When she sat down, he was introduced to her face, which was stunning. With shoulder-length hair partially covering one eye, it was clear that she was channeling Veronica Lake. She looked Asian with an exquisitely beautiful face and a body to be noticed.

"What's your name, and what would you like to sing?" asked Ken.

"My name is Wen Lee, and just for the record, I do not fancy myself a chanteuse. I'm not really a singer. I like to sing, but my instrument is the harp. I've been playing my entire life. Jazz has invaded my ears, and my body and mind are learning to embrace it. I think singing will help me."

"I happen to agree, Wen Lee. So you, like me, are a musician. Good! What would you like to sing? I might be able to play it."

"Do you know Lil Armstrong's 'Just for a Thrill'?"

"I'm impressed," said Ken.

"Why?"

"One, because few people know who she is, and two, because of the people who have heard of her, even fewer know she wrote that song."

After they chose the key and the tempo, Ken played a simple intro before Wen Lee hit an Armstrong-inspired "Just for a Thrill" with a blues inflection that stopped all conversation and gave Ken great phrasing to improvise behind. It was a stunning surprise, a moment that would transform Fat John's corner dive into a legitimate jazz spot and establish a relationship between Wen Lee and Ken that would last a lifetime.

Because of that night, Fat John gave the place a fresh coat of paint, hung pictures of jazz greats on the walls, stopped watering down drinks, and had an open mic for singers on Wednesdays and Sundays. With some prodding, he hired Ken as the house piano player on open mic nights. On other nights, he booked young instrumentalists and gave groups a chance to play for modest pay. Fat John's became the place to hear up and coming talent. On Wednesday nights, it was always crowded because that was the night when Ken Carle and Wen Lee would put their musical love affair on display for all to see. In an obtuse reference to Charley Chan, Fat John always referred to Wen Lee and Ken Carle as number one daughter and number one son.

When Ken was not playing at Fat John's, two evenings a week were spent eight blocks away playing at an upscale Italian restaurant called Fiori Di Campo. The restaurant was a family-owned and operated business for thirty years, but time had tired the first generation, and the children were now running it. The food continued to be old-world excellent; however, the children wanted to update the atmosphere and décor. Along with the decorative changes, a piano was added.

Shortly after Ken moved to New York from Hartford, his mother visited from Maryland. She made reservations at Fiori Di Campo on the recommendation of a friend, and there they greeted each other. She told him of the plans to sell the farm and move. Yes, it was a difficult decision, but she and Ken's father had passed the time in their lives when the farm was neither an important asset or a joy. William, Ken's brother, had started his career as a lawyer on the West Coast, and he, Ken, was now in New York pursuing a career in music. Life had changed, as it most often does, and it was now time for them to prepare for that change. The details would unfold in time. As for Ken's current state of affairs?

"No, Mother, I don't need any money. So far, I'm doing okay."

"Are you sure, sweetheart?" She reached into her purse.

"Mother, stop. I appreciate how you feel and I love you for it, but at the moment, I need no help. If I ever do, you and Father will be the first to know."

"Kenneth? Have you found a lady friend?"

"I may not be ready for a girlfriend, Mother. But I have found someone I'm quite fond of."

"What's her name?"

"Her name is Lee, and she is a harp player of extraordinary ability."

The next hour was filled with more mother-son chatter, and eventually it became clear that the loving guidance and care that had been the center of their relationship had come to an end. What Ken's mother knew how to say to her son was no longer relevant or welcome. This fact was almost impossible to accept, but being a realistic woman, she rose to embrace Ken's reality, hugged her son, and taxied back to her life without him. As she traveled back to the St. Regis, the city seemed silent and dull, as if in mourning. While she prepared for an evening at the opera, she became fully aware that she had just crossed the threshold to a new stage in her life. Her primary focus would have to change.

*****

As his mother stepped into the cab to leave, Ken walked back into Fiori Di Campo and asked if they needed a piano player.

"The boss is not here, but if you want to wait, she'll be here in a minute."

Ken sat at the four-stool bar next to the piano and sipped a beer. Before long, the manager of Fiori di Campo strolled into the restaurant and said a word to the maître d', who nodded in Ken's direction.

"Hi! I'm Maria Fattore. This is my family's restaurant. I manage it. What can I do for you?"

"I'm Ken Carle, a piano player. You have an instrument, and nobody is playing it. Would you like someone to play it?"

"We put the piano in hoping to have live music, but we have not gotten around to it yet. We don't even know what kind of music we want."

"I can play almost any kind of music. So I'll make you a deal. If I can play the music that blends with your idea of what would be nice in the restaurant, you will hire me two nights a week. However, if I can find music that fills the tables, you'll give me a bonus." Ken smiled at his own brazenness.

"I'll first have to hear you play, Mr. Carle."

"Is now an appropriate time, Ms. Fattore? Tell you what, I'll play a tune of your choosing and then take requests from the few diners still here. If you and the diners like what you hear, we'll talk further. If not, let me know."

"First of all, my name is Maria, and I got two conditions that need to be satisfied. I got to like the music, and it's got to get asses in the seats."

"Give me a month working two nights a week. If business in general picks up enough to cover my pay or if it's better the nights I play, you keep me on. If nothing changes, you don't need me."

"All this sounds very reasonable," said Maria. "But I don't want any contracts or written agreements. If you can agree to that, we've got a deal."

The next few minutes were spent negotiating Ken's nightly pay. Finally he sat at the piano and for thirty minutes played in a variety of styles. He took requests and got applause from an audience that was thankful for the addition of Ken's abilities and taste. Over the course of a few weeks, Fiori Di Campo doubled its traffic, and patrons were treated to melodies originally sung by the great Italian American crooners like Sinatra, Martin, Bennett, and Damone, all of whom were hip to the creative influence of jazz. Soon Fat John's and Fiori Di Campo stabilized Ken's financial life and provided the opportunity for him to move beyond the periphery of the lower east side music scene and slowly introduce himself to some of the more important music venues.

5

Coming of Age

David Walton procured work as a part-time janitor for Heron Designs, a small engineering firm located a few blocks from his neighborhood and far enough away to be immune to the dangers his neighborhood generated. He liked the job because he was treated with respect, even though the work was menial. One afternoon, while cleaning the men's room, David had a brief conversation with a man who ultimately turned out to be the boss.

"Hi, I haven't seen you around here before, but I think I recognize you. I think I've seen you playing baseball at Siler's Field. I'm a fan, and once a week, I watch some of the local teams play. Don't you play for the Hawks?" asked the man.

"Yeah, I play with the Hawks."

"Well, from what I can see, you're one hell of a player. You play both shortstop and center field, don't you?"

David nodded.

"Man, you've got one hell of an arm. With a man on second, a long high ball was hit into center field. The man on second stole third and tried to steal home. I think it was you who threw a line drive from center field to the catcher at home plate who tagged the runner out. I've been playing and watching baseball for a long time but have never seen a player your age throw like that. I was impressed. You also hold your league's home run record this year, don't you?"

"Yeah."

"Personally, I think you might have a future. Keep playing like that and colleges will be interested in you."

"Yeah?"

"My secretary told me she hired a new part-time janitor."

"I just started working here. My name is David. I'm in high school."

"High school, huh?" he said, as if taking a moment to acknowledge the passage of time since he was in school. "What do you learn in high school these days? Anything useful?"

"Like what?" David asked.

"Like, what is the Pythagorean Theorem?" The man wanted to see what the kid knew.

David answered correctly, but the man persisted. "Have you had Algebra 2 or Trig?"

"Yes," answered David. "I've had both."

The man knew that most high school students did not make it that far in the math and science curriculum. So again, he persisted.

"Did you find those courses easy?"

"I didn't find them that easy, but I found them fun."

He had never heard a high school kid say that math was fun. He wondered who this kid was. Was he lying or was he telling the truth?

The man finished washing his hands and turned to leave. Standing there with a mop in his hand, David asked the man his name.

"My name is Johnathan. Maybe I'll see you around." And with that, he turned and left.

The next day, Johnathan made some calls to the school and found out about David's home life, sports history, and academics. He was not impressed by his school record. Everything was mediocre except his math and English grades. Much to his surprise, he was in accelerated classes in both and had gotten A's in every class.

Two weeks later, David was called in by the secretary who hired him.

"Mr. McKoy would like to see you in his office, David."

"Do you know what he wants?" asked David, showing a little concern that there may be trouble.

"I don't know," she answered. "I'm just delivering the message."

When David knocked on the boss' office door and entered, there sat Johnathan, the man he'd met in the men's room. He was sitting behind a wide desk covered with papers and drawings. His face was serious but transformed into a smile when he saw David. With that, David thought he wanted to talk about sports, but to his surprise, this was not the case.

"David, I've been thinking. How would you like to put away your janitor's mop and come to work for me a few hours a day? You seem like an intelligent boy who could benefit from the kind of work we do here. There are also things that you could learn quickly if you apply yourself. Your assistance would free some of the engineers to concentrate on other things. It would be an immense help to the firm's bottom line. So what d'ya say? If you're willing, I'll double your hourly wage, as long as you stay in school."

David was shocked. Why such a decision would be made confused him, and even though the offer was attractive, he was suspicious. He thought it might be just another example of white hyperliberalism trying to assuage some perceived guilt for the country's original sin.

"Why are you offering this to me? Why don't you hire someone who has engineering experience? I'm just a high school student."

Johnathan flashed a quick thoughtful smile and then answered. "This, in part, is a practical decision for me. Yes, I could hire someone to do this work. However, it most likely would have to be a full-time position with a full-time salary. We would have to pay health care benefits and vacation pay. It would be a costly proposition. Or I could hire someone like you. Someone smart enough to do the work and motivated and presentable enough to fit into a professional organization. We would save a great deal of money. I think you would be happy to make more money than you could anywhere else in an after-school job. And if I'm correct about you, you're going to love what you will learn."

If all this was true, he could not tell. Maybe Johnathan was nice because he was nice. Maybe he wanted to give an athletic kid from the neighborhood a boost. Whatever was true, after hearing the answer to his question and thinking for a moment more, David answered yes.

"I don't know what to say," said David. "I'm beginning to get excited. No, that's wrong. I *am* excited, but I would like you to know that I have a standing commitment every Tuesday at three o'clock. If you can work around that and if you're really going to do this for me, I promise I will give you and the work you want me to do my full attention. I'll try my best to do a good job."

"I think we can work around your previous commitment, and I'm sure you will make a real effort to try," said Johnathan.

"I don't mean to sound greedy, but if it's not too much to ask, I would like to pick my replacement custodian. A friend of mine could use the job."

"That's fine with me. But, I'll have to interview him first. You should tell him there might be a part-time job opening as a custodian. In the meantime, I do have expectations of you. You will have to wear a shirt and tie. You will have to come to work on time. Be here by three thirty. And there will be Saturdays when you will be asked to work, especially when a big project is about to be finalized and another is about to begin. The most important requirement is that you remain in school and graduate."

David's mind was racing. This kind of thing had never happened to him, and he was shaken by the opportunity. He had to tell his friend how to behave and what to expect. He had just enough money to buy a couple of shirts and ties and enough to give his father a few bucks. The thing he thought about most was the requirement to stay in school. He had not been the best student, and the idea of being a good student seemed to run against his current emotional fabric. He didn't care about sitting in classes, listening to twenty-three-year-old teachers read out of a book that he could have read without their assistance. Neither did he want to listen to the older teachers waste time controlling the class with inane tasks or coming down to the level of students so they might relate to them better. The only classes he liked were Math and English, and he had taken all of them. The rest he thought could be done without instruction and without much effort. As far as he could see, treating school the way he was already treating it did not have to change. What he did have to do was commit to learning the things Johnathan wanted him to learn.

Within a few days, Johnathan gave him the task of becoming familiar with the cast of engineers; who they were, what projects they were working on, and what they liked best about engineering. All of them welcomed him with a surprising ease that made David want to learn as much as he could. He immersed himself in studying the mathematical and logistical problems that needed to be worked out and resolved so real work could take place. He learned that nobody could complete an engineering project by himself; teamwork was necessary. Almost every task needed to be approached analytically with a high level of attention to detail, and that detail is always important. Johnathan taught him that strong communication skills and a desire to learn were necessary to be a good leader. Not only was Johnathan the owner of the firm, but he also possessed leadership skills his employees respected. He was the boss. And save for the higher mathematics, David soaked up the attitude and processes that made the firm run smoothly and within six months could be helpful to the ancillary needs of the engineers. In short, he was welcomed as part of the team. Johnathan made the right decision by embracing him, and David would never be the same. The job gave him invaluable experience, and it also gave him more money than he ever had. Until then, sports and his father were what consumed most of his time. Now that he had money in his pocket and was old enough to get a driver's license, the magic door to girls opened wide, and David walked through, smiling.

Saturday night, David went to a dance on the west side of town and met Alice Blackwell, a girl who, because of her looks, was admired by a number of guys. Inviting him to visit her one afternoon, he took a bus that got him a few blocks from her house. Anticipating another encounter, his spirits were up, and as he crossed Park Street, which separated the east and west end of town, a group of boys he barely knew from high school stopped him and asked him what he was doing on their side of town.

"I don't understand your question?" answered David. Of course, he knew exactly what was meant and readied himself for the fight to come.

"We know who you are and we don't want you on this side of town," said Claude, the leader of the four boys.

"Claude, I know who you are, and if for some reason you want to fight me, be a man about it and fight me. If you only have courage enough to fight me when you're surrounded by three other guys to protect you, then I say you're a punk." Then he said, "If you guys are gonna let a punk lead you, you ought to be ashamed."

The three followers saw that David had gotten angry and was ready to fight. The one remaining was Claude, who was too stupid to back down. David stepped toward Claude and punched him hard in the face. He went down. He then turned to the other three, and they walked away. As Claude was getting up, he grabbed for David's legs to tackle him. But what he got was a knee in the face, and he went down again. By now, David was out of control and wanted to really hurt Claude. Fortunately for David and Claude, a policeman saw the whole encounter from an unmarked car and stopped David from hurting the bully. With Claude lying on the ground, the cop said to David, "I've been watching this guy and his friends intimidating kids for an hour. I think their reign is over. Here's my card. If anybody asks, tell them to talk to me. Now get out of here. I'll take care of the punk." By the time he reached Alice Blackwell's house, the intensity of anger he felt during the encounter with the four troublemakers had slowly dissipated. She was waiting for him on her porch, and when he walked up the steps and greeted her, he was offered something cool to drink. But instead of a pleasant teenage afternoon discussing high school, most of the time was spent talking about what happened and how David's anger might need to be controlled.

*****

One afternoon, when he should have been in school, David looked at his father and asked the question he always wanted to ask but never did for fear it would send his father into one of his frequent depressions that could last for days. The morning had been good, and conversation between father and son was animated.

"I know you don't talk about it much and I guess it's 'cause of my nervous condition and my state. I saw cripple Henry down the hall dis mornin', and he was tauk'en 'bout you. I played like I knew it all and I guess I do, but he did say something I didn't know. He told me that you was 'bout to break the Queen City League home run record. Dat record was set by Johnny Davis twenty years ago, and it ain't never been broke. Is it true dat you 'bout to break it?"

"Yeah, Pop, it's true. I didn't tell you because I didn't want to give you false hopes."

"I know I ain't much, son, but I know things 'bout you dat you don't know. Like you is both me and your mama when we was young. I can't tell you how I know, but you is the best of what we coulda' been. Maybe it's my Alma lookin' down on you. She thought you was a gift from God, and if she got anything to do with it, you'll break that record, Son."

David leaned with one hand on the faded red corduroy chair that he had scrubbed more than once. Across the dimly lit room, an unlikely breeze fluttered the living room curtains that fell on the couch's arm and cooled the normally warm room. John Walton lay prone on the matching red couch, looking twenty-five years older than he was, the position that, for a number of the past years, had defined his frame of mind.

"Pop, I care more about you than I do about baseball. You know I love you, don't you?"

"Yeah, I know. You been takin' care of me since you was six years old. I was da one who taught you to love baseball. Me an' you sittin' on dis here couch, lisn'n to da games on radio and watchin' um on TV. Dat's what we did, ain't it?"

"It's true. You did teach me the game, but how come you never came to see me play, Pop?"

"I don't know, son. I guess it was my condition. But I knew you could play good even if I didn't see you."

David instinctively knew that this was a rationalization. Just as instinctively, he also knew that giving his father room to be right was more important than what some would consider the truth. David had something else on his mind. Something that shaped his psychology and its suppression energized motivations that helped determine the person he was. After a lifetime of wondering and not knowing the combination that would unlock the door behind what he needed could be found, David finally got the nerve to ask.

Between exhaling his last breath and inhaling the courage to ask his father about the ghost that haunted them both for as far back as he could remember, the tape that recorded his lifetime search for answers ran through his memory. Those echoes that start when memory plays an old-time tune on the heart can be cruelly sweet. Everything anyone said about his mother was remembered. And when the conjoined twins of imagination and memory work their magic, a deep abiding longing or aversion might attach itself and persist. Vague memories of half-forgotten or half-imagined things, not true or false, can leave a permanent mark. David was infected with persistent longing for a mother he never knew but only imagined.

At five and six years old, Ms. Bell down the hall would sit for him while his father was working. An enormous woman who could not move fast enough to catch him when he resisted being bathed or dressed, was his primary caretaker. Around kitchen chairs and under the table he would dash to escape her. He could still hear her high-pitched voice. "Get over here you little rapscallion and eat this food so I can dress you." David remembers her eating all the time. When she wasn't eating, her husband, Jessie, who always dressed in cowboy clothes, would bring food. The food was always greasy, and the image he had was of her sitting with her giant arms and elbows resting on the table eating meat out of a bowl with one hand as she wiped the grease running down her forearm with the other.

He always remembered the days and nights when Miss Bell's kitchen was full of women getting their hair done or having her sew their clothes. The chatter was constant, and sometimes when he was put down to nap, loud talk kept him awake. The drinking, smoking, and laughing were a constant presence at night. But among the things he remembered most was the smell of burning hair mixed with Dixie Peach, the hair pomade used to stop the hair from burning and to keep it straight after the hot comb was heated on the stove and carefully run through the hair.

On one occasion, he asked Miss Allene if she would be his mommy. Startled but amused, she declined.

"Will you be my mommy? David asked as he looked hopefully at the attractive lady sitting in the kitchen, waiting for her hair to be straightened.

"I'm sorry, little David, I can't be your mommy. You already have one. She had to go away and she is now with God."

"But where is God? I want God to give my mommy back," cried David.

"Your mommy brought you to us, and we're gonna always love you." Deeply sympathetic arms reached down and gently embraced him. I love you, David," said Miss Allene.

The room was quiet and attentive, and one by one, the woman in his life followed suit and embraced him, letting him know they were there for him and he was loved. Miss Bell said it was time for a nap. She picked him up and carefully carried him to the bedroom and laid him down.

"You have a nice nap, David. Okay?"

"Okay. I'm gonna wait for my mommy."

In the limitless time that can exist in a second, David remembered Miss Bell and his life long yearning for his Mother. It was time for his Father to tell David of their loss and his great sorrow.

"Pop, I've got a question I've never had answered. How come you never talked about my mother? I don't really know the circumstances of her death or anything about her. I used to ask some of the women your age in the neighborhood, but I never got a real answer. Please, Pop, tell me about her."

Lying silently on the couch, John Walton looked at his son and cast his eyes down on the old worn carpet under the coffee table and on the dirty linoleum floor. His visage took a deeply mournful expression. In a few moments, he began to weep, and the sound that came from him was of a sorrow so deep it could have held the broken dreams of the entire world. David kneeled next to his father. Cradling him in his arms, he waited for the weeping to pass.

"Tell me about my mother, Pop. Who was she? Where did she come from? How did you meet? And how did she die?" asked David.

"Okay," he said with painful resignation as he wiped away tears and began to tell his son what he should have always known. "Me and your mama growed up in McKinney, Virginia, and went to the same one-room schoolhouse and worked in the same baca' fields 'til we was old enough to run away together. We loved each other since we was three years old. I can't remember life without her. When we was little bitty kids, we would cry when we wasn't together. Both of us liked school, and we made it as number one and number two in eighth-grade graduation. I was good with numbers, and she was good with words. I found out as we got older that she was a good-looking person and we was both good at sports and such. We lived in the country where farm life was hard, and it was made harder by the white folks who always found a way to hurt us. It was always 'Nigga dis' or 'Nigga dat.'

"I remember the week before we left in the spring of 1932, when we got on a train and came here. Dat was the week we said goodbye to everybody. We said goodbye to all our relatives and friends and to our special places. Dar was a big hill about a mile away, and if you walked through the woods a bit, you could climb the hill. On the top, there was a great walnut tree, and the ground around it had spring wildflowers. From that hill, you could see all around for five or ten miles. We liked to go up there and hug and kiss. That last time was when Alma told me that she loved me and I told her the same thing. She told me her favorite song was called 'Body and Soul.' She said she heard it on the radio at Mister Wilson's store and that it was always singing in her ears. She told me she belonged to me with all her body and soul. And she took my face between her two hands and made me believe it. It had turned cloudy, and when she did dat, the sun came out, and she told me it was a sign from God. I told her I would give up my life for her, and I meant it. I guess I'll carry the memory of that walnut tree to my grave."

"All we wanted was a little slice of freedom and respect and room to grow. I don't guess I'll ever forget that train ride. Sittin' on that train for all those hours, I found a ring stuffed in the back of the seat. We later found out it was a diamond, and we took the stone out and made a new ring your mama wore. Dat ring was special to her. She all the time would hold it to the light an' say 'Dis ring gonna make our future.' Dat's right, we was going to get our life started in a new place. A place to work in peace, a decent roof over our heads, but, most of all, a place that let us hope. For us, tomorrow was full of hope. We was so happy, David. Your Mama Alma got a job as a cook, and I got a job fixin' things for the bus company. We only had two rooms, but we was in love and we was happy. I loved your mother so much that I would sometimes sit and cry about it. She was my life and reason for being alive. As the years passed, we loved each other more. Then one day, she told me she was going to have a baby. We was sure 'nough happy 'bout it. That was you. Before you was born, she named you David, after the one who killed the giant in the Bible. She said she was gonna give you the stone in her ring 'cause a stone was all David needed."

"So what happened to my mother?"

"When it was time for the baby to come, the doctor said there was a problem and I should wait in the outside room until he came to get me. When the doctor did come, he handed me the baby and told me that Alma didn't make it. At that instant, time stood still, and it felt like that moment lasted a year, and in that moment, my heart broke into a thousand pieces and it ain't never mended."

John Walton began to convulse and cry again.

"Oh, David, I'm so sad. I miss her so much. Even after all dees years, I miss my Alma like it was yestaday."

For the first time, David got some insight into his father's years of depression, and he began to cry with him. His mother was godsent and became part of his father's soul. They were one and together held the talisman of happiness, and through no fault of his own, he lost half his soul. David now understood multiple dimensions of his father's life. He sat with his arms around him and thanked him for being his father through all the years of trouble and heartbreak. David didn't question why his father carried such pain for so many years. He knew there was no answer and that any attempt to find an answer would lead to more pain. This was not a problem of rethinking or retraining. This was not a psychiatric problem. Talk therapy would have made it worse. Bad learning was not at issue either. This blow went beyond human understanding and entered a realm that few could understand. His father lost half his soul, and it was irretrievable. For him, it was not a metaphor; it was a reality. David thought that not turning to sin or bringing his life to an end took more than a Herculean effort. He respected that effort and loved his father more because of it.

"I don't know how in the Lord's name I got you. I spect' dar's things work'n I don't know noth'n about. With your mama bein' gone an' da world fallen in on me, an me spendin' most of my life lyin' round dis here place, it's a wonder dat you turned out. I'm sorry for being half a father. You been more than a good son. Without you, I swear I woulda disappeared into dust."

*****

The next day, John Walton was up early making breakfast. David thought maybe his father had been unburdened by yesterday's talk. This time, he need not take a reading of his father's mood. What was true of John Walton was also true of his son. Something important had happened yesterday. He felt that somewhere a hole had been filled. A need had been satisfied. A prayer had been answered. The inhibition that helped define their relationship had been reduced, and it was now possible to ask some questions differently. Not in a way that protected but in a way that informed. David felt free to expose his true self in the presence of his father and desperately wanted to do so. As he looked around the small galley kitchen, he seemed to see it anew. For the first time, he saw the Maxwell house coffee can full of bacon grease as an eyesore. The Formica top on the kitchen table had begun to separate from the substrate, and the yellow plastic upholstery on the three kitchen chairs had cracked, and the stuffing was coming out. The dirty floor screamed out to be mopped. The green paint on the wall over the stove was peeling, and grease-infused dust particles stuck to the wall around the still working but noisy exhaust fan, making him cringe. Even though he lived with the greasy filth, he now made a silent vow to do something about it. Last night's conversation with his father had partially fixed something broken and given him reason to hope and maybe even a reason to aspire. For David, living in the conditions that allowed these things to happen could no longer be tolerated.

"Pop, can I ask you a question?" This instigated a troubled look and a change in his father's aspect. A slight alteration in his face suggested paranoia or defensiveness, and David knew he should tread lightly.

"What?" answered his father.

"Are you still interested in watching sports?" David could see his father's face relax and return to its normal state.

"I watch it on TV sometimes, but I never watch a whole game. So I guess I ain't that interested. Why do you ask?"

"Well, Saturday might be the final game of the Queen City playoff. The Bears are playing the Hawks again. It was the best two out of three games. Each team has won a game. If we win Saturday, it will be the first time the Hawks will have won the Queen City championship. If we lose, then there's always next year. Come on out and watch the game, Pop. I'll be playing center field. So wa' da' ya' say, Pop? It would mean a lot to me."

"I don't know, David. It's been a while since I been out like dat. I'll think about it."

"Okay, Pop, I'm going to school."

*****

Friday came and the town's baseball-loving population chatted endlessly about which team would win the final game of the Queen City Championship. It seemed the west end of town wanted the Bears and the east end of town wanted the Hawks. The fire and police departments ran pools. Diners and restaurants all over town were crowded with people who wanted to talk about the game.

"Dammit, Vic," said little Joe Turner in angry opposition. "You don't know what the fuck you talkin' about. If David gets a good pitch, he'll knock it out of the park. I don't care who the pitcher is."

"I agree that he got some power, but if that Sandy Hanks throws his knuckleball, can't nobody hit it. Walton or anybody else."

"Man, I'll bet you ten bucks that if David comes up against Hanks, Johnny Davis is gonna have to share that record. It may even be broken."

"You ain't even got ten bucks," yelled Vic so that the other guys in the diner could hear, and maybe even get in on the action. "Hey, Wanda," he yelled across the counter to the waitress who was taking orders from other locals who were also talking about the game. "You got a pen and paper so we can make dis bet official? Joe don't know what he's talkin' about."

And so it went. On stoops, at kitchen tables, in eating establishments all over town, the conversation was the same. In the high school, students were so excited with all the buzz about the game that nothing of substance took place. They were so distracted that the principal, after serious deliberation, gave them the afternoon off.

The local newspaper had three lengthy stories about the upcoming game. There was a story about the Bears' history and the team's talented players, listing the stats on each player, the coaches, and what their strategies might be. The story about the Hawks was equally long with all the same discussion about their lineup. The third story was about local baseball legend Johnny Davis, who, along with a .345 batting average, has held the home run record of 20 for a single season for twenty-two years. The story went on to say how Davis left town, went on to college, and was drafted by the majors. During his first year as a pro and before he had time to find his footing, he was hit by a car that ended his life. Since then, nobody has come close to his level of play until now.

> The gifted athlete David Walton is the first to challenge the legacy of Johnny Davis. Walton, the center fielder for the Hawks, currently has a batting average of .349 and is on his way to breaking Johnny Davis's home run record. Currently, Walton has smashed 19 homers, some beyond the Siler's Field fence, and with a possible two games left in the season, there will be ample opportunity to hit two more.

*****

The weather on game day was as anticipated. The sun broke through the clouds early, warming the atmosphere and drying the infield and grass so regular play could take place. The town added folding bleachers to better accommodate the expected throng and a dozen auxiliary police for crowd control. Siler's Field had not seen this kind of Saturday attendance in its entire history as a playing field. The game was scheduled to start at noon, but people began to arrive at ten o'clock. Baseball fans, friends, family, and fans of Johnny Davis, those who wanted to see David Walton break the record, and those who just wanted to be in the mix of the excited movement showed up. A crowd as large as this had not been seen, and for many it was thrilling.

"Don't be in such a hurry, you'll get there," said Glenn Wilson to the man behind him, who was pushing in assertive anticipation. After another push that drove him into a lady in front of him, he began to get annoyed.

"Look, man, the people in the ticket booth are working as fast as they can. Please don't shove me again." When it happened again, Glenn threw a punch.

Another part of the noisy crowd trying to squeeze into a two-person ticket lane knocked an elderly lady onto the ground, where she lay under the feet of a crowd that seemed at first not to care. "Would you please make room for this lady to get up off the ground?" shouted a man trying to help her and push back bodies so that she could breathe and get to her feet. Because of these and other potential dangers, the rescue squad and emergency medical technicians were present and ready to serve people in need.

By eleven o'clock, many of the players had arrived, and some were on the field warming up. Some were shagging fly balls. Others were scooping up fast-moving ground balls, and still others were warming up their arms. Even though the crowd was still arriving, people knew that it would not be long before the game would start. Most of the Hawks were in uniform and by eleven thirty were beginning to wonder where their star player was.

David had not yet left for the field. He had spent most of the morning scraping the peeling paint and trying to clean greasy walls in his kitchen. He knew the game started at twelve but wanted to do as much as possible before he left for the game. He also knew that much of the town's excitement had to do with him, but in typical David fashion, his priorities were not always those of the crowd. He wanted a clean kitchen, and for once, just this one time, he wanted his father to come to the game. He would soon graduate from school and would likely be somewhere else before long. Time with the father he had cared for most of his life was ending, and before it did, he wanted to give him something special.

John Walton was lying on his couch with his eyes closed. "Pop. Pop. Are you awake? The last game of the season might be today. I would like you to come."

"I don't know son, I ain't feeling so good today. I think I might just lie here and dream about the places I'll never get to see."

"Please, Pop. I really want you to come to the field and see the game. I'll be playing."

"Okay, David. I'll try but I can't promise. Only if I'm feeling better."

David knew not to push his father, so he asked no more. If history was a predictor, he knew that the probabilities were not in his favor. But he also knew that like himself, his father might have been unburdened by their talk and found the emotional space to get beyond himself and appear in public.

Arriving at the field house, David went into the locker room and changed into his uniform. Tony Scakit, the first baseman, was also late. "Do you believe the size of the crowd? This crowd is even bigger than last week's game," said Tony. "All the guys know you don't like to talk about it, but the crowd is here for you. Even the kids from the west side who want the Bears to win would like to see you break the record. I think you got the juice. You'll do it. Let's just play a good game," said Scakit.

"Thanks for the encouragement, Tony. I'm a little nervous Sca', but let's go have some fun."

"Let's get out there and warm up. We don't have much time," said Scakit. David and Tony joined their teammates and had only a few minutes to warm up before things started. The umpire announced that because Siler's Field was the home field for the Bears and the Hawks and because the Hawks had the better record, the Hawks would bat second.

"Play ball!" screamed the ump', and the game began.

The Bears got two runs in the first inning, and in the third they drove in another run. With two outs, the Bears' power hitter struck out, and the sides retired. The Hawks sent three men to the plate. Two popped up, and one struck out. By the fourth inning, nothing had changed. David would periodically look at the bleachers to see if his father had decided to come. His presence at this game would have been the most crucial event in his young life. After striking out his last time at bat, looking at the bleachers did reveal the presence of Johnathan McKoy and some of the other engineers from Heron Designs. Of course, he was glad to see them and pleased they thought well enough of him to come to the game. Some of them even had their families, who waved enthusiastically, but he could not detect the presence of his father. In the bottom of the fifth, the batter at the top of the lineup hit a single to left field right down the third base line. With one man on, the second batter struck out, looking. With one man on and one out, the third batter hit a line drive over the second baseman's head. Two men on, first and second base. A timeout was called because of debris on the field, and David, who batted cleanup, warmed up with a heavier bat and looked around at the crowd in the bleachers.

"Play ball!" yelled the umpire.

David stepped to the plate. He now faced Sandy Hanks, the pitcher whose knuckleball nobody could hit. Hanks was taking his time, leaned down to chalk his hand, and then bent to read the signal from the pitcher, and with his hand first in his glove, wound up and threw. David saw the ball leave the pitcher's hand and tried to follow it, but when he swung, it was not where he anticipated it would be. "Strike one!" signaled the umpire. The crowd was quiet in anticipation of what might happen next. Knocking the clay off his shoes and oblivious to the weight of the bat, he stepped to the plate a second time. Feeling a slight breeze on his neck and the muffled sound of random voices saying, "Come on, David," he relaxed and settled down.

"I told you he couldn't hit dat knuckleball," said Vic Hatchet. "I think you gonna owe me ten bucks."

"Dis guys gonna get cocky and get his head handed to him. I ain't given up on Walton yet. It ain't over till it's over," said Joe Turner.

Hanks wound up and threw again. David swung and missed again. The crowd was now making a lot of noise. Cheerleaders for each team jumped and waved in encouragement. But it looked as if David would strike out again. Some were saying that the record set by Johnny Davis would not fall today. The count was 2 and 0. David readied himself and tried to relax, making himself believe that this was just a game and it would not define him. Yes, he did want the Hawks to win, but if they didn't...

He turned to face the crowd, and there at the end of the bleachers, almost hiding, was a slight figure with a wrinkled shirt and a bow tie he recognized—the only tie his father ever owned. It was Pop. He had come. His father had come to see him play on the day when the home run record could be broken. David turned from the plate, filled with the kind of joy he rarely experienced. He teared and tried to hide by feigning something in his eyes. Stalling for time, David readied himself again and stepped to the plate. He allowed himself to feel the pride he wanted his father to feel, and it filled him with power. All the visual and reflexive sharpness he trained for in sports and his secret aikido training became heightened and focused.

The pitch was thrown, a knuckleball. The whole thing seemed to be happening in slow motion. He followed the ball as it approached the plate, and when he swung, the power with which he hit it was focused with pinpoint accuracy. The ball flew off the bat with a cracking sound that predicted it would leave the field. The crowd stood and watched the center fielder run in vain to catch it. In that moment anticipation of the crowd was palpable. When it was clear the ball would clear the fence, the crowd went wild. David rounded the bases at a slow jog and tried to absorb all the goodwill he could feel from his teammates and the crowd. As he reached second base, he could see his father standing with his arms straight up in the air. No feeling in the world could have surpassed that. The score had just changed from Bears 3, Hawks 0 to Bears 3, Hawks 3. The next batter for the Hawks was tagged out at first. David had tied the home run record, and he thought he had nothing to prove. Then in the bottom of the ninth, Jimmy Ellis, the Hawks' third baseman hit a low floater over the first baseman's head. With the score tied in the bottom of the ninth and with two outs and one man on base, the game was all up to David. If he could drive in a run, the Hawks would win the championship. The pressure was like nothing he ever experienced. Like the crowd, he knew this time at bat might be his last. He sensed that what happened now would be the capstone of his youth. A few minutes would determine how he would be remembered. Reluctantly picking up a bat, David stepped to the plate with a level of concentration he rarely achieved. He was now so internally focused he did not hear his teammates or the hopes and goodwill offered by his supporters in the bleachers. He was in the world alone with nothing but his talent and the grace of fate.

Sandy Hanks stood tall on the mound glancing at Jimmy Ellis who had taken a long lead off first base. If he could throw Ellis out, they would have to play another game. Winding up, Hanks threw to first base hoping to catch Ellis, too late. With the ball back in his glove, Hanks bent to read the catchers' signal. Winding up, he threw his fabled knuckleball again. David connected. The ball travelled over the left field fence. He rounded the bases to the adulation of his team and his fans, who crowded onto the field, lifted him like a triumphant hero, and paraded him around to cheers and high-fives, handshakes, and congratulations for what seemed to him like an eternity. Looking toward the bleachers, a banner he had not previously seen read, "ENGINEERS FOR WALTON." He waved so they knew he'd seen the banner and appreciated their support. David knew he had done something special. Not only had the Hawks won the championship, but he had also broken the home run record. He was filled with pride for himself and his teammates.

After a brief locker room celebration, David found his father, who was still sitting in the bleachers waiting for him with a few other scattered well-wishers. John Walton stood and raised his arms straight above his head with his index fingers pointing toward the sky. He enfolded his son in a silent embrace and finally said, "If I pass tomorrow, it will be with pride that I'm your father."

"Thanks for coming, Pop. It wouldn't have been the same without you."

As they left the field together, the remaining fans cheered again, and John and David Walton walked the long way home with congratulations following them. Fall weather had come and leaves from deciduous trees were covering the sidewalks and lawns that ran through the upper middle-class neighborhoods through which they had to walk. The crackle and rustle sound made by the fallen leaves underfoot made music with the dappled light floating through the leaves still desperately clinging to trees. The ups and downs of sidewalk sections lifted by the roots of mature oaks, maples, and sycamores slowed their progress but added character and a sense of adventure to the walk. For the first time in a long while, they enjoyed each other as they moved through the world. The afternoon was beautiful and made even more so by the well-kempt Victorian homes that lined the streets. It was the kind of housing that was foreign, mysterious, and coveted by people like the Waltons, who could only guess what living in a house like that would be. But David had gotten much closer to knowing than his father. He actually knew some kids who lived in this and other neighborhoods like it. He had been in classes with them and gleaned their values, speech, and their dress. John Walton knew very little of that world and never would. But what he did know was that his son would one day get there. He knew that if he played life like he played ball, he could make it. He knew because he knew Alma was with him.

Walking into their apartment and closing the door, Pop threw his arms around David, and when he released, put something in David's hand.

"This is your mama's ring, the one that holds the stone she wanted you to have. Keep it and she will always be with you."

While looking at his father, David's hand tightly gripped the ring and shoved it deep into his pocket. It was one of the only heartfelt things he had received from his father. Straining to hold back the deep well of emotion that fought to bubble up, he thanked his father for the gift and embraced him. It was not just a gift. It was the baton being passed into his hands from a generation whose blood and history ran through his veins. It was the screams and cries emerging from slave ships. It was the tortured moans of whipped runaways who were caught searching for light at the end of the tunnel. It was the dream of two kids from Virginia who almost tasted the milk and honey on the other side. For David, it was the essence of the promise John and Alma made to each other. It was his mother's dream for him. He would not let it go. It was all he needed.

6

Phat City

The 1960s

With two nights at Fat Joe's and two evenings at Fiori di Campo, Ken was beginning to see himself as a working musician. His days were spent with practice, musical exploration, and the requirements of daily life in New York. Nights at Fat Joe's were more musically exciting. His creative juices flowed in the company of other musicians, and he could not wait to play for the singers, many of whom were also seasoned musicians in their own right, and came because of the high level of play. In addition to the music and the money, Ken never missed a night because of Wen Lee's likely presence. One night a week, she would wake up in Ken's arms, and they would thank the fates for bringing them together and then say goodbye.

Much more money was made at Fiori di Campo playing Italian American songs sprinkled with the jazzed-up pop tunes of the day. The restaurant was pricey, the food was excellent, and the good old boys were sure to show up when Ken played. Out-of-towners were treated to traditional ethnic New York cuisine, and politicians who wanted to be away from the spotlight showed up regularly. Gentlemen and ladies were expected to be dressed up, and inappropriate behavior was not tolerated. Maria ran a classy place, and because her clientele was from both sides of the law, it would remain that way. To bring Ken in line with her vision, she replaced his oversized tip jar with an elegant black walnut tea box with a folded card that discreetly read *Tips*. It was almost as if the good fellows and the politicians were required to tip, and boy, did they.

"Hey, kid!" Ken would sometimes hear when he took a break and headed to the men's room past one of their tables.

When he approached the table, he'd hear, "You play good music, keep it up. We like you." He would then be slipped a fifty or a hundred-dollar bill on the QT. Shoving it into his pocket, he would always ask for a request. They would always say, "Let the visitors make a request. We're family." The politicians seemed to take a cue from the good old boys by putting something in the tip box, and the tourists followed suit. On a good night, he could almost make his monthly rent. The icing on the cake was that he and Marie got along famously.

Making enough money to satisfy the demands of his current lifestyle, Ken was free to visit the popular clubs. And although he listened and played throughout Manhattan, he spent most of his time in Greenwich Village. At the club called The Half Note, Cannonball Adderley, Zoot Sims, John Coltrane, Bob Brookmeyer, Art Farmer, and Clark Terry could be heard. At The Five Spot, an incredible array of talent both performed and dropped by, including Thelonious Monk. Bradley's exposed Ken to a raft of creative post-bop piano and bass players who could weave magic with jaw-dropping ability. Players like Hank Jones, John Hicks, Tommy Flanagan, Kenny Barron, and Kirk Lightsey were just a few. At the Village Gate on Bleeker Street, he could hear Herbie Mann, Miles Davis, and Roland Kirk. On any given night, he could wander into The Blue Note, Arthur's,

The 55 Bar, and Sweet Basil's and often end up at the Village Vanguard, arguably the most celebrated jazz club in the city. Here, iconic music by Sonny Rollins, The Bill Evans Trio, and John Coltrane would be recorded. Ken was where he wanted to be, and he inhaled as much of it as he could.

One night, Ken walked into an uptown Third Avenue bar. There at a double table sat four older gentlemen, one of whom looked familiar. He could not place the man, so he nodded hello and sat at the bar in front of their table to have a drink. It wasn't long before he felt a light tap on his shoulder.

"Please excuse my interrupting, but aren't you Ken Carle who plays Fiori de Campo?"

"'Tis I," said Ken, a bit surprised. People downtown recognized him some time, but it had never happened uptown.

"We thought that was you. There's another chair at our table. It would please us greatly if you joined us. Please join us."

Ken graciously agreed, gathered up his drink, and turned to sit with his hosts.

"Ken, can I call you Ken? My name is Saul. These three mugs are James, Clarence, and Herve. We been listening to jazz all our lives and sometimes we go down to di Campo to hear you play. Word gets around, you know."

"I'm flattered, gentleman."

"Don't be flattered, kid. You got the goods," said Clarence.

"We see that you do pretty good down there," added Herve.

"Now I know," Ken declared. "It's James that I recognized when I walked in. He never takes that hat off. And it's a great hat."

"That's right, Ken. You got good taste, kid. And I always walk up and make a deposit."

"And," said Ken, "I always see you do it."

"Where'd you learn to play the piano like that? It sounds kind of familiar to me."

"Yeah, James, you heard it from the last time we was there." Saul laughed.

"Saul's been try'n to be a comedian for fifty years, and he always falls flat," added Herve.

"Clarence, don't Ken remind you of somebody else? We been try'n to figure it out," said James. "I'm gonna ask again. Where did you learn to play? I think it's the left hand, and Clarence agrees."

"It's those extra little figures you do with your thumb and middle finger. I haven't heard that for a long time. The interesting thing is that it informs your right hand in a way that makes it timeless," added Clarence.

"I had a wonderful—let me rephrase that—I had an extraordinary teacher," said Ken.

"What is his or her name?"

"His name is Bootsy Johnson."

The talkative old men said nothing. They just sat there looking at each other with gap-mouthed expressions on their faces.

"You knew Bootsy Johnson?" asked Herve.

"You ain't old enough to know Bootsy Johnson! Stop kidding us," said Clarence.

Ken knew that if they were friends of Bootsy, they were friends of his, so he decided to give them the scoop.

"I know him. He was my teacher and friend until I left for college. He's an old man now and doesn't play very often. Some of the old stuff is still there. But he's retired now."

"It must be close to forty years since the scene was graced with a talent like that. I remember some of the talk. He just disappeared. I think there were articles in a couple of the jazz magazines. He walked away. Some said he wasn't cut out to take the crap musicians of that era had to take, especially black ones," said Saul.

"Man, I loved his playing. He could make the rain stop and the sun come out," added James.

"He went home to Maryland and stopped appearing publicly. He worked as a stableman for my father until he met me. I was eleven. No one knew about his extraordinary talent. When we found out, my family hired him as my teacher and promised to take care of him. I've recorded some private sessions with him and some with both of us. One day, I'll try to release them. He only plays at home now, but to me, he's a god."

"Bootsy Johnson, that's what drew us to you. You make us feel the way he made us feel when we was teenagers," added Clarence.

The conversations continued as two more rounds of drinks were downed and memories were shared. When Ken left his newfound friends, he floated down Third Avenue with Bootsy, spirit lifted and proud to be a part of such an important legacy.

7

High School

David's stellar reputation as an athlete did not change the opinion many of his teachers had of him. He spent most of his time avoiding teachers and ditching classes. When he was present, he was accused of arguing with teachers and challenging their knowledge bases and assumptions. His aim was not to bait his instructors. He merely wanted clarification or more information that would help him understand better. Sadly, most of his teachers could not provide that information and often saw his persistence as a polemic or a challenge to their authority. For many of the teachers, he was a wiseass and a troublemaker. This was bad enough, but what made it worse was his dark skin, a sure sign there was something suspicious and nefarious about his motives. During those years, if one raised the question of racial prejudice, it was denied, and he or she were called hypersensitive. In truth, most Negro males in particular felt the result of these attitudes but did not protest because they often could not defend themselves against the biased treatment or articulate it for what it was. Those who could had very little support and thus were on the losing end of a biased transaction that was built into the American psyche. There were, however, some enlightened teachers who thought David was one of the few students who could challenge the school's orthodoxy, especially as it related to racial prejudice. For them, he was not just seen as an out of control athlete trading on his physical gifts but instead as an intelligent person who should be taken seriously.

One of many incidents occurred in a mandatory nineteenth century history class that David seldom attended. The reason for his absence had little to do with disdain for the study of the past and much to do either with what he perceived as the school's attempt to consciously eliminate the Negro's contribution to the dynamic nineteenth century or with the utter ignorance displayed by those given the license to educate. One of the many picture books David's father had in the house was *A Pictorial History of the Negro in America*, written by Langston Hughes, and consequently this provided a real sense his ancestors had played some role in defining what America is. Negroes were never mentioned in history class except as slaves in the cabins surrounding the mansions of antebellum slaveholders, singing spirituals and playing the banjo. They happily spent their time slaving away for the master and giving songwriters like Stephen Foster the fuel to write all the degrading songs about the Negro that helped shape America's utterly false assumptions about who the Negro was. David also knew that in his everyday life Negroes were not present except in their own communities and people who looked like him were invisible in daily life except as servants, maids, or other workers doing jobs that required little intelligence. He knew his father's unfortunate life would have been different without those assumptions, and even as a teenager, he rejected the possibility that the myth would guide his life. David's need for respectability, which was sometimes handled without tact, often caused him to challenge authority in a way that ruffled feathers.

"To pass this class, you must write a ten-page term paper. Its structure must be the standard format you learned in your

English class. It must be historically accurate with at least six references. It is due two weeks before the term ends." Miss Milanafey spoke in a serious tone.

"Miss Milanafey? What subject do you want us to write about?" asked Harriet Millbrook.

"You may write about anything you choose, Harriet," answered Miss Milanafey. Other students raised their hands with questions about the term paper, and Miss Milanafey provided the necessary information. Then David Walton raised his hand, and when he did, Miss Milanafey tried to ignore him as if he wasn't there. She finally allowed a question when he persisted.

"Are you sure we can write on anything as long as it is about history?" asked David.

"This question has been asked and answered, but I'll answer it again!" she said, showing obvious impatience. "You may write on any historical subject you wish."

David had never written a paper as long as ten pages. He needed help and he got it from the engineers at his job. He wanted to do something meaningful and remembered the picture he saw of black soldiers in a picture book.

"Get as much information as you can about your soldiers and, before you write a word, teach us about what you've learned." So at the end of the workday, the engineers gathered and listened to David teach them about a part of American history about which they knew nothing. They asked questions, tested his facts and organization, and treated him as they would any professional. By the time he sat down to write the paper, he was an expert, and the paper flowed from his pen and extended to more than twenty pages. The boss' secretary even typed it for him, but it was not ready the day it was due.

Two weeks before the term ended, the students in Miss Milanafey's history class turned in their history term papers.

All but a few made the deadline. David was among those who didn't. Coming to class late, he pleaded with her to give him one more day. She finally agreed to only one. Fortunately, he got it in on time. Miss Milanafay read the title: "Buffalo Soldiers: Unsung American Heroes." Accepting the paper and feeling its heft made her curious about what David was trying to pull on her. This paper was expertly typed and with many more pages than required. She could not wait to read it.

"I don't know where you got this paper, but it is clearly something a fiction writer produced. It's not true. There was no such thing as a buffalo soldier. The things they supposedly did were made up by someone cleverer than you. It is clear to me that you didn't write it. I don't know where it came from, but it will be marked *Plagiarized*. You will receive a failing grade for the paper. Along with your many absences, you will receive a failing grade for the class. I want you to come with me to the vice principal's office, where you will be disciplined for being such a cad." At the vice principal's office, Miss Milanafey and David waited to be seen by the high school disciplinarian so it could be decided what punishment would be meted out for flagrantly violating the rules of academic honesty.

"David Walton, you are no stranger to me. Arrogant, argumentative, and absent," said the vice principal. "What do you have to say about the current charges?" The disciplinarian's accusatory attitude was partially true and the part that wasn't angered and strengthened David's resolve.

"I say that once again I'm being accused of something I didn't do." Being somewhat frightened by the vice principal and the office that held the ultimate authority, David was nervous and slightly intimidated, but slowly steadied himself.

"Are you telling me that Miss Milanafey is charging you with plagiarism and you are not guilty?"

"That's right. Can I speak honestly?"

"Be my guest, young man."

"Miss Milanafey is under the impression that because she is a teacher, she has to behave as if she knows everything. The truth is, there are many things she is ignorant of. And most of all, she is ignorant about who and what I am. People with her kind of prejudice should not be allowed to teach. She thinks I'm stupid and ignorant, but let me answer the question you want answered. Yes, black people made significant contributions in every decade of the nineteenth century. Black soldiers of the 10th US Cavalry were pivotal in winning the West. A monument to the buffalo soldiers stands proudly in the quad at West Point. I could give a half-hour-long presentation on these brave men, and she still wouldn't believe it. The real issue is whether I wrote the paper. The answer is yes. I could write it almost word for word again. Test me. That's the only way to prove it."

"That's quite a speech. What do you have to say, Miss Milanafey?"

"I know that he's a cheater. It's consistent with everything we know about him. This time he won't get away with it."

"Not only did what she just say support the fact that she is prejudging me in some ways, but she still has not provided proof other than her prejudice that I didn't write my paper. How does she know that there was no such thing as a buffalo soldier? So I'll request this of Miss Milanafey directly—prove that they did not exist. I want you to discredit all the references in my paper and those that I did not include."

"Well, I never!" she said as if her exasperation was evidence of her correctness.

"You never what? Encountered information that you didn't know? Made an incorrect judgment about a person and admitted it? Or maybe you have never apologized for being wrong. Or maybe my blackness has you twisted in a knot."

David knew he had won, and the personal strength derived from the whole episode gave him insight into surprising aspects of his own character. The importance of hard work and standing up for your work until proven wrong was clearly demonstrated. He also saw quite clearly that the anger he usually felt when he was wronged, like Miss Milanafey had wronged him, was not necessary if you could win without it. This one experience drove Sensei Kim's lesson about anger in further than would have been the case without it. This was an important part of the meditation he practiced with aikido. Anger interferes with technique, blinds you to your opponent's approach, and interferes with winning.

*****

David's final year in high school was tumultuous. Unlike many of his friends, school was not the center of his life. Work at Heron Designs had become almost routine, but because of his boss Johnathan's erudition, David convinced himself he was not ready for college until he acquired some of his boss' gifts. Somehow thinking he would need a presentable style before a college would seriously consider him, the work of shaping his character into one that was presentable would take a great deal of discipline before he applied. David was driven to go to college but was held back from applying by his fear of failing. There was the typical vacillation. He would approach the idea of college and then become anxious about not being accepted. To reduce the discomfort caused by the conflict, he would opt out and stop thinking about it. College was put on the back burner because his head was in a proverbial hole. David let time make the inevitable decision. College would have to wait. He still had ample money from working at Heron Designs, but this part-time job would not last after high school graduation.

He was watching over his father, enjoying an active social life, and practicing aikido. It could not be said that David lived a dull life. Romance was at the top of his agenda, and there was never a time when he needed companionship. Always discreet, he never waved the flag of conquest publicly or showed any disrespect toward the young girls with whom he kept company. Sampling the nectar of every flower that came his way, he never deceived, hid in the shadows, or treated companions with imprudence. But he did, however, look through an unconscious imaginary lens, hoping to find the lady his father married. A lens that never closed.

Playing baseball as often as he could, the admiration of the sports community continued. Taking the lessons he learned from the engineers at Heron, he was always a modest team player and an example of what a sportsman should be. As the year came to an end, his father, John, became very ill. Refusing medical attention, John Walton died on his couch of poverty, a broken heart and a medication that did more harm than good. His only joy was the hope he had for his son.

David was devastated. He lost the only family he was aware of. Now in the world by himself, David felt alone. The one thing that defined home for him was gone. Without his father, the emotional history they built in their shared space lost its power. Memories connected to every corner, door, and leaky bathroom faucet meant little unless it could be shared. The one person who gave his life meaning was gone, and he could not help being angry. Angry at life and a system that allowed a good man like his father to suffer and die the way he did. He blamed himself for not doing enough to help solve his father's problems. And among those blamed was the Tremont Pharmaceutical Company that David believed made and sold the antidepressant drug Lopresid that sent his father into a downward spiral ending in death. He believed they made a poison medication for his father to take and acted like they had no idea that something was wrong. They knew and did nothing about it. The only thing they cared about was profit. So back to the library he went and tracked down the Tremont Pharmaceutical Company, its CEO, and Dr. Wayne Moore, the pharmacologist who designed the drug and was primarily responsible for its distribution. Discovering his notes from his first stumbling into the article on Lopresid, he now was able to communicate with Miller and Bradford, the receptive law firm collecting the stories from complainants. David was added to the list and was sent the paperwork necessary to join a potential class action suit.

*****

David barely graduated from high school when he was faced with having to leave Heron Designs. Johnathan McKoy made it very clear that when high school was over, David's work at the engineering firm would be over too.

"Haven't I done the kind of job you needed and wanted?" David asked. "Is there anything that I could have done better? Is it possible to get one more year to organize my life so that I have a chance to think about my future?"

"David, I can't tell you how fond we are of you and how pleased we are with your work. You have learned far more than any of us expected. We have come to the conclusion that you would make a fine engineer." Johnathan knew since the day he hired David that his home environment did not provide the kind of support and advice he needed now. Over the last two years, he had always made an effort to help him stay on the path to responsible adulthood. Now with the two of them sitting on the edge of his spacious desk, Johnathan knew it was time to cut the umbilical cord. Oddly and unexpectedly, he felt a surge of real emotion and attachment, and as he wrapped an affectionate arm around David's shoulder, he knew he would have to let him go.

"I don't think I'll be able to replace you, son." And with that, David knew he had lost his bid for another year. He knew Johnathan was also feeling what he was feeling. It made him happy to know the tall, elegant man who hired him felt enough affection to call him son.

Releasing his arm from David and walking around to the front of his desk, Johnathan opened a side drawer, removed a package, and handed it to him.

"It's something that serves two purposes. First, it's a thank-you present for allowing us to try to seduce you into the field of engineering. Second, it's a going-away present I think will be a beacon of encouragement. It is obviously a book. I hope you will one day read it."

"Do I have to open it now?" asked David.

"No," answered Johnathan. He opened the door, and they both walked out of his office. Nobody was in their offices or at drawing tables. As the two turned to leave, David suddenly heard "Surprise!" coming out of the library. It was everybody. All the engineers, the secretaries, and even his friend Larry, who he recommended to replace him as the part-time janitor. They were all there to bid him goodbye and express their good wishes.

David never had a party and did not know how to translate his feelings into the words that would have expressed his gratitude. He only had his beliefs and an abiding hope that he would one day have them all know that the kindness they had shown him would not be wasted. As David left to walk home, he felt a profound sense of loss that made him stop, lean against a factory wall, and wipe his eyes. For the first time in his life, a kindness shown by white people washed over him and caused a deep emotional reaction. He knew he could not return the favor by letting them down. In considering his options, he was left with only two alternatives. Either he could get a dead-end factory job, which was not at all appealing, or he could join the military and hope for the best.

8

Being Judged Worthy

The following day, David made a visit to the local Army recruiter where he was given the standard travel and training speech. It was suggested he return so his aptitude for various kinds of training might be assessed. After some initial recruitment testing, in which he scored high in some areas, the recruiter strongly suggested he receive further testing after boot camp. In boot camp, he became a platoon leader and was recognized by his drill and combat instructors as a standout recruit. When he finally took the advanced Armed Service Vocational Aptitude Battery (ASVAB) to determine job suitability, David scored high on memory, language, and math potential. After reviewing the test results, the sergeant who proctored and scored the test made a comment to the officer heading the testing unit.

"Excuse me, Major Ellis, sir, I've got a ringer here," said Sergeant DeQuallo.

"What do you mean, Sergeant?"

"Well sir, Private Walton, a black kid, just scored off the charts in some areas. In memory, language, and math, he was in the ninety-eighth percentile. Scoring that high in one is not that unusual, but scoring that high in three different areas is almost unheard of."

"What should we do with this Private Walton, Sergeant?"

"I'm not sure sir, but I do know what we should not recommend," said DeQuallo emphatically.

"Do you mean he should not be assigned to an infantry battalion? Maybe we should alert the CO and let him decide where the Army could best use him," said Major Ellis.

On Friday of the next week, Major Ellis came to work with, among other things, a thin folder on Private David Walton. After reading the comments and reviews written by his recruiter and those by his boot camp drill instructor, he knew Walton was the real thing. With his ASVAB scores, along with the reports written by his boot camp instructors, Major Ellis determined David would be a prime candidate for military intelligence, a job for which the recruit appeared well suited. Because David only had a high school education, there was some initial hesitation, but because he was one of the few black men considered for such a highly sensitive classified section, he became somewhat of a bureaucratic experiment. So David was first sent to Fort Holabird in the City of Baltimore, where he studied for eight weeks and was introduced to the basics of intelligence training, and then on to Fort Huachuca, Arizona, for specialized training as an intelligence analyst, where he spent a year and became a member of the Military Intelligence Corps. David knew an intelligence analyst with his training provided support in operations, planning, and decision-making. His work would have an impact on military and national security and the political and public relations of the government. The primary responsibilities of his intelligence duties would be to recognize and analyze information likely to affect military operations and national policies, to operate and manage information technology systems, and to advise and plan the employment of sophisticated intelligence collection and surveillance systems. After a little more than sixteen months of training, he received orders to report to the Pentagon in Washington, DC.

Intelligence analysts work in the US and in embassies and military bases across the globe, and they often have to coordinate with other intelligence programs and help gather information. Because of his aptitude, skills, and temperament, David would have no trouble spending time far away from the base, and because of his martial arts skills, could handle himself in dangerous situations. When he received orders for the Pentagon, he was ecstatic, knowing he would soon be in the middle of a hotbed of intelligence and that his life, at least while in the military, would be interesting. Or at least that's what he thought.

With his father gone and no one else to tell of his progress since leaving home, David sent a brief note to Johnathan Heron telling of his achievements and progress. It wasn't long before a letter came in return mail, saying how proud he and all the engineers were of what he'd been able to accomplish. Knowing David's father had passed, Johnathan also knew how important it is for a "kid" to share the good things with someone who cared. He encouraged David to write often.

*****

It took a while to acclimate to the environment and security demands of the Pentagon, but in a few months, he was able to perform his job competently and have time for a social life. Sharing an apartment with Henry Wilson, a soldier he befriended who worked in security at the Pentagon, the quality of his day-to-day home life far exceeded life in the Plainview projects. A two-bedroom, two-bathroom space with an eat-in kitchen and a large living room with a large balcony was certainly better than a barracks or a shared apartment on base. Like David, Henry was athletic, and together they spent many weekend hours playing sports and enjoying the outdoor life in Maryland and the Chesapeake Bay area. His community included people of every race, color, and creed, including many military families. For David, the arrangement was perfect, and because most of the residents were relatively young, it was easy to make friends with individuals and families.

"Hi! My name is Rich, Rich Lee. This is my wife, Annabelle. We live on the first floor in number 168. We just moved in from Colorado a week ago. I've seen you around a couple of times since we moved in." Rich extended his hand and he and David greeted each other easily.

"I'm David. My roommate, Henry and I live in the building with the long front walkway with no parking. We've only been here a few months and we love it. I'm sure you and Annabelle will like it too."

"I like it already," said Annabelle, piping up with a cheery perkiness that was immediately attractive. "And what I like the most is that this small community is hidden from the road and that great shopping area with its funky little shops and grocery store by that dense stand of trees you cannot see through. It reminds me of home. It reminds me of a little of Colorado. I think we are going to like it here. Do you like trees, David?"

"I guess I like them well enough." *What an odd question to be asked by someone you've known for five minutes*, thought David.

"I happen to be very fond of trees and I'm always ready to talk about them and their relationship to a quality lifestyle. I am a professional arborist and will soon be looking for a job, or might even chance to start my own business. So if you know any landscapers or landscape architects, you might mention them to me or me to them."

"What do you do, Rich?"

D. A. GREY

"I studied electrical engineering at the University of Colorado and have been hired by a local company that is designing and manufacturing semiconductors."

"I worked for a small engineering company when I was in high school," said David.

"You worked for an engineering company in high school?" Rich asked with a legitimate amount of incredulity. "You can't be too long out of high school now. What did you do for them?"

"I started as a janitor and then began to assist the engineers who were mostly mechanical and civil. I learned to help with drawing and with some of the trig and calculus problems. It was a life-changing experience."

"For a high school student to be doing that kind of stuff is amazing. You were incredibly lucky."

"David, we have to go. Let's exchange phone numbers. We'll be in touch so we might finish the conversation." Each wrote down their numbers and exchanged them with every intention to follow through.

"Well, it was nice to meet you both, Annabelle and Rich," said David as he practiced the names of his new neighbors. "I hope to see you soon."

On his way back home, David thought about how much his experience had changed in the brief time he'd been away from home. He was now finding it increasingly easy to meet people, a social skill he had never been good at. It seemed to him that people who grew up in urban environments, and especially in the projects, on the whole saw the world in a different way than those who grew up in suburban or rural environments. David's experience was bracketed and defined by little space. Little space for clean or dirty clothes, for pots and pans and room to cook, for space on benches and space to walk without being harassed, or the space not to dodge the constant flow of people moving through. There were too many people, so he

92

learned to shut them out, to become blind to them so they would not be in his space, or challenge his sense of right and wrong or his personhood or his individual rights with violence or groupthink. He could not hide from the sound of the all too frequent police, fire, and ambulance sirens that constantly thundered back and forth, and the irrational horn honking that continued from early morning to late in the day, filling his emotional and mental space.

Snapping out of his free-associating reverie, David looked around and saw space. The trees, the lawn, the ability to take a walk all by yourself without having to spend energy ignoring the beggar or the hustler. He told the truth. He was really pleased to have met Rich and Annabelle. The environment made it easy. He was glad to be working for the Army and living where he was. Walking up his sidewalk, he opened his door and settled into a clean and comfortable chair. Taking a breath and without the pressure of necessity, he thought of the giftbook given to him by his unlikely friends at Heron Designs. *Where did I put it?* he asked himself. He then quit the chair, rummaged through his belongings, and retrieved the unopened package. For some reason, he had never been curious about the contents, but now he felt the urge. When he opened the package, the cover read *The Souls of Black Folk* by W.E.B. Du Bois. David heard of Du Bois, but if truth be told, he knew little or nothing about him or what he said, no more than he had known about the buffalo soldiers before he spent the time and energy finding out. More than that, here he was, a black man-child who knew nothing of how his own people thought about who he was. At home, he never really stopped to listen to the street-corner preachers who sometimes talked about the necessity of knowing your people's history or the teachers in high school who would say things like "If you don't know where you came from, you won't know where you're going." He never had even the slightest impulse to really think about these things.

As he opened the book, he saw a handwritten dedication by Johnathan.

> What follows is the story of a people and a great mind with the desire to carry the hopes of his people in his heart and his work. There will be others with his intelligence, strength of character, and commitment. We believe you could be one of them.

David was stunned. He sat there looking at the dedication, not knowing what to think or feel.

How could Johnathan have thought such a thing? How could he have thought I could carry the hopes of people I didn't even know? What he said was nice, but that is who he is. He always went out of his way to give me a boost. To make me feel I was doing an acceptable job. But this is different.

He felt no call to do the work of civil rights. Did Johnathan really mean what he said? David didn't know.

What David did know was that he would make an effort to become acquainted with Du Bois and what he thought. He opened the book to the preface and started to read.

As time passed, the inevitable formation of day-to-day habits eased David's and Henry's life as soldiers and friends. The energy required to adjust to military and social demands abated and left room for other things. There were disagreements and earnest talks about household responsibilities but none that went beyond what their military training had taught them. David and Henry were learning to live together without incident. Each assumed their respective duties without complaint. Henry was the consummate outdoorsman, and in the evenings after work, he would ride his bike, hike, or play basketball with others in the apartment complex. David spent considerable time in the evenings reading or hanging out with Henry when it was convenient. On Saturdays, they would play friendly baseball games against teams from other apartment complexes.

"David!" said Henry. "I want to remind you that we have a baseball game Saturday at ten o'clock with a team from the apartments on Red Admiral Way."

"I'll be ready to play," said David.

"If you've got your head in one of those books, I'll be sure to remind you." With David not mentioning he held the home run record in the town league during high school, Henry thought the triple David hit the previous week after striking out his first up to bat was a lucky hit. After all, Henry had organized the team, named it "The Rockets" and assumed the job of captain. He thought of himself as the real jock on the team and acted that way. He had not yet come to grips with the breadth of David's physical talents.

"I'll be sure to respond to your call," said David.

David woke early Saturday morning, made breakfast, and then sat down to read. After a night out, Henry woke up late and then scrambled to make it to the ball field on time.

"David!" said Henry as he hurried to ready himself. "It's time to go. Remember the game?"

"Okay, I'm ready."

They left the apartment together and made it to the field with enough time to warm up. Rich and other players from their complex were there, along with their wives and kids. It was thought that last week's game was won because of a fluke triple hit in the later innings. So the wives and kids came to give their team as much encouragement as possible, and that would require a great deal of rooting and cheering for support. The team they were playing called themselves the Yankees and had the reputation of being a good team that played with serious intensity and aggressiveness. By ten o'clock, the game began. The Rockets would bat first.

The first inning came and went, and by the end of the second inning, the Yankees were up by three runs. At the top of the third inning with two men on, David came to the plate and hit a home run down the third baseline and tied the score. Annabelle, who had gone to the dollar store and purchased some pom-poms that she shared with the Rockets' cheering section, went wild with enthusiasm and taunted the Yankees a little. In addition to an enthusiastic thank you for getting the Rockets back in the game, Henry and the others would say how lucky David was to again make a game-changing hit. The score was now tied, 3 to 3. With two more hits and a bobbled ball in center field, the man on third scored. The Rockets went up by one. Again, Annabelle and her confederates cheered wildly and taunted the Yankees. Henry could see the Yankees were getting bothered by Annabelle's jeers. Coupled with the fact that they were losing and getting frustrated, he asked her to dial it back a little, but she would not relent. By the bottom of the eighth, the Rockets were up by two, and the Yankees were making mistakes that were the cause of even more frustration. Annabelle continued to tease the Yankees players.

"Would you shut that bitch up?" said one of the Yankees pointing to Annabelle. She had really gotten under his skin.

Rich heard it and, in defense of his wife, approached the offender.

"First of all, she is not doing anything that would violate the rules of baseball. Second, the lady you were referring to is my wife. I think you owe her an apology for referring to her in those terms."

"Go fuck yourself and the boat you came in on, pal."

"I'm gonna ask you once more. Apologize to the lady."

"The bitch needs to shut up," he said again.

By this time, players had gathered around Rich and his adversary. A few of the Yankees were supporting their teammate's unwillingness to apologize for his slight. Tempers flared, and a tall muscular Yankee pushed Rich to the ground. Henry and David moved in close, trying to defuse the situation.

"Please, please stop," said Henry, holding up his hands in an attempt to prevent a violent altercation. "Let's forget it and finish the game." However, the aggressor had reached a level of anger that would not allow him to stop.

"You want some too?" said the aggressor, not knowing that Henry was in military security. When the man reached to hit him, Henry subdued him with a move that put his face in the dirt. Three others came after Henry, and David reflexively reacted. He dislocated the arm of one, slammed another to the ground with such speed and ferocity he could not breathe, and the third backed off and threatened from a distance with a bat. When he gathered his nerve and raised the bat to hit David, what he discovered after he was left helpless on the ground was that he was completely out of his league.

David turned to Rich and asked, "Rich, do you still want an apology?" Nodding in the affirmative, David grabbed the offender by the arm and then walked/dragged the man over to Annabelle, and she got an apology.

"I'm sorry, ma'am," he said as he sheepishly stared at the ground like a prepubescent offender.

Members of the Yankee team who had not been subdued were cowed and watched helplessly. At that point, it was clear to the Yankees that the Rockets would not be frightened or bullied by them. Without much discussion, everyone agreed the game was over and the Rockets had won.

Upon returning home from the game, the roommates talked about what had happened. Neither was happy about how they were forced to handle themselves. Both had been exposed in a way that might have a bearing on their jobs and the potential for disciplinary action. Neither wanted a reputation as a person with fighting skills because public knowledge of those skills might draw challenges. This kind of situation was probably unlikely, but talk of it would make it more likely. That evening, at a gathering of those at the game, there was a celebration for winning the game and much discussion about how the aggressors were left on the field licking their wounds. Then after all the conversation and expressions of amazement about how chivalrous Rich was and how amazingly Henry and David had handled themselves, Henry asked for everybody's attention so he might say a word and share his thinking. David was quiet.

"I know this is a party, but I have a couple of things I want to say and some I need to say. So can I please have your attention?" said Henry. The noise level abated, and those needing to finish speaking an idea or tell the punchline of a joke slowly settled down.

"First, let me say how pleased I am to be in a community that feels as good as this one does and being with people who I can easily call friends. I still think David's two home runs were lucky hits. I just can't imagine that someone who keeps his head in a book can also hit a baseball. Everything that happened today was a team effort, and we all need to be congratulated for being a team, including Annabelle who knows how to drive our opponents mad. So I lift my glass to the future success of the Rockets and to our community. It's important that we stay together and support each other in all the things that count. Finally, and I really need you to hear me on this." The noise caused by the good feelings and sense of comradery stopped, and everyone attended to Henry. "I need you to take what I'm about to say very seriously because it is in no way a joke. What happened this morning should not have happened. None of us wanted it to happen. People could have been badly hurt. Except for a dislocated arm, everybody walked away healthy. Some hurt feelings but healthy. It did not have to happen that way. It should be clear to you that David and I are trained. We are soldiers. We do not want to fight at home. We want to relax and be with our friends. We do not need people looking to fight us. There are a lot of crazy people in the world who want to fight because they have nothing else. It's like the old cowboy pictures, the fast gun shoots the bully. Others find out about it and want to challenge the fast gun, and another fight starts. Please, please don't mention what happened this morning to anyone. Don't talk about it. Deny you saw it or know anything about it. Call it an urban myth. It is important that you do this because David and I could find ourselves in trouble on the job. So I ask you for a vow of silence about what you saw." The room was silent. He asked again, "Will you vow before your friends not to mention a word of what happened?" He looked around the room into all the faces of their community.

"Is there anyone not willing to take such a vow?" Nobody raised a hand.

9

Valerie

The morning was filled with a few chores and some necessary errands if taken one at a time would seem small but taken together would consume considerable time. The screw that fits the nut that held the box holding the mail, the stamp that posted the mail, the items needed to repair the toilet, the return of a late library book, getting fresh uniforms from the cleaners, and buying dessert to take to today's community picnic all conspired to devour David's weekend morning. He recently received an invitation to join Annabelle and others at an afternoon gathering being held in honor of a friend who just moved to the Washington area.

The morning had been spent, and David was going to arrive late to the gathering. Still a young man, David had not yet developed the social maturity not to be agitated by a late arrival. The invitation said the party would start at two o'clock.

"Shit, I'm going to be late," he said, hurrying to bring his Saturday chores to completion. He looked at his watch. It read two fifteen, and he would still have to go home and prepare to attend. Because Henry was scheduled to work, David would be attending the party alone, and when he left the apartment, his watch read three o'clock.

Upon his arrival, he greeted the gathering and was well received by a group of men standing by the barbecue grill talking about sports. He waved to Annabelle, who caught his eye. It had been almost nine months since the incident with the Yankees, and as Henry had asked, no one ever talked about it. Nonetheless, an understated deference and respect were afforded to both Henry and him. They could see it. Never failing to wave or say hello, their neighbors often went out of their way to be nice, even when it was unnecessary or inappropriate. Both Henry and David enjoyed the attention and, when possible, returned with the same. It was much like a mutual admiration society. Once, after a few drinks, Henry said, "Check this out, it's like a family dog that enjoys being petted and cared for. The dog could be counted on to defend. You know, like what they call a quid pro quo. Take care of me, I'll take care of you."

David responded, "I don't like the canine example but I get your point, Henry. Still, the logic of the analogy is fairly accurate."

Annabelle and some of the other women transformed the yard and made it an attractive party place. Colorful crepe paper, balloons, paper tablecloths, and plenty of inviting things to eat festooned the space. As David stood with both hands supporting a large covered strawberry shortcake, one of the wives approached and guided him to a table so he could free his hands.

"How've you been, Claire? I haven't seen you for a while," said David.

"Well, I finally found a job as a research assistant at NIH. I have to get up early so I can beat the heavy traffic on the Beltway, and sometimes I have to stay a little late, so by the time I get home, all I want to do is sit down." Claire took a breath and a sip of her drink and started talking again. "I don't want to work, but if we are ever going to get that house we want, I have to work. And I don't know when we'll have time, energy, and money to start a family with Jeff working all the time too. You know, he should really slow down or he'll burn himself out. And…"

At that moment, Annabelle put her arm in David's, politely begged Claire's pardon, and walked David toward the other side of the yard.

"Did Claire drag you into every corner of her life?"

"She snagged me and was getting wound up when you saved me." David laughed. "She's got a real talent."

"I'm sure that one day you'll have the pleasure of knowing just how talented she is, but right now, I would like to take a stroll around the yard and talk to other people. Will you join me?" Before he could answer, Annabelle said, "I think I'd like a drink! How about you, David?"

"A drink would be nice. What do you want?"

"How about a beer?"

David walked to the cooler, reached to the bottom, and pulled out a very cold beer and a coke for himself. Together they walked and talked as Annabelle drank. Above the music and other conversation, David heard Rich's voice from across the yard saying, "Remember, David, she's taken. Unless you're really serious." They laughed and continued strolling until they stopped a short distance from a woman David had never seen before.

"David, have you met Valerie yet?" asked Annabelle.

"No," he answered, but when he saw her, his response was visceral.

As they approached, Valerie sensed that Annabelle was about to introduce her to the man she was walking with and was suspicious about her motives.

"David," she said. "I'd like you to meet my friend Valerie from Colorado. She came to DC to see if she could get some traction but has not yet decided where to live. She's been here a few weeks and has not met many people, so I thought I would introduce her to some."

He extended his hand as if it were an offering. "Hello Valerie. It's a pleasure. It is nice to have friends like Annabelle to help make hard transitions easier. Did you come because of a job?"

"No David. It is David?" He nodded in the affirmative. "No, I don't have a job. Maybe that would have been a better strategy. Instead, I came hoping to find one, but I have not really started looking yet."

"Are you trained in something specific? Or are you interested in anything in particular?"

"I'm from Colorado, so my interests tend to lean in the direction of outdoor activities. You know, biking, hiking, skiing, rafting, that kind of stuff. I just graduated from college with a political science degree but really have no idea what to do with it."

"I've always played sports," said David, "but I don't know if it could be considered an interest. They were just always there. My roommate Henry is also into the outdoors. I've started hanging with Henry and have come to like that stuff. And maybe I've come to see outdoors activities as sport."

"Where I come from, most people do some kind of out-of-doors activity. I think they consider it sport," said Valerie.

"In fact," added David, "We're going canoeing on the Chesapeake next week. Would you like to come? Annabelle, if you and Rich are available, it would be great if you could come along."

"Valerie! We even have a neighborhood baseball team. You should come out sometime. It's a lot of fun. David and Henry are great." Giving Valerie the eye, Annabelle bumped into David and said, "Carry on, bro," and excused herself to talk to another guest, leaving David and Valerie to get to know each other.

"You're a very interesting-looking woman," said David. Valerie was in shape and had long semicurly hair, a smooth ruddy complexion, and high cheekbones that would draw anyone's attention.

Valerie bristled, as if David had uttered a profanity that she despised.

"No, no. I don't think you understand. Of course, you're beautiful, but that's not what I meant. I meant that I'm having trouble putting you in an ethnic category." He was initially disconcerted by Valerie's flash of anger but immediately understood it and recovered.

"Believe me, it was not a vacuous pickup line. It was honest curiosity. Look at the variety of people at the party. We seem to represent a lot of different ethnic histories. I'm told, for example, that my mother was beautiful. She was half Native American and half black. My father's mother was black. I look the way I do because of it. Your look is interesting in the same way."

"I apologize for the flare-up, David. Ever since I was a teenager, men of all kinds have been after me because of the way I look. Over time, I've become very defensive and often nasty when it happens. I'm sorry you had to see that part of my experience."

"Don't give it another thought. I'm still interested in your ethnic background."

"Okay, here it is. My mother was a full-blooded Arapaho Indian, and my father is the son of a black cowboy. I was raised on the reservation until I was ten years old. My Mother called me Supriya, which means beloved. When my mother died, I moved to Denver with my father and his wife. My father is a mining engineer and civil rights advocate, and she heads up a small foundation that provides educational and travel grants for Native Americans."

"Somehow I can see political science in your future. By the way, would you like a beer or a drink of some kind?"

Valerie smiled at the thought of a beer. David went to the cooler, grabbed two beers, and snagged two chairs along the way. After a satisfying swig of her beer, Valerie suggested that she and David's mother had something in common. They were both Native American and black. She also wondered if David's mother identified as Native American or black. Or as both, as she did.

"I don't really know. I never met her. If I had to guess, it was likely black. She always lived as a black person, and given the history of racism in the country, I don't think she had a choice."

"She died in childbirth with me. My father took me home from the hospital and he never left me."

She paid close attention to his expression and the way he phrased his relationship with his father and intuitively knew there were painful things in David's childhood that he felt the need to obfuscate.

"I did love my father, but he's also gone. I lost him soon after I finished high school."

"I'm sorry to hear that. Losing a parent you love can be devastating. Different people deal with it differently. My mother's culture is a family-orientated one. People work hard to recoup a family if they have lost one. Having a partner is very important."

In the family culture where Valerie was raised, woman talked a lot about how to get a man. She in some ways was preprogrammed to ask the question she thought might be inappropriate in the present circumstance. Nonetheless, she could not stop herself from asking. Also aware she would in part be fulfilling Annabelle's motivations, she asked, anyway.

"David, how do you feel about marriage?"

Noticeably retracting, he felt repelled.

"That seemed to come out of the blue," said David. "What do you mean? We just met. I have no intentions or any reason to feel any way about marriage." David was surprised by the question. It didn't seem to have a foundation, and he was disturbed by it. He had been here before. *All women think about is marriage*, he thought.

"I didn't mean relative to me. It was a general question and aimed at no one in particular. If you had ever considered it, I thought it might be interesting. Please don't be upset. I was not collecting data. I was simply being conversational."

"Growing up as I did offered no opportunity to see marriage up close and personal. To use your words, I have little data for or against. I have never witnessed the textures and contours of it. Except for very few examples, most of the marriages I've seen have been unhealthy ones. So how do you feel about it?"

"My girlfriends never believed me, but I don't think I ever want to be married," said Valerie.

"Now that's different!" said David. "Very different."

Sitting in low chairs with legs and feet stretched out on the grass, they sat quietly and, for a few moments, enjoyed the atmosphere and watched the kids throw balls and parents practice parenting. They watched as ketchup and mustard were applied to burgers and hot dogs, half eaten and dropped on the ground. Teetering cups of whatever there was to drink competed with watermelon seeds being spat as loud laughter and earnest conversation spilled their textures into the ether, supplying the ingredients for the elixir that filled the late afternoon with a relaxing blanket of joy.

"Welcome to Washington, Valerie. By the way, what is your last name?"

"It's Olephant, Valerie Olephant. And what's yours?"

"Walton, David Walton."

"I'm going to give you my number, Valerie Olephant. Call, whatever the reason, and let me know if it's okay for me to call you. Also, remember to check with Annabelle about canoeing."

David lifted himself off the lawn chair and turned to offer Valerie a hand. "This is the second time today you've offered me your hand." David searched for meaning in what she said. At that moment, he could find none. He helped Valerie to her feet, and together they walked toward a small group of adults and joined the conversation. As they turned their attention to the people in attendance, the day dangled in twilight, enriched by party lights that embraced the two strangers and their friends.

10

A Serious Challenge

"Captain, you wanted to see me?"

"Come in, Walton." Standing behind his desk, Captain Higgs looked stern and harried, in contrast to his normal look—serious with a smile. "As you know, we have been shorthanded for a month now, and it will be another few weeks before we are returned to our full complement of analysts. We got Sergeant Cohan sent over by headquarters, but he will be here for only a few more weeks. What makes matters worse is that I requested and have been granted a furlough to resolve some pressing family matters. I've asked that you be put in charge of keeping this unit running smoothly with the same degree of diligence I would expect. This is a very serious responsibility, but I think you can handle it. Are you up for the challenge?"

"Yes sir." David responded with a crisp salute. "You can count on me sir, and I hope for your swift return."

"Walton, this is a lot of responsibility for an E-4. Some are betting against you," he said with a look intended to suggest a challenge. "Is there anything you would like from me before I leave?"

"Yes, Captain. There are those in the department who out-rank me. I would like you to speak to the unit and inform them of my primacy in your absence."

During the next week and beyond, David was in a state of strained attention, hyper aware of every piece of collected information that might link in some direct, tangential, or predictive way. Information that might shape or begin to shape a pattern of activity or concern that needed attention. He came early and stayed late, communicating with analysts and meeting with others with whom he might share the benefits of cross-fertilization.

When pulling a file needed to investigate political activity between two countries in the Middle East, it became apparent to David that the ME-6 file he needed for his investigation was incomplete, as some materials were missing. Consequently, he had to shelve that investigation and turn to another until the material he needed was found.

That evening, David returned home with much on his mind.

"You seem to be distracted, David. Is there something on your mind?" Have you had a bad day?"

Addressing her as Miss Olephant, David said, "I've had a busy day and encountered a problem that concerns me, but there's no reason to give my temporary distraction a second thought. Tonight, what I would like best is to concentrate on you."

"David Walton, you talk differently than any man I have ever met. You're so formal. Sometimes when you talk with me, I feel like I'm the heroine in a Henry James novel. But it's no criticism," she said.

"I love it when our conversations sound like that. It makes me feel valued and respected. Those are the times when I want you most," she said in a semi come-hither way. Then with her eyes resting softly on his, she forgot her dinner and moved toward him with a face and body expression that let him know that all she was belonged to him. Sitting sideways on David's lap, she gently wrapped her arms around his neck and kissed him on the nose. Of all the attractive attributes Valerie had, her style of flirting and sincere coquettishness always connected with David easily. It always seduced him into a happy pursuit.

"If you keep it up, we'll have to speed up the consumption of this lovely dinner."

"I wouldn't object to that," said Valerie.

"The sound of 'we' does no harm to my sensibilities," said David as he put down his fork and tried to look through Valerie's eyes and into her heart. Not just a look into her heart, but it was an effort to decode the depths of his own heart. The only person he had loved unconditionally was his father, but his father's love was not actively demonstrable. It was assumed because it was there and because he was there, steadfast and ever-present. Might that kind of love be different than the love you have for a woman? He never knew his mother, so he never felt the daily impact of a mother's love or the daily expression of that love and the thousand ways it showed itself in kindness, style, and discipline. He never learned to carry or give that kind of love and he wondered if the kindness and physical attraction he and Valerie clearly showed each other was the kind of love that would last.

"What were you thinking just now, David?"

"Only how much I adore you and what that means for me." David would have to find out the answers to his questions for himself; divulging them would only confuse Valerie.

The next day, David sat at his station contemplating the missing material from the ME-6 file that he had been unable to find the day before. However, when he opened the file, there it was, not organized according to protocol but there. His immediate supposition that a filing mistake had been made and corrected, but he later thought to check who had used the file and to check their understanding of how and when information should be returned. When he inquired into who used the file, he found that no one had used it. He then walked back to his desk and noted his potential misperception.

On Thursday of the next week, another ME file was reported incomplete by another analyst. And as before, when the file was pulled the next day, the material was there in the appropriate format. This second incident was recorded with the first. David's suspicion grew, and he was sure someone in his unit was the culprit. To find out, he trained a hidden camera directly on the filing kiosk.

At the end of the following day, Sergeant Cohen said he would be leaving late because he had a few things to clean up. When David checked the footage in the morning, he saw Sergeant Cohen pulling a file and putting it in his pants, covering it with his shirt, and walking out without a briefcase. The next morning, David checked with security and discovered Cohen had reentered the building, stating he had forgotten his briefcase and needed to retrieve it. Not knowing if Cohen was using his pants or his briefcase to transport files was immaterial to David. His sense of intrigue and fearlessness got the best of him, so rather than reporting it right away, he decided to follow Cohen. But before he did, he took notes on what he'd discovered and backed them up with the film footage he had of Cohen taking files clandestinely.

David rented a car and enlisted the help of his ex roommate Henry, and they staked out Cohen's apartment for the weekend. Though Saturday saw no movement in or out, at nine fifteen Sunday morning, Sergeant Cohen left his apartment. David followed him to a converted government warehouse now called the People's Temple of the Worldwide Pentecost. Because Cohen did not know David's roommate, Henry followed him into the church service and sat directly behind him. The sanctuary was a large space that quickly filled with people of many backgrounds and ages from all over the Capitol area. The first service lasted for seventy-five minutes with the vice ministers, choir, and musicians seated behind the lectern. As the parishioners filed out, Henry followed Cohen, who stopped and nodded to one of the vice ministers. People were swarming, but the crowd slowly began to file out.

"May I help you, sir?" asked the vice minister while standing alongside Cohen as bodies with choir robes moved back and forth.

Henry groped for an answer and immediately said, "No, I'm waiting for Sister Evege." He took a chance that there was no woman named Evege in the congregation. There was also a very good chance that if there was, neither one of them would know it. After all, he thought, the likelihood that the vice minister would concentrate more on the business of the church and less on knowing every member of the congregation was pretty good. "I'm supposed to meet her around here. I'll just wait until she comes. That was a great service. I saw you sitting behind the minister. Do you also preach?"

"I'm glad you enjoyed it. My name is Reverend Wilcox, and I preach sometimes." Even in his robe, one could clearly see that Reverend Wilcox was a well-dressed man with a baritone voice that had a practiced sound. You could tell he had spent many years influencing people or spreading the Gospel or both. He paused and then said, "I'm sure Sister Evege will be around presently." The focus was now on the reverend, and even though the chances that he knew a Sister Evege were small, faking a knowledge of her supported the illusion that he knew his parishioners.

To get something observable to give to David, Henry said, "Can I get a picture of you, Reverend Wilcox? Sir"—he motioned to Cohen—"you can get in the picture too." Cohen was pleased to accommodate.

Both stood smiling as Henry took the picture. He found it difficult to comprehend the thoughtless hubris required to allow such a photograph. "Thank you, gentlemen," said Henry, trying to feign some semblance of graciousness and eliminate any suspicion, though what he felt was quite different. His mind was on what his next move would be if there was suspicion.

As the two men turned and moved toward a room, Henry waited. Soon he could hear a copy machine, followed by Cohen walking out of the room with telltale papers visibly protruding out of a pocket that his jacket failed to cover. Henry walked in the other direction, through the front door of the church, and alerted David to watch for Wilcox as people streamed out of the church. Given the description, David waited and watched as the good reverend entered his car with a manila folder and a Bible under his arm as if it was just another Sunday. David followed Wilcox for thirty minutes until Wilcox stopped his car half a block from the Israeli embassy. Before long, a well-dressed man walked out of the embassy toward the car Reverend Wilcox was driving. The man smiled as he reached through the open driver's side window and Wilcox handed the man the folder. David snapped a picture. The man said a few words and quickly walked away.

On Monday morning, David was lucky enough to get a meeting with the appropriate brass. Lieutenant Colonel Howie, Captain Higgs, and two other officers walked into the conference room without fanfare and sat down.

"What's so important, son? Why did you interrupt my morning?" said Colonel Howie.

"Well, sir, let me get right to the point." He cleared his throat and began to report what he'd discovered. He covered every detail of the espionage, leaving nothing out, including names, locations, and pictures from the theft of the file to the delivery of the specific file to the man who turned out to be the administrative secretary at the Israeli embassy.

"Is anyone else aware of what you've discovered?" asked Colonel Howie.

"The only other person who knows anything about what I've reported to you is my roommate, Sgt. Henry Wilson, who works in Pentagon Security. Without him, I would not have been able to follow my hunch."

"Captain!" said Colonel Howie, speaking to his staff officer. "Bring Sergeant Wilson to my office immediately."

"Does anyone who works in your unit know anything about this, son?"

"Not a soul, sir."

"Listen, Walton, you are to carry on as if nothing has changed since before your foolish investigation. Do not share a word of what you discovered. If you do, trouble will find you. Also, I'm sure you understand that following the perpetrators was unwise, not only because it was extremely dangerous but also because it may have violated the chain of command. You should have reported it immediately upon suspicion. We know of your martial arts skills, Walton. However, I know nothing of your skill with small arms. So just in case you decide to ignore me and go off on another unsanctioned investigation, I want you to report to the pistol range at least twice a week and develop respectable skills. Captain Higgs will handle the details."

"Yes, sir," answered David.

"Thank you for your good work, Corporal Walton. You are excused."

David stood, saluted, did an about-face, and left the room.

*****

Summer had all but ended, and David could begin to feel the shorter days and cooler air threatening to paint the foliage. Time had changed the atmosphere that rolled across the Chesapeake and began to bring the long hot days of the Washington summers to an end. The seasonal crowds diminished, and the denizens of government could be seen more clearly without being masked by the virus of visitors who fueled the city's economy and helped make it a destination. The summer months had been transformational in the life of David Walton. And like the season, his life was about to settle down. But among those things not changing was his single-minded commitment to the pistol range and the laser-like focus he gave to aikido.

*****

When Valerie plopped down on the couch, she leaned forward so David could place a pillow behind her for more support and then lifted her legs so she could stretch out. David got up to get something cool to drink from the kitchen.

"Have you heard from Henry?" she asked from the couch.

"It's strange that you ask. I forgot to tell you I heard from him yesterday. He said he's still flying high because of the promotion and pay increase. He's really enjoying the time with his family and went on and on about not being here today. A little bird told me when he comes back, he'll be reassigned and will wind up in an administrative job. Maybe in LA or NYC."

"Who told you that, Sergeant Walton?"

"Divulging secrets, I can't do, Miss Olephant."

"Sgt. David Walton. Now that has a nice sound. Almost as nice as Daddy. And how many kids will have a father who has received the Army Distinguished Service Medal?" said Valerie.

"While standing there listening to the wonderful things Colonel Howie and others said about my work ethic, integrity, and patriotism, I started to get a little nervous. They couldn't have been talking about me. And when he pinned this medal on me?" David looked down at his breast and fingered the medal with his right hand. "I felt unworthy. All we did was follow an avaricious asshole to church. But when I saw you in the audience smiling, I have to admit, I was filled with pride and wanted you to be proud." He thought of his father standing on the bleachers with his arms straight up in the air and his fingers pointed toward the sky and could hardly hold back his emotions and deep spiritual wish that he could let his father know that the medal was given in recognition of his achievement.

"I was about to burst with pride," Valerie said as David handed her a glass of iced tea.

"Thanks for the drink David. What a week we spent in New York. Your commendation, promotion, and medal will be one of the high points, and that first visit to New York will always be a standout memory for me. It all seems like a dream. It was spring, and I wasn't showing then. Other than DC, Denver was the only city I'd seen. Without the opportunity to leave Colorado, I'd built my images and understanding of Manhattan on pictures, but the reality of it was astonishing. There are places in Colorado where nature wraps itself around you, and somehow you become integrated and part of it. The only other time in my life I've felt that way about humanity's integration into nature as being a beautiful thing was in Central Park."

"I suspect what you're talking about is something that has to be seen and then felt," said David, who felt himself admiring the emotional sensitivity that he had heard comes with pregnancy.

"I don't know. I've gotten it while reading works from some writers."

"Like who?" asked David, whose interest in reading worthwhile writers had grown immensely. He had developed the habit of investigating writers he thought he should know. Valerie was well read. He adored her for that, and he wondered if what she was reading might be interesting or informative for him. Or might it be something that had to do with pregnancy or delivery? Was pregnancy affecting her choice of reading material?

Valerie began to talk about John Muir, the environmental philosopher who could pour the wonder of nature onto your eyes and have it leave a lasting impression on your heart and some of the poems by people like James Whitcomb Riley, who could take an ordinary fall day with a pumpkin and turn it into a hymn or meditation that produced a breathless romantic experience.

"Those are cases in which the individual is titillated into a state of rapture. That day in Central Park was different. It was magical and held the wide-eyed hopes of humanity in its arms. It was not an individual thing. The park itself held our good and essential nature and let it unfold for all to see. It made us all a part of it. A dozen distinct cultures in their native dress strolled together and watched with welcoming eyes as they were being watched. There is wisdom to be found in mature elms, oaks, and a hundred other hardwood varieties as they spread their massive limbs to embrace us. On that day, the dappled sunlight provided a spiritual texture to the malls and lanes that led to fountains, lakes, statues and the history of nature and art," she said.

"If I never return, I will still carry a piece of it with me always."

"Wow, you got all of that from sitting in Central Park?"

"And more," said Valerie.

"How are your legs feeling, sweetheart?" David asked. He lacked a male role model to show him how to behave, but he had seen characters on TV behave that way toward their pregnant wives.

"My legs are fine," she said.

David sighed. "While I was thinking about Central Park, I felt it might be nice to spend a few hours at the National Mall and read a little about some of the wonderful buildings and scenes around us. The beach chairs are in the car, and all we need is a blanket in case it gets nippy and some grub. What d'ya say? You in?"

David's broad smile was all she needed, and he walked while she waddled to the car, and they drove to the mall and talked as they read about the history of the Washington Monument and the Lincoln Memorial.

"History is fine," said David, "but I think it's time to think about the new addition to our relationship. It's time to start turning the second bedroom into a nursery. We will need a great many things. It's funny how I still think of it as Henry's room, but it will soon belong to a brand new Walton."

"I think it might be time to talk about names. I haven't thought about it in any meaningful way," said David."

"If you have no objection, I always thought that if I ever had a boy, I would want to name it after my maternal grandfather," said Valerie.

"It depends. I don't think I want a son called Geronimo."

"Don't be silly, you nut. Why would I name a child Geronimo? Unless I, like you, were a little nuts. By the way, Geronimo was Chiricahua Apache. My family is Arapaho.

"Of course, you know I was joking."

"In the Arapaho pueblo where I lived with my mother and grandparents, my grandfather was a tribal elder and was respected by everybody. His name was Joshua Walkingstick, and I loved him very much. He was the keeper of the pueblo's tradition, and I thought Joshua would be a nice name for our son."

"If I followed your lead and suggested the name of a person I loved or respected, two names come to mind. My father, John, would be one. Another would be the mentor who taught me how to think about being focused. His name is Johnathan," said David.

"It seems you have two Johns," said Valerie. "You do know that Johnathan is a contraction of John and Nathan?"

"I never thought of it like that. So if you combined our suggestions, what we have is Joshua John Walton. What do you think?"

"It's a great name, David. Anyway, this is going to be a great kid. And a rose by any other name…," she said.

"I love our optimism," said David. "By the time this kid is ten, he'll be enrolled at Princeton."

"What a great notion. But I want to warn you. Every ten-year-old I knew in college, and I've known two, have been a little different," she said sarcastically.

As they sat on the grass-covered mall looking toward the Lincoln Memorial, the sun moved slowly toward the horizon, cooling the late afternoon as they, like a few others, admired the majesty of the memorial.

"A penny for your thoughts?" asked David.

A loud silence hung in the space before she spoke. Then she answered.

"I am a Native American woman. I am a black woman. I am the remains of an attempted extermination and a product of complete domination and abuse. I am what most white people want to forget. They want to forget their selfish greed and justifications for enslaving a people "by any means necessary." For me, it's impossible not to be constantly aware of who

I am. America's original sins have deeply scared my conscious and unconscious life. If there is a Great Spirit or a God, I hope they bless America and its hopeful continuation toward a more perfect union."

For a few minutes, all that could be heard was the ambient sounds of the surrounding streets. David hung his head, trying to process the profound things Valerie just articulated. She was right about who she was, and he had never seen that truth as clearly as she just spoke it. Discomfort was the least of what he felt, and he knew his job was to fill in the gaps in his ignorance.

"What do you feel when you see that great memorial David?"

A thoughtful moment passed.

"I like you have heard Lincoln's words almost all of my life, but I have come to know this country has not dedicated itself to the proposition that all men are created equal. It is a myth, not a fact. It is carved in the granite of the memorial as if it were the truth. Many Americans and nearly half the politicians in the US Congress don't really believe it and yet, we like to repeat the myth and wave it like a flag. Like Lincoln, I do hope that those who have given their lives to make the myth a reality did not die in vain."

Grasping hands, the two of them sat on the grass looking at the memorial, quietly pondering whether the strength of the sentiment it expresses would ever become a reality.

Driving home, the conversation continued and then shifted to the baby's bedroom.

"I think the crib should not be put on the windowed wall. Maybe it should be on the adjacent wall with a changing table next to the bed. The dresser might be best on the opposite wall. We could put up some colorful pictures and other baby things," suggested Valerie.

"I have no experience with any of this, so I'll follow your lead Valerie. If I do have a suggestion, I'll let you know," said David.

"What I do know is that it's time to get ready. We only have six weeks before I deliver."

What Valerie didn't know was that their friend Annabelle had already organized a baby shower that David hoped would supply many of their needs. He also hoped he had not given Valerie a reason to suspect the surprise.

*****

Josh was less than a year old when Valerie announced she was pregnant again. The year had passed quickly. Josh was now walking and Valerie found a job. Annabelle and two other women in the apartment complex took care of babies and kids under five years old, making the potential expense and inconvenience of day care a non issue. For Valerie and David, all of the specific and amorphous dreams they could muster poured into the daily life of Joshua John Walton. He, like the two of them, was loved unconditionally and attended to when the need arose. And now the family would be expecting another member. Josh would have a brother, someone else with whom he could negotiate the life of the family and the world outside. He would not be alone or without guidance or someone he could play with. Josh would have a brother and he would be called Lynn after his maternal grandfather, Lynn Olephant.

11

The Job

David walked out of the bathroom half-dressed and with toilet paper stuck to his face to stop the bleeding caused by recklessly shaving in a hurry. He wanted to see Valerie before she left for her first day at her new job at the Kirkland Publishing Company. As she prepared to leave, David said, "You are a remarkable sight. If looks were all that counted, you would be the president of the company in a year."

"You always say that kind of thing David, but seriously, how do I look?"

"Valerie, you will definitely be noticed. I can't imagine anyone more attractive than you."

"I just hope my boss thinks I'm dressed okay for the job. I really don't know what to expect."

"Unlike the military, I don't think you have a serious dress code, and given that the publication you will be working for has an out-of-doors, nature-type orientation, I'll bet you will find a culture that is a little less formal than you think. But whatever happens with how you dress, I'm sure you will do just fine being who you are."

"Remember, I'll only be the secretary to one of the editors."

"Yeah, but everybody has to start somewhere, and when they find out how much you know, that job title won't last long."

"Well, I want to get an early start, so if travel takes longer than I think, I'll be on time."

David kissed Valerie, wished her luck, gave her a hug, and watched her leave. He finished the morning prep with the kids and followed her out the door a half hour later.

The large sign reading "Kirkland Publishing Company" was visible above the building's entrance at least two blocks away. As Valerie approached, not knowing what to expect, she was anxious. The initial interview had gone well, and the second interview went even better.

I don't know why I'm feeling anxiety like this, she said to herself while walking. *I liked the people and they seemed to like me. But why this nervousness? Maybe because it's my first real job as a college graduate. My life as a professional will begin today.* And with that, she composed herself, entered the building, and walked toward the first gatekeeper.

"Good morning. My name is Valerie Olephant. This is my first day of work, and I was told to come here and there would be a package waiting for me with instructions as to what to do next."

"Welcome to Kirkland, Ms. Olephant. You are in the right place. Here is your employment portfolio. Your next stop will be a visit to Human Resources. We hope you like it here."

The receptionist looked to be about Valerie's age and had a flair for seriousness and sophistication that would make a newcomer to Kirkland leave their casual foolishness behind and behave like a professional. When she arrived at HR, she was greeted by another receptionist who asked her to take a seat and said someone would be with her soon.

"Valerie Olephant?" inquired the well-dressed woman who approached her with a pleasant smile. Extending her hand in welcome, she said, "My name is Ann Magillacutty. I will be with you most of today and in the future. If you need HR for any reason, I will be the person you consult with." With that, the two ladies walked into an adjoining room, and the business of the day began. Valerie sat all day filling out the information thought necessary. The next day, she would spend time with her boss, Jocelyn Miller, editor of *Outdoor Adventures*.

Later Valerie told David that Jocelyn Miller thought of herself as an educator, and belived a significantly difficult and enjoyable experience of any kind helps transform a person or helps to clarify what it is they do not wish to do again. Equally important, demanding physical experience helps an individual understand their ability to expand limits and push through to a stated goal. The underlying assumption of the magazine was pushing physical limits can often teach more than academic learning. A "can do" spirit learned from physical challenges can help achieve success in any endeavor. *Outdoor Adventures* was the vehicle she wanted to use to get that message to the general population.

After a few months of working at Kirkland Publishing and getting to know her boss and the company culture, Valerie's boss, Jocelyn Miller, called.

"Valerie, did you get the response from the Teton climbers? They will have to get the final draft back by week's end, or the article will not make it into the spring edition."

"Boss, I sent that letter out last week, and I'm waiting for a response."

"Valerie, if you don't stop calling me boss, I'm gonna banish you to the mail room."

"Maybe it's time for us to be assertive and give the guy a call. You do have his number, don't you? And if you do, why don't I have it? Look, boss, I am here to do the stuff that will make your job easier. But you've got to share information with me so I can push the right buttons when they need to be pushed. If you don't work at helping me, I can't help you and maybe I belong in the mail room."

"Here's the number," said Jocelyn, as if exasperated. "And please stop the melodrama. It's so beneath you. There's a folder in the second drawer of my desk," she said as she hurried from her office on her way to the weekly editorial meeting. "There are two letters from people who would like us to cover them on some proposed adventures. Call them and make appointments. I'll see you when I get back."

Jocelyn was not a relaxed person, and no matter how hard Valerie tried to slow her down, the next day was always more of the same. But somehow, with Valerie's assistance, every two months, the magazine was published on time. The subscription base was burgeoning, and the newsstands and bookstores sent very few copies back. From all industry accounts, *Outdoor Adventures* under Jocelyn's leadership had become a successful publication with credit given to the team of people that made it possible. This included Valerie Olephant who, because of her natural inclination toward the outdoors, was beginning to participate as an on-site coordinator for potential stories for the magazine.

*****

Dinner was done and the children were getting ready for bed when Valerie said, "David, I have a surprise for you, and you're gonna love this one."

"Please don't tell me you're pregnant."

"Honey, that's the last thing I'd tell you. If it were true, I would have already done something about it."

"You, my dear, are a most sensible woman!" David said with a broad smile, kissing her on the forehead.

"You couldn't possibly guess, so I'll just tell you." But before she could tell him, David ventured a guess.

"I know. Your parents are coming."

"No, that's not it. It's much better," she said with a level of excitement she could hardly contain. "Jocelyn walked into the office today and handed me an envelope. I thought it was something she wanted me to follow up on. I was busy, so I laid the envelope on the desk and continued working. Jocelyn left the room, and an hour later, I opened the envelope. You would not believe what I found."

"What? What?" David asked. "I can't stand the suspense. What was in the envelope?"

Valerie reached into her pocket and handed David a folded envelope with a letter inside. David opened the letter and skimmed what was written. "Dear Valerie, because you have been much more than I expected, your job title and responsibilities will change, and you will receive a twenty-percent increase in salary."

David stood holding the letter while showing genuine happiness and pride he could not contain. He leaned back against the wall and pulled Valerie into his arms.

"You are much more than I could have ever expected," he said with the letter in hand as he enfolded Valerie in a gentle hug. "I knew sooner or later, Jocelyn would come to appreciate what I have known since we first met. She is lucky to have you, and so am I."

Valerie stepped back from David and, with a finger slightly touching her lip, smiled a childlike smile. She was amazing, and to him, that moment was truly heaven-sent.

Nine months later

"Valerie, I've been talking to a couple of river rats who want to start a white-water rafting company. They've both rafted the world's great rivers and have also done a great deal of rock climbing with instructor certification in both. They need a boost to kick-start their new commercial endeavor. They think our publication would be just the right vehicle to illuminate their approach as an educational adventure. They have two ideas. One is to advertise a raffle for adults who have little or no experience with river rafting or rock climbing. Sixteen winners will embark together with instructors on a ten day river-rafting and rock climbing adventure. I like the idea because it dovetails nicely with my thinking about how adventure based learning is a powerful tool that supports other kinds of learning. The second idea is to write a piece about how the trip was experienced. The testimonials we get after the experience might help give the rafting company a boost getting their business started. It might also be good for the magazine. With your experience, I think you should go along and take notes on what a trip with them would actually be like. I'll be sending a writer/photographer along who will compose the article for possible publication. You will support him in every way you can. The entire trip should take ten days or so. Consider it a vacation."

"But what about David and the children?" she asked.

"We have two months before plans are finalized. See if you can arrange something. Let me know as soon as you can. Such a trip will put you in good stead professionally."

"I'll see what I can do, Jocelyn."

Valerie told David of her conversation with Jocelyn, and they discussed how they might make it happen. As usual, childcare days would be covered by their friend and neighbor, Annabelle. Annabelle agreed to watch the children until David got home from the Pentagon, even if he ran late. David would care for them in the evening and deliver them to Annabelle again in the morning. The weekend presented no problem because David would be home.

Two weeks later, preparations for the white-water rafting trip were complete. David was excited that Valerie could now travel for her job. She read Jocelyn's final note to the entire staff out loud to David. "The excursion will take six rafts, including two supply rafts, each with a professional guide. Representing *Outdoor Adventures*, Valerie Olephant and writer/photographer Tony Batone will join the party. Let's hope this one is a home run."

"By the way," David asked, "who is Tony Batone?"

"I never met him, but he's a freelancer with a great reputation. I read one of his articles published in the Smithsonian and thought it was really well done."

"He sounds like a real pro. Being able to work with someone like that is a stroke of luck," said David.

"I think Valerie wants me to watch and learn. You know, I was a fairly good notetaker in college, but I've never taken notes about how nature makes you feel. I think Jocelyn is looking for a female perspective."

"If I had to guess, I would say she's probably looking for material that will draw people toward the possibility of going on a trip with the rafting company. Female or not, you have the ability to bring a love of the natural world into the human perspective and give the relationship between people and nature added value. However, if I remember correctly from one of our previous conversations, Jocelyn wants the experience to be in part educational. Whatever else she wants, make sure you do that. It sounds like the adventure will not be easy, and when people come through difficult experiences, it changes them. It gives them a certain kind of power or wisdom. Tony, whatever his name is, will likely find that he lucked out working with you."

"You are so sweet, David." Then getting back to her more immediate concern, she said, "Are you going to take care of my babies and be good while I'm gone?"

Valerie returned eleven days later with two notebooks full of written material that, once partially cleaned and organized, provided some of the raw material for her contribution to the article. David knew Valerie would regale him with the details of her adventure, but for that, he could wait until she was rested and ready. For now, he wanted to skim what she had written and talk about her collaboration with the photo journalist. With some hesitation, she handed over the notebook. With the notebook in hand, David asked about her partner on the trip.

"So how was Tony Matain?" he asked.

"His name is Tony Batone," said Valerie in a tone that might have had an almost imperceptible edge. David noticed but said nothing and waited for an answer. When none came, he opened the notebooks to scan what she had written. It was clear that the speed required to write what was happening at the moment produced almost illegible script. But in the short time since packing up and returning, Valerie had rewritten some of her observations and made them legible and coherent. She finished enough for David to achieve a glimpse into what had been experienced. But by no means did she finish the job of transposing all she had written. Adjusting to her writing required some effort, but soon what looked like scribbles began to take on meaning. It was clear from the heft of the notebooks that she had taken her job seriously. Some of the notebook had descriptions of what the rafters experienced. Other parts recorded how participants felt about the experience.

> Single-engine flights between Salt Lake City and Brown's Landing. Bumpy flight/a few people got sick in transit (Picture of brown's landing)
> Instructors are lovely people, articulate, warm, smart, considerable teaching abil-

ity, and humor enough to make everybody comfortable.

Four rafts and four people in each raft, each raft scheduled for KP duty and biv-ouacking. First evening—long and tiring. Uncomfortable gear, hard ground, but with luminous sun and a sky infinitely garnished by twinkling stars. (Picture, night sky)

First morning: awake at 5:00 AM, break-fast, pack dunnage bags, which will keep personal items dry over next 10 days.

Learn fundamentals of rafting through deep canyons—imagination of participants outclassed by surrounding canyons.

After lunch: 10-20 knot upstream wind, fighting hard for every yard gained. Three sets of difficult and dangerous rapids. Requires considerable effort. (Picture negoti-ating Rapids)

In upstream estuary by 7:00 PM, take cold bath in river, night is cold, bodies are sore with a few cuts and scratches. Sleep on hard ground but thankful for it.

Second morning: woke at 5:00 AM, eat, pack, prepare rafts.

Tough stretch of white water called Desperation Rapids—we stopped to scout what John Wesson Powell in 1869 called Hell's Half Mile. This half-mile stretch of river twists and snarls at the raft, bathing us with a constant deluge of water. We strain our muscles to the limit of our endurance but are triumphant. (Picture of Hell's Half Mile taken from above)

Fifth morning: we look for portage near the confluence of the Green and Yampa rivers. At a magnificent point called steamboat rock, we disembark and prepare for a day of climbing.

The rock face is steep and scary. Everyone is horrified. The instructor makes the first climb. We are all horrified but afraid to say so.

Terry (a housewife) said, "The tremendous amount of energy it took to make progress tore at the muscles of my hands, arms, shoulders, and legs. My feet failed to find a foothold, and I belly slid five feet down the rock face, scraping my body and holding on tight to the progress I made." (Picture of Terry climbing)

John (an accountant) said, "My muscles screamed with pain. The effort dug into parts of my character I didn't know existed." Male or female, everyone was game and willing, and everybody made it.

More river rafting and rock climbing for five days. (Pictures available) Complete questions and answers available.

Question: Richard, what did you get from your rafting adventure? Answer: It was the hardest thing I could have done. I loved it. I learned a lot about self and I'd like to do it again.

Question: Peggy, what do you think about the trip? Answer: It was hard. I did things I never thought I would do. Not only did I do them, I liked doing them. Sleeping outside on the ground and not bathing. Now I know that I can go beyond my comfort zone.

Question: Glenn, was it a good trip? Answer: I never expected to do that kind of thing. I was more physical than I've ever been. The river rapids scared me silly, but I did it, and now that it's over, I can tell you that I liked it and will do it again. The climbing was way beyond me, but I did that too.

As he read, grains of sand and dirt were falling out of the notebooks. David stopped for a moment and shook the pages to free the grit. Continuing to read, he realized the rafting trip was something he would love to do. Sharing that realization with Valerie brightened her.

After he read enough to get the flavor of her snapshots, he slowly closed the book and handed it back to her.

"As soon as you can, you'll have to give me the whole story. I can't wait. I do know that you'll want to decompress. If you want some space, I'll take the kids out for a while."

"That would be great. I'll take a nice long bath and unwind."

While gathering the kids, there was very little conversation between David and Valerie. David could detect a nearly subliminal restraint, a certain defensive inhibition that was barely noticeable. It was as subtle as a whispering flea, so he shrugged it off as his imagination. Nonetheless, in the spaces of his mind, forgotten by habit and blanketed by hope, a feeling of foreboding hid.

During the next week, Valerie transformed her handwritten notes into a first draft article that she shared with her collaborator, Tony Batone. It was not quite what he envisioned and made changes where he thought appropriate. They then shared the article with the guides leading the rafting experience who made a few suggestions. When shown to Jocelyn, her major complaint was that Valerie might have spent more time describing what she felt and less of what she did. The behavioral requirements for such a trip might best be described by a member of the rafting company or by writer/photographer Tony Batone. Incorporating Jocelyn's suggestions made the piece better, and when the last edit before reaching Jocelyn's desk was complete, the rafting company was pleased with what Valerie and Tony had done. With those changes made, the piece was given to Jocelyn and accepted. Valerie was ecstatic and began to think of herself less as a secretary and more as a writer for an outdoor magazine. For the first time, the word *professional* could apply to her life. For Valerie, the collaboration with Tony was just as exciting as the actual experience. Their interest overlapped. He loved the outdoors like she loved the outdoors. He was acquainted with the same books she had read. The way he talked and what he talked about excited her. The things he loved to do, she wanted to do. They each wanted another assignment together.

12

Decorated and Dropped

David's military career had been going well. Few soldiers achieved as much at twenty-five. He had been promoted twice and was now a staff sergeant with a uniform adorned with ribbons that made him proud. Most of all, he was proud of the Army Distinguished Service Medal and other citations received for exemplary service as an intelligence analyst. No longer a smart young recruit, he had grown into a disciplined man and a talented professional deserving of respect and on whom others depended. The Army wanted men like him within their ranks and did what it could to provide the necessary incentives for him to continue being a military man. David knew he was being offered the possibility of a career that would have been challenging and diverse with the added benefit of never having to worry about basic needs. However, something in David sensed a future that could only be satisfied by something he could not articulate. Some yearning connected to his past or to something dreamt or wished. Or something that might have been delusional in nature but carried the feeling now guiding his decision not to extend his career with the Army. He searched but could not find the reason he resisted. Looking through the stories told by his father and the stories of his own past, he found nothing. Yes, there were holes, both psychological and informational, that needed to be filled, but none could account for him wanting to move on. So with considerable difficulty, David capitulated to the demands of an unidentified desire. One that would cause unpredictability and a greater acceptance of life without a tether.

*****

Dinner was finished, and the two kids had their bedtime stories and were tucked in. Valerie was working on her latest project and being clearly disturbed by what she was faced with. Since she went to work for the magazine, David noticed a change in her. She was more frequently impatient, not as playful and certainly much less romantic than she had previously been. But after inquiring into what he saw as unusual behavior, any foreboding he might have had came out of the shadows. As much as he fought such a thought, he could not help but be mildly suspicious. But of what?

Deep in a reverie that included Valerie, David felt her hand rest softly on his arm as she sat down next to him on the couch. She did not speak. He could sense her breathing. He listened and said nothing. Then she spoke in a low mournful voice.

"David, would you sit with me for a while? I need to talk."

Halfway in his subconscious, David heard something in Valerie's voice that seemed ominous. And with the set of her jaw and downcast eyes and chin, he knew instinctively that what she had to say would not be good. He did not know what it could be, so he braced himself and waited.

Valerie stumbled through a couple of starts. Looking as if she might be close to a breakdown of some kind, she composed herself and said, "I know this is not what we planned, but I've fallen in love with another man and want to be with him. Please don't think this has anything to do with you. It doesn't. You are one of the best things that happened to me, and I promise I will never do anything to harm you in any way." As her words washed over him, David sat in paralyzed silence, unable to think or move any part of his body. He was dumbstruck by the glaring difference between his perceived realities, the one he was building his future on and the one being foisted on him by a woman he trusted and who had born two children who made them happy.

Without a word, David entered a state of rage neither one of them had ever experienced. Opening his mouth, a noise as ancient and primal as the beginning of time sprang from his throat and filled the room with the pain of a thousand mourners having just looked death in the face. He settled into deep sorrow with mildly heaving contortions that allowed his eyes to weep an endless stream of tears. "Who is it?" he raged.

"You know who it is!" she answered, her voice suggesting that she believed he knew.

"Who is it?" he screamed again. "Say the name. Say the goddamn name," he demanded.

"Tony Batone, the photographer at the magazine," she answered.

David stood motionless, not knowing what to do or which way to turn to make what was happening go away. Like he was being turned inside out, feelings he had not had since childhood overwhelmed him. *"Where is my mommy? Why has she left me?"* David was dragged into a state of infantile loss that caused him to regress into a lost motherless child who needed to be cared for. *"Why did you leave me if you loved me?"*

Valerie instinctively knew what was happening inside David's heart, but there was nothing she knew how to do about it. What do you say to soothe a cut so deep it endangers the essence of one's soul?

"Oh, David," she said. "I'm so sorry. I've hurt you, I'm so sorry." She also began to cry, and just for a moment, they held each other and cried together.

In short order, he pushed her out of his private space and moved away. He stood looking at her, not knowing what to say or do. But a silent recognition began to wash over him. He and Valerie never married. He had never promised undying, everlasting love to Valerie, and she had never promised it to him. But who they were as people made it easy for them to be together. They liked each other and they looked good together. Their friends thought they made a great couple, and Valerie's father and David got along famously. Mr. Olephant became the kind of father he never had. They read together and talked often. He had recently introduced David to Khalil Gibran, the Lebanese American poet and artist who penned *The Prophet*, in which he opined on love, saying:

> "When love beckons to you, follow him
> though his ways are hard and steep.
> And when his wings enfold you yield to
> him,
> though the sword hidden among his
> pinions may wound you.
> And when he speaks to you believe in
> him,
> though his voice may shatter your
> dreams
> as the north wind lays waste the garden."

Over and over, the verses rang in his memory until he saw them in a new light. He began to understand that for as much as he was being ravaged on the threshing floor by what he had just been told, Valerie had made a choice that he would not have been able to make if the shoe were on the other foot. His inability to make such a choice was not due to lack of backbone but due to his strong commitment to the idea of children and family and not to passionate love. Even so, there was a contained emotional collapse that he could not control, and that left him speechless. The knowledge that life would not always do his bidding had just become a reality. It washed over him like a wave of freezing water.

"And what about our babies?" David asked in a pleading request as he unconsciously fingered his mother's stone in the ring on his right hand.

"I know how much you love the kids and I would do nothing to take them from you. I've given a great deal of thought to what would be the best way for them to have a normal life. If you're willing to listen, I'll tell you what I think."

"Go ahead," David said.

"Tony has asked me to marry him. He is a writer and can work anywhere. You should find a place where you want to be, and I will move close enough so the kids can be with either one of us without having to travel too far. Does that sound okay?"

"Look, we have two beautiful boys together. If we were going to be married, it would have happened by now. I'm not mad at you. I just want to get on with my life. It's also time for you to get on with yours."

David blinked helplessly, and the aching, empty pit that had opened in his understanding versus how things were, swallowed him in a timeless trap of sorrow.

13

Going Home

The day David was discharged from the military, he had one thing in mind: going home. He had never taken the opportunity to visit before. But now that things in his life had changed so dramatically, home might be the best place for him. Most recruits went home after being discharged. This was also true for David. Both of his parents had passed, and many of the friends he grew up with had moved away, disappeared into the background of life, were struggling to keep a nose above poverty, or had met an ignominious end. Even though he was not sentimental about his formative years, he was in part sculpted by those years and he needed a touchstone to help him stay balanced as he thought about negotiating an uncertain future.

As he drove his rental car toward Plainville, seeing familiar landmarks along Route 22 increased his anticipation and triggered good and bad memories of the people and places he used to know. As he turned off the highway and drove up North Drive toward Richmond Street, little had changed. The old buildings and houses looked older than they did before he left. Then, noisy children gave life to the neighborhood as they played on the tree-lined streets leading directly into the center of town. Unfortunately, things were different now. The scene changed when he crossed over the Greenbrook Bridge heading to Richmond Street, which was situated in the middle of town, equidistant from the outer boundaries of both the east and west ends of the city. The kids who lived on the five or six streets that intersected Richmond thought of themselves as the Richmond Street Boys. The neighborhood was a true melting pot and had been that way from the time of the city charter in the nineteenth century. Black, Italian, Jewish, and Irish families found themselves in the same boat. Everyone was largely poor and hopeful. The sandlot sports teams were always integrated, and even though the kids fought each other, there was a strong bond between the boys and girls of Richmond Street. David's baseball teams were drawn from this population. However, the integration of the races only persisted until the neighborhood kids reached puberty. During the magical teen years, things changed in a hundred ways. White parents and their sons did everything possible to keep their daughters and sisters from mixing with black boys, a reality accepted by all and which mostly separated the races when the kids were not in school.

An Italian bakery serviced the neighborhood and many of the surrounding towns. In the evening, David and his friends would sit on the curb with a canister of cold beer that someone of age had purchased for a buck and waited for the freshly baked bread to come out of the oven. The beer was cold, the bread was hot, and each of David's senses carried a vivid memory of those warm summer nights. There was a butcher shop where freshly plucked fowl could be purchased. Any cut of chicken, beef, pork, or lamb could be had. Two blocks away from each other on Richmond Street, a Jewish and an Irish grocery store would keep running tabs and feed the neighborhood. "I'll pay you on Tuesday, Abby," or "I'll pay you Friday, Mr. Mac," were promises familiar to everybody. Two barbershops and two bars brought good and bad men of every background into the fold and helped tag the neighborhood as a rough place to live. The housing projects could be seen from every perspective.

Before David parked the car to walk the street, he took a nostalgic ride. It had only been a few years, but in that time, things had changed enough for him to be alarmed. Since he had been away, the town now felt much smaller than he remembered. Businesses that were his touchstones no longer existed. Without them, he wasn't always sure where he was. Streets that went in one direction had now reversed. The elegant Park Hotel was now a home for the mentally ill. The Victoria Hotel across from the main fire department was gone, and in its place was new low-income housing. The neighborhoods that housed the guys and girls he remembered now seemed different. They seemed less welcoming and intimate; in some instances, he could not see himself spending time in such places. Especially now that his father was gone, he no longer felt an emotional attachment to the place. It was just a place he once knew.

After touring the town, David finally parked his car on Richmond Street and began to walk. Most everything was gone, even the railroad bridge looked small and old. As he walked beneath it, he remembered his father's voice saying, "David, you got to be out of this house by the seven forty-five train, or you won't make it to school on time." Or "David, when you hear that six o'clock train, you better get your butt home." When he passed under the bridge, he saw a man building a wall between two buildings to keep rats out of the vacant lot. The man had a body type he recognized and handled blocks like he was born knowing how.

"Willie, is that you?"

"Who's asking?" the man said without turning around, not wanting to be interrupted.

"It's David, David Walton."

"The same David Walton that got killed in the service?"

"Willie, do I look dead?

The mason turned around and looked at him for the first time. His perennially red eyes from an ample intake of Jack Daniels brightened as he realized it was indeed David. The David who was the best athlete in town. The David who everybody respected. The David he had taken as a brother, fought with, chased girls with, and cracked the doors of maturity with. The David who died while protecting American interests was there standing before him very much alive. Excited, Willie jumped up to face this man who he'd loved and lost to the unpredictability of time.

"My god, David. It really is you. Everybody thought you was gone. Killed in the war. Look at you. Looking strong and healthy and alive. Thank God. Are you back?"

Just as glad to see Willie, David finally felt he was home.

"It's good to see you, man! How you been?" asked David.

"You know, David, I'm still poor and black and working hard to get the jobs I need to pay the rent and keep my truck running. Things haven't changed much. It's about the same."

"How's your parents, Willie?" David asked.

"Mom died of cancer two years ago. My father had a stroke and moved in with me."

"I'm really sorry to hear that, Willie. I liked being around your parents. It was like watching something I never had and knew nothing about," said David.

"Yea, it's just me and him now. My marriage didn't work out, so I take care of my father. It's hard but I can do it. Social Services help a little, and I'm glad to have the support."

"I know about how hard it is, Willie. I took care of my father all my life."

"Everybody knew it was tough for you, David. But you know something?"

"What?"

"One of the reasons people in the neighborhood respected you so much and why the bad guys left you alone, other than the fact that they was scared of you, is 'cause they knew you had it hard."

David reached out, put his hand on Willie's shoulder, and said, "Do you remember the time you and me took Myra Johnson and Cynthia Nelson to Surprise Lake for some stargazing?"

"I remember that it wasn't for no stargazing. I remember those white cops caught us doing the 'nasties' and threatened to arrest us for something like indecent exposure. We ran and they couldn't find us in all that wilderness up there."

"Man, that was some funny stuff." David laughed.

"Did you get married David?"

"I had a couple of kids by the same woman, but I didn't get married."

Willie could see the pain in David's face and let the marriage questions go.

"Look here David," said Willie. "I've got to finish this job, so I'll see you tonight." Willie reached out and grabbed David's arms and made him promise he would come to the weekly fish fry and say hello to all the fellows who were still in town. "You can't say no. I'm gonna tell everybody I see that you're back in town. If you don't come, there's gonna be a lot of disappointed folks."

David left Willie and spent the rest of the afternoon walking the streets, where memories could be found at almost every intersection, hedgerow, or Victorian house, all of which were old enough to have seen better days. For reasons he could not explain, he did not visit the engineers.

As he strolled through the neighborhood looking for people he knew or those who knew him, he found himself in front of the Ragland house where he'd spent many hours learning survival skills. Built on one side of a double lot, Mr. Ragland built a shop in the back of the second lot where he could work on the variety of small jobs he hired himself out to do when he was not working on the assembly line at Ford Motors. His son Billy was not at all interested in learning the skills of a handyman and instead was seduced by the lure of the streets. David, however, spent many hours learning enough about electricity, carpentry, and plumbing to prepare him for working with a handyman if he had to. He was only in his early teens, but because David's father couldn't help, Mr. Ragland was helping to prepare David for the life he might lead. Wanting to tell Mr. Ragland what he was doing with his life, he knocked on the door, and eventually a young lady in a housedress and head scarf appeared.

"Hi, my name is David Walton. I used to live in the projects down the street. I was very close to the Raglands and wanted to say hello."

"I'm sorry, Mr. Walton, but the Raglands have passed on. My name is Ruby Chandler. The house and property now belonged me and my husband, John."

David was stunned and just stood there, not knowing what to do or say.

When Ruby saw the intensity of his reaction to the news, she invited him in.

"Thank you for the invitation, Mrs. Chandler, but I'm in town for a short time and I've got a lot of ground to cover." With that, he turned away and walked down the steps to the sidewalk and down the street.

The afternoon was winding down, and David began to move toward Willie's backyard fish fry.

David walked up the driveway past the dilapidated house and into the backyard, which was mostly shaded by thirty-foot white oaks. There was no lawn to speak of, but a number of derelict chairs and a couple of picnic tables were scattered around. Country soul music was playing on the boom box, and a man with his back turned was connecting a propane line to a burner under a ten-gallon pot filled with the oil that would fry the coolers of fish soon to arrive with the men who caught them. It was George Shorter, aka Chicken.

"Chicken, you know what you doin'?" asked David.

"Who wants to know?"

"Somebody who's known you long enough to know your real name."

Chicken George turned, and David could see that little had changed in his life. By the way he was dressed, it was clear he was as marginal as he'd ever been. Working for Willie pouring sidewalks and cement floors and blacktopping driveways, he always looked dirty even when he wasn't. His hair now was mixed gray and as always, he looked unkempt with a constant smile that exposed missing teeth that seemed to move around in his mouth randomly. Pound for pound, Chicken was one of the funniest human beings David had ever known. He came to Plainville as a freshman in high school, and because he was so funny, quickly became one of the guys. Raised on a chicken farm in rural Georgia, he was always talking about the farm until he acclimated to his new home. The kids liked him and gave him the moniker Chicken to let him know he was one of the boys.

"David!" he joyfully yelled. "We thought you was killed. But here you is, alive. Lord have mercy. Come here man." Chicken put down his tools and ran across the yard and gave David a hug and would not let go. And true to his character, he began to make ridiculous jokes.

"I seen dead folks before, but none of um looked as good as you."

"Chicken, stop lying. You ain't never seen a walkin dead man," Thurman said as he walked into the yard, not really knowing who Chicken was talking to. Thurman had been drinking hard since he was a teenager, and nothing had changed. If you let him tell it, he and his brothers were a family of rustlers who had to leave Texas in a hurry.

"Shut up, Thurman, and look who it is."

A few minutes before, Willie came into the yard and was now sitting quietly on the bench he'd been sitting on since they were kids. He stood up and embraced David from behind. Meanwhile, the glass of Jack Daniels he held in his hand never lost a drop. When Thurman stopped and saw it was David, he yelled, "Man, where you been? We talk about you all the time. Some thought you was dead, but I knowed you wasn't. Did you drive here? Man, I'm gonna play your plate number tomorrow in the lottery. You want to see my new truck? Come on over here and check it out. Ain't nobody from this town gonna ever hit a baseball like you or do any sports like you."

David was being treated like a returning conquering hero. For him, it was just good being home. He thought of his father.

As they moved toward the truck, more old friends walked up the driveway carrying coolers full of catfish and porgies into the tree-shaded backyard. Chicken George had the frying oil ready, more friends came, the music was turned up, and the weekly fish fry began. Two half-gallon bottles of Jack Daniels were placed on the tables, along with ample beer, and the jubilant crowd opened the weekend's front door. The joint began to rock. To David, it was like he'd never left. The laughing, greeting, and remembering transformed the hard lives that many of these people lived. David flung himself into the evening and embraced this part of his past with all cylinders firing. He was fully aware that the joy he felt would be short-lived and that his life's trajectory was now different. Unpredictable, to be sure, and different. The deep affection he shared with these people would always be with him, but tomorrow he would go back to a life where who a person was could be masked by who they wanted to be. Here on Richmond Street, what you see is what you usually got. Whether it revealed the good or the bad, honesty was easy because mostly there was nothing to lose.

Morning came and David drove back to Washington with the Jack Daniels still running its course. His head felt as if it was the size of a pumpkin and throbbed like a drum. As he drove, there was irony in knowing his hangover and his military service would both be ending. What also occurred to him was that for the first time, he was not subject to an authority. He was no longer his father's child, nor was he under the care of the military, who gave him orders that must be followed. He now was free to set his own sails and could truly be master of his own fate, and his aspirations would be his only boundaries.

*****

David had done well, and when his military service ended, the CIA recruited him to be an analyst and field operative. To avoid putting more pressure on his disintegrating family and because he had nothing else to do and nowhere else to go, he accepted the CIA's offer without much consideration. David joined the CIA and was trained to detect foreign and home-grown terrorists. It was not long before he was evaluating information from worldwide sources. He collected data from satellites, foreign newspapers, foreign broadcasts, and human contacts. Since data could be unreliable or incomplete, it was his job to sift through the information and either discard what was irrelevant or finish putting the pieces of a puzzle together.

The people recruited with him included a puzzle master and mathematician named Ken Carle. Ken was a little older than David, with an aristocratic air and urban hipness that David found interesting and attractive. Ken was comfortable in the dens of the wealthy, the absurd fantasies of the rich and famous, or in a neighborhood bar. He called himself a nocturnal chameleon. The two shared a mutual attraction, and during orientation and training, became friends. Ken, a jazz lover, exposed David to the sound and taught him to appreciate the music in a way that made him a fan. David also discovered Ken was an extremely talented piano player who would work for the "Company," but who would continue to play professionally as his cover. With his musical skills and name recognition, he could be placed almost anywhere for short or extended periods of time. When asked how he wound up in the CIA, Ken told him his father knew people and he then dropped the subject.

After the initial training, David Walton, decorated Army analyst, small arms expert, and aikido master, was paired with musician, mathematician, and puzzle master Ken Carle. The work they did together bore fruit and the agency didn't question their level of commitment or their analytic or field skills.

In his quiet moments David thought about how far he had come since high school and his father. He thought his army experience had given him discipline and regularity. His partnership with Valerie taught him some rules about romantic engagement, and his two children were teaching him about the realities of parenting. These things alone changed him irrevocably. However, because what he did for the CIA was very similar to what he did for the army, he wondered if the CIA would ever satisfy the undefined yearning he sometimes felt. A yearning that over time would become stronger.

14

The CIA

"**L**ieutenant, have you heard from Langley yet? I'm expecting a communique."

"It's coming in now, sir. It's cryptic, but here is the essence of the intelligence. It seems that for the third time this year, our shipment to the Sudanese resistance never reached its intended destination. After it left Chad, the rebels never got the goods. We flew it into Abéché on a private Nigerian carrier with whom we have ties. According to the pilots, the cargo was unloaded and handed off to a transporter, who made the three-hundred-mile trek across southern Chad to connect with the Sudanese rebels. The ball was fumbled somewhere in Chad. We have no idea who took the goods or where they are."

"What a fucking mess," said the general.

Even when operation HELP was first proposed, General Davis did not like the complexity of the plan to arm the Sudanese resistance. "There are too many junctions with too many people involved. I don't think it will work" were the words he used when unnamed members of the government wanted to give Sudanese supporters military assistance. "If our involvement with rebel forces is detected by political adversaries, we will have hell to pay," he said.

The general sat on the edge of his desk, took out a cigarette, and stared into the bottom of the glass that usually held scotch of some kind. Maybe he would find some wisdom there. He thought conferring with his political advisers and the CIA director before moving forward was both necessary and prudent. If the unspoken support for the resistance was to continue, the current plan required some alteration. He turned to his aide-de-camp, Lieutenant Coit, and requested he convene the decision makers so everyone is aware of the plans. "Try to schedule for Friday afternoon," the general said to Lieutenant Coit.

Two weeks later, the general, Senator Mark Wilkins from the Senate Intelligence Committee, Deputy Director of the CIA Kent Williams, and a senior official from the National Security Agency met at the Pentagon to review the status of the operation and what to do next.

"We can't continue to support the Sudanese rebels if we got no idea where that support is going," said Senator Wilkins, in a permanent Southern drawl that rolled off the end of the cigar plugging the left side of his mouth.

"Senator Wilkins is right. If our support is discovered, there will be political bedlam. The Russians, the Chinese, and the Iranians will eat our lunch and make us into hypocrites in the eyes of the world. We can't allow that to happen," said Senator Wilkins.

"In the last three months, we've wasted treasure and spent the energy of critical assets trying to find out what is happening on the ground with no actionable intelligence. The more the CIA exposes itself, the closer our adversaries will get to our plan," added Williams.

"We can't keep shooting blind with no results. I think the best strategy for us at the moment is to scrap the program and reevaluate. It is, however, important that we find where the leak is. Someone in our ranks is a foreign agent and is passing on critical information about arms shipments. We have to find out where the chain is being compromised and neutralize the mole," said Senator Wilkins.

Deputy Director Kent Williams, who didn't share all Wilkins' opinions, considered who might do the job most effectively and had some ideas. "I would like to see a clean slate immediately, and we can start again when we have plugged the leak," he said. The others agreed.

By Monday morning, the clandestine operation HELP was completely shut down, and all traces of its existence were eliminated. Cargo manifests, fictitious dock records, and individuals who were in any way connected to the intercepted shipments disappeared. Internal documents also disappeared from the records in various US agencies. The operation was washed out of existence. All that was left was finding the mole and eliminating any contacts made by that person.

It had been almost a year since David and Valerie had gone their separate ways. So that no rash decisions were made, she declined the invitation to move in with Tony Batone, the writer/photographer. They would have to nurture the relationship to ensure that living together would be healthy for David and the kids. Instead, Valerie and the kids moved into an apartment in the district, near her office. David found a small apartment in Fairfax, Virginia, and was there mostly on the weekends when the kids were with him. He furnished it the best he could, but it was really for the kids. He loaded the house with the things kids like so they would want to spend time there; toys, books, games, and big TVs filled their time together, and they always wanted to come and play with their daddy. It worked perfectly, and he loved them unconditionally. Valerie had been true to her word, and she never used the kids to strike at David. After all, she had left him.

Upon opening his mail one evening, he found an envelope that had the size and shape of an invitation. When opened, there was an invitation from Kent Williams, Deputy Director of the CIA. The invitation was not job-related; it was personal.

"You and a guest are invited for dinner and cocktails on Saturday, the eighth of June, at 7:00 p.m. RSVP at..."

David was surprised. He had never been invited to an event by a senior officer at the CIA. Of the hundreds of agents who had worked at Langley, he did not know anyone who had been invited. The next few days he asked and listened closely, and nobody at his level had been invited to a social evening by one of the agency's directors. He heard nothing about anyone being invited. The only person who might be able to help was his friend Ken Carle, but he was away on assignment and out of contact. David was savvy enough not to refuse an invitation from a CIA director. The only problem was who he would bring as a guest. There were not a lot of options. The only realistic possibility was Ruthann Johnson, a lady in his aikido dojo with whom he had connected and on two occasions had shared a beer. She was tough, conversational, informed, and attractive. When he asked her, she was quick to say yes, and after some jocular conversation, both left looking forward to an evening neither one of them would have ever anticipated. David was relieved.

On the evening of June eighth, David picked up his date, and together they drove to the Kalorama neighborhood of Washington DC.

"Where are you taking me, David?"

"I told you. One of my bosses is having a few people over for dinner and drinks."

"Who is your boss? I've been paying attention, and we just passed President Carter's House. I thought you were in the

Army and worked at the Pentagon? How do you find yourself in cotton this high? This is where the important players live."

"I simply got an invitation in the mail and RSVP'd. I'm as much in the dark as you are. Let's just go and have a good time. We'll figure out the details along the way."

David parked the car on the street and opened the door for his date. Together they walked past a couple of well-kept mansions with beautiful gardens. As they approached the address, a suited greeter asked to see their invitation and escorted them to the front door. When the door opened, the invitation was passed to another suit, and they were graciously welcomed by their host, Deputy Director Kent Williams.

"Welcome, David. This must be the lovely Ruthann Johnson. Please come in and join the rest of my guests."

"Ruthann, this is our host, Dep—" Before David could finish, he was interrupted by their host who said that everybody was there to enjoy themselves and titles should not be used.

David began again. "This is Kent Williams, our host." Ruthann had no idea who he was, and because she was not impressed by titles, she really couldn't care less.

As they crossed the threshold, David could hear the jazz stylings of a piano player who sounded like someone he knew. Looking across the room, he could see the blissful face of his friend Ken Carle, who he could see through the raised lid of the piano, wearing a tux and doing what he loved best. As David and Ruthann moved toward the piano, servers plied them with hors d'oeuvres and champagne.

"I thought you were on assignment, Ken. But here you are, showing off again."

"I wouldn't have missed this one for the world," said Ken. Smiling at Ruthann, he said, "If I had not come, I would have missed the opportunity to meet Miss Johnson."

"David describes you as charming Mr. Carle, but tonight there will be no formalities. You'll have to call me Ruthann, and I'll call you Ken. So, Ken, before the evening is over, you'll have to play a song for me."

David did not have eyes for his friend Ruthann, but on two occasions, he'd mentioned her to Ken. He'd also described Ken Carle to Ruthann in the hope they would one day meet. There was no intention to matchmake, but with what he knew of them, an eventual meeting might spark a friendship.

"Given that I have not been hired to play this gig, it won't be long before we have a chance to chat," said Ken. "But before that, what would you like to hear?"

"Well, let's see." Ruthann scanned what turned out to be a considerable knowledge of the American Songbook and then said, "I like Count Basie, and though I know that Paris is at its loveliest in May, I'll take the tune 'April in Paris,' please." Ken played an interesting introduction, and without any shyness or hesitation, Ruthann began to sing. David was shocked. The lady had a voice, and she began to lead Ken through the song with her own vocal stylings. The guests could not help but be drawn to the music, and as they began to gravitate near the piano, the party was on. Half-filled champagne glasses, broad smiles, and a love for good music transformed Director Williams' beautiful house into an evening of music, joy, and loss of some restraint.

David felt an arm hook into his and heard a playful voice saying hello. "I'm so glad you decided to come, David. I'm Kent's wife, Amber, and I'm sorry I missed you when you came in." Looking over at the piano, she said, "Your date, Ruthann, and Ken Carle have transformed what might have been an otherwise sedate gathering."

Something caught Amber's attention. "I'll catch up with you a little later." She moved toward the piano and chatted freely with her guests. When the song was finished, the whole party clapped and begged for another. Ken was in his element, and Ruthann was trapped by the insistence of the crowd to do one more. "Do another, do another," chanted a few who stood around the piano. From across the large room, someone yelled, "Do 'A Sunday Kind of Love.'"

"That's a good one. Do that!" yelled a woman who was standing with Senator Burgess, the Virginia Republican known for reaching across the aisle. Ken provided an introduction, and Ruthann joined him in her pitch-perfect voice.

When the song was over and with a promise to return, Ruthann joined David, who was mingling with a group of women. Before long, Ken Carle joined the group, and after a few minutes, Ruthann drifted away to get drinks. Ken and David stood alone.

"It's good to see you David. I assume we are still working for the same company. Are you still competing as an alternate on the US aikido team? I hope so. You seem to really enjoy it."

"I do enjoy it. It keeps me youthful. Why don't you come to one of the practices? You might enjoy it. It's all about technique. Like playing the piano and now that you've met Ruthann, she might also enjoy your coming."

"You'll have to tell me an occasion that works for you," said Ken.

"In fact, the team is training hard for a series of matches and tournaments across North Africa and Europe. I'm hoping I'll be given the time to participate in some of them. But in general, things are going well."

"How are you doing?" asked David.

"As you might well know, my musical career is thriving in other parts of the world. I'm getting the chance to really concentrate on the music. Exclusive clubs, mostly throughout Europe and some in Southeast Asia. My bookings are made by people we both know. I meet all kinds of people, assess information, and pass it along to our friends. The money and tips are great," he said, trying to make a long story short without implicating his work with the agency for those with big ears who might be standing nearby.

"I understand completely," said David, who changed the subject and spoke under his breath.

"Why were we invited to this party, Ken?"

"I've considered that and I think we'll find out soon. Just be patient."

When the clock struck one, it was clear to all the party had gone well. Ken and Ruthann did another two songs, and during the second one, an older lady said to David, "I just love your wife. She and the piano player added sparkle to the evening. You are a very lucky man."

As Ken and Ruthann entertained their audience with music perfect for their musical sensibilities, David took a comfortable seat and sipped a drink. Two ladies standing near joined him and talked about places in the world they loved. Because he was not well traveled, David could join in by asking questions and telling cute jokes. After hearing the wife of Oklahoma Congressman Hadley talk lovingly about Paris, David said, "Did you hear about the Frenchman who jumped into the river in Paris? He was declared to be in Seine."

"That's cute!" said Mrs. Hadley, who smiled and said, "I've heard some more risqué jokes about the French that I like more." Then she said, "The French and the British decided to have two cats swim a race across the English Channel. They imaginatively named the French cat *Un Deux Trois* cat and the British One Two Three cat. Which cat made it across first?" She paused. "The British cat because everyone knows that *Un Deux Trois* cat *cinq.*"

Without smiling, David looked at Mrs. Hadley and said, "That would not be considered risqué, and I will always consider you a lady because of your tasteful sensibilities. But I will never tell a joke with you again." With that, the two ladies laughed, smiled at David, and walked away. As the guests began to leave, their host motioned to David and Ken.

"Thanks for coming, guys. Both of you helped make it a memorable evening. I'd like to spend more time talking, so if you aren't currently in a critical part of an ongoing investigation, I'd like both of you to meet me in my office at ten o'clock Monday morning."

15

A Ticket to Africa

By ten o'clock Monday morning, both Ken and David stood talking in the waiting area outside of Kent Williams's office. Ken had just returned from an assignment and thought his presence at Kent's door had something to do with that. David had no idea why he was asked there, so he burned with anticipation. After a twenty-minute wait, one of the secretaries appeared and hustled the two of them in to see the deputy director. She shut the door behind them.

"That was a very unusual DC party, and you two, along with the talented and beautiful Ruthann Johnson, were the main ingredients," said Kent.

"A good time was had by all," Ken said with David nodding in agreement.

"Let me get right to the point. Because time is of the essence, I needed to see you together in a social situation. There are others who say you work well together, but I wanted to see for myself. Now that I have, I want both of you to meet with Senator Mark Wilkins. He'll be expecting you. Please solve this problem. It would mean a great deal to me and others who are well positioned. You will not be assigned until I hear from Senator Wilkins. Is there anything else, gentlemen?"

"We understand sir," said David, and they left.

A message was left at Senator Wilkins's office, saying he would be gone for a week and David and Ken would be scheduled for the Monday of his return. With a week before the meeting would take place, Ken suggested they could spend a few days fishing the Chesapeake and relaxing in the Carle family cottage on its banks. There was a sailboat, fishing gear, and a nearby store for supplies. Although David had done some canoeing with his ex-roommate, Henry, he could not know the Chesapeake like Ken Carle, who spent many blissful nights sitting on his family's cottage porch after a day full of fishing, crabbing, and digging for oysters. Ken called ahead to have a local caretaker air the cottage out and prepare the boat for use.

Before they left, David wanted to spend a few hours at the gym watching the aikido team training for the upcoming matches. Although he trained on a regular basis with the team, he had no real plans to compete. He might have other things to do. A few times in the past week, Ken asked David about aikido and wondered how it looked while being practiced. Of course, he had seen other martial arts being practiced on TV and wondered if aikido looked anything like what he had seen.

"I've briefly watched the characters in movies fight using martial arts. If you ask me, what I see on television is fake. If men were hit and kicked like that, they could not survive the blows. Fortunately I've never been kicked, hit, or hurt in any way as an adult."

"I know what you mean," added David. "What you see at the movies and on TV is not real martial arts. What you see are actors demonstrating rehearsed dance moves. Often they do them so well it looks like a real fight."

"Nevertheless, when I hear martial arts discussed, I'm curious."

"There are a few aikido dojos close by. You might like to see how a fight between a trained and an untrained fighter would really look. You could also compare that to a match between two trained fighters," added David.

"There is a very active dojo in Alexandria where I sometimes go to get away from the usual. If you're not busy Wednesday night, I'll take you over to watch how skilled aikido practitioners engage their art."

"I think I'd like to see the real stuff in action," said Ken as he, with both hands and arms flying, mimicked the movements of a martial artist in combat while he made aggressive grunts with his voice. David thought Ken's demonstration was hilarious and slowed down to let a full-throated uncontrollable laugh escape his belly.

"Kenneth," said David, using Ken's full name to emphasize the seriousness of his next comment. "Don't ever do that again. Unless your intention is to produce high comedy. If people saw you do something like that, they'd wonder if their assessment of you as a serious upper middle-class Yale guy who is intelligent, sophisticated, and musically talented was accurate."

"Isn't that how you do it?" asked Ken, knowing full well what he had just done was ridiculous. They both laughed again, enjoying the knowledge that their relationship had matured enough to behave in unguarded ways.

Wednesday after work, David drove to Ken's apartment to pick him up for an evening of martial arts. Ken had been waiting eagerly for the past hour, and when David honked his horn, Ken was in the car without making David wait. Most of the commuter traffic around Washington had petered out, and the time it took to reach their destination did not cause complaint. When the two CIA agents walked into the training facility, they were greeted by others who knew and respected David.

"What is that I smell, David?" asked Ken with a facial gesture indicating his displeasure.

"You're smelling the salves and creams applied by most athletes to soothe and loosen muscles. It's generally referred to as Heat but is called different things by different manufacturers. Some use it more than others, but at one time or another, everybody uses it. Let's sit in the bleachers so we can get a bird's-eye view of the action. Actual practice will start in a few minutes."

Ken could see a number of men milling around the four large mats that were the practice areas. All dressed in the white gi with different colored sashes, men readied themselves by stretching their muscles and practicing the fall to get their mind and body prepared to hit the mat. Not long after, a small group of beginners took the mat and listened to an instructor talk about the "the reverse wrist throw." To demonstrate for the beginners, a more advanced student approached the instructor with his hand out to push the instructor. The instructor somehow locked the aggressor's wrist and, without much effort, threw the assailant to his back.

"My god," said Ken. "That was so quick. Could the aggressor stop the reverse wrist lock?"

"It happens so fast an unexpectant aggressor is caught off guard," said David.

"That was impressive," said Ken as he watched the maneuver demonstrated twice more.

Next was a demonstration of the head throw. Once again, the attacker lunged at the instructor. Stepping aside, the instructor blocked the aggressor's hand while continuing to hold it and while simultaneously grabbing the back of the head and turning in a circle and then threw the assailant using his own momentum and strength. Again, Ken was as impressed as a wide-eyed child. Joint locks, armlocks, and others were demonstrated as Ken watched in amazement, constantly looking in David's direction to show his interest. After a half hour or so, the demonstrations for the beginners were over and followed by real practice matches between trained competitors. These matches were quite different without the dramatic holds and throws. The main reason being that those trained in aikido knew how to avoid the competitor's skills. Unlike the dramatic effect of various throws, the combatants pushed each other around the mat, trying to grab the opponent's gi or appendage in a way that would allow a throw or provide an advantage. Pushing and shoving did not give Ken the kind of excitement he wanted, and soon he began to lose interest.

"I can see that someone trained in aikido has a great advantage over an untrained person," said Ken. "But equally skilled opponents have a much more difficult time in an encounter."

"That's right," responded David. "But when a trained person is out in the world, it is unlikely that they will ever be accosted by someone with fighting skills. This is mainly true because in aikido, we are trained to avoid physical encounters. Have you seen enough, Ken?"

*****

Off they went to spend a week on Tilghman Island, Maryland. Ken taught David to handle a skiff and to fish and crab. On one special day, the two spent the entire afternoon in the town of Easton, Maryland, the ancestral home of the celebrated abolitionist, Frederick Douglass. There, once a year, historians, political activists, and celebrants from all social classes crowded the town to listen to speeches about Douglass and historians who talked about his impact on the abolition of slavery and his hope for the Negro in America. Others drank beer and stuffed themselves with seafood, oblivious to the import of the celebration. David and Ken heard of Douglass and vaguely knew who he was, so they both bought a copy of his book, *Narrative of the Life of Frederick Douglass*, and sat on the cottage porch and read it. Their evenings were informed by Frederick Douglass' life and mellowed by the cool bay air carrying a hint of salinity. Reading Douglass, they were both students of America's glaring hypocrisy and greatest shame. But there they were, from two completely different backgrounds—one privileged and one poor, each trying to find the paths to an understanding that would support a lasting friendship. Their conversations were honest but relaxed. David spoke of how invisibility drove people to think, feel, and behave in ways that Ken never considered. Ken spoke of how his privilege allowed him to be deaf, dumb, and blind to the plight of others, even though he had early contact with another talented luminary from Maryland in the person of Bootsy Johnson.

"Have I ever told you of how I came to play piano and why I love jazz the way I do?" David listened with great interest as Ken told of Bootsy Johnson, the black stableman and genius piano player who transformed his life. David told of his impoverished single-parent childhood, what people thought of his athletic ability, his disinterest in pursuing a life in sports, how technical things came easier to him, and how the engineers helped him see a different future. The two friends came to know each other like never before, and the seeds of an even greater friendship were planted. David would later become a student of Frederick Douglass and, because of it, would never forget his week with Ken and the time he spent at the cottage on Tilghman Island, Maryland.

A week later, David Walton and Kenneth Carle sat waiting for Senator Wilkins. Their anticipatory state lasted for an hour as they watched others enter and leave the senator's inner sanctum. While waiting, Ken excused himself and found the closest men's room down the hall from the senator's office. Waiting for Ken to return, a recognizable face passed by, but David was not surprised to see his aikido teammate, Wagner Gerald, whose name came up quite frequently when the policy wonks got together to talk about who had power and who didn't. He worked for and with Senator Wilkins. He filled the roles of Wilkins's adviser, aide, and constant companion.

"Wagner Gerald, is that you?" asked David.

"Well, I'll be darned," answered Wagner. "What in the world are you doing here, Walton? You're still in the Army, right?"

Not wanting to expose the real reason he was seeing the senator, David ignored the question and said that he was hoping Senator Wilkins could help him get furloughed so that he could join the US aikido team in the upcoming international aikido matches.

"I didn't know that was possible," said Wagner Gerald in a tone that suggested some incredulity. "I've been working with the senator for almost three years, and I can't remember a single time when he was asked to consider such a request. I wish you luck with that, David."

"Thanks, Wagner, I'm gonna need it. Oh, by the way, you *are* going to fight with the team on the upcoming trip?"

"So far I've been lucky and have made almost every trip. I've even made it to some boxing and track and field. So far it looks like I'm going. At least, I'm getting ready to go. As you know, I've been training pretty hard."

Wagner continued. "You may not know this, but the senator is an ex-Olympic judo team member. I think he hired me because of my martial arts skills. When he hired me, there was an understanding that I could be a participant in the team events."

Wagner hesitated and said, "Let me ask you something, David. Why do you choose to be an alternate on the team when everybody knows your skills are superior?"

"The answer is simple, Wagner. I've got children, and the time required to participate on the level that you do is simply not possible for me. But this time, I'd like to go and see what the world competition looks and feels like. To breathe the air and rub shoulders with the participants would make it real."

"I've got to go, David. Good luck with the senator. Either way, I hope to see you at practice." As he walked away, he turned and smiled and said, "Washington is really a small place, isn't it?"

It was not long before Ken returned from the men's room and they were both invited into the senator's office.

"Gentlemen, the senator will see you now," announced another of his assistants, who walked into the office after them.

Nodding to his assistant and waving her off with his cigar-wielding hand, the senator said, "We do not want to be disturbed under any circumstances. I will not be available unless there's an emergency."

Senator Wilkins walked behind his broad desk and looked out of his window onto the street below in still contemplation. He was known to be a prudent man who thought before he spoke and who clarified his thinking with constant feedback from his staff. He slowly turned to face his visitors.

"I'd like to thank you boys for coming. Your boss and others think that you are the perfect two to find a solution to a problem this government is having internationally. The President and members of the intelligence community decided the world would be a more peaceful place if the current government of Sudan were a more democratic government. For the past two years, we have been supporting Sudanese rebels who could bring that much-needed democratic change. However, a serious problem has arisen. Three of the last shipments of money and weapons to the rebels have been intercepted somewhere in eastern Chad or Western Sudan. We have consequently dismantled the program."

David listened carefully as the senator continued to explain, but he could not stop himself from considering how he might approach a solution. Ken's puzzle-oriented mind waited for more information in which a key to discovery might be found in the information to come.

"What we know is that the weapons we send clandestinely are being intercepted and sold on the open arms market to the highest bidder. What we need to know is, one, who is the dealer? Two, who is intercepting the shipments and what is the path to the dealer? And three, who is the mole and where are they getting information about the shipments? Gentlemen, we must make this problem go away. East African peace talks are being organized. When they start, the world will need a strong democratic contingent from the Sudan. They need our help, and the world political apparatus can't know about it."

He continued, "It's been agreed by the necessary authorities that you now work for me. You will use any technology you need at CIA headquarters or from the NSA. However, financial or personal assistance will come from this office. You will answer to me and nobody else." Sitting in his desk chair, the senator reached to open one of his locked desk drawers. Fumbling with keys, he eventually opened the drawer and extracted two small boxes. Each contained two items.

"Here are your new cell phones. Pressing the number five will get you directly to me. Pressing number one is an emergency call for help. Someone will find you. Here is an ATM card for each of you with a fifty-thousand draw per month. Don't get carried away but spend what you need to get the job done. When in doubt, check in. When in trouble, check in."

After a moment of silence, the senator asked, "Do either of you have any questions?"

David and Ken stood processing what they just heard, each wondering what they had just been recruited to do and how dangerous it might be. They also appreciated the need for utter and absolute secrecy.

"I ran into Wagner Gerald in your outer office. We are both on the US aikido team. I suggested that I was here to see if you could help me get a furlough so I might join the team on their next sweep through North Africa and the Middle East. He thinks I'm still in the Army and should keep thinking that. Also, no one should know of anything we ask of you. Our plans and communications with you should be absolutely secret," said David.

"Don't forget that I'm an active senator, and working out the details of every problem that comes up is impossible. You will be largely on your own. But I can promise this, only Kent Williams will know anything about what we speak of here and he will know the details of your assignment and how your work is unfolding. Who you are will never be known by anyone but me and Director Williams."

Agent Carle then chimed in, "I think David and I agree that a relationship with you is nonexistent from this day forward. You will only hear from us clandestinely. To do this job, the basic requirement is absolute secrecy. Nobody but the four of us should know what we are doing and why. Otherwise, what's the point?"

"All Wagner Gerald needs to know is that you have agreed to try to help me with a furlough. What does he do for you?" asked David.

"Gerald is one of my best assistants. He is a smart adviser and an effective strategist. He, like you and I, is a fighter and he helps me keep my fingers into that world that I love so much.

He helps to keep my office orderly, but in essence, he's a glorified briefcase carrier who loves the power, access, and attention. I need him. He'd be hard to replace."

"He's a good fighter," said David, and with body language intended to change the subject, he added, "We have our instructions, Senator, and we will do our best to find what you need." Ken nodded in agreement.

"Please leave through the side door that opens onto the busy entrance hallway and avoids my outer office. I will not be seen with you publicly again."

When they left, Senator Wilkins buzzed his secretary and asked that Wagner Gerald come in. "Wagner, what do you know about this David Walton?"

"I know that he's military. I know he's a nice guy. I know he is one of the best fighters on the team but only wants to be an alternate. I know he wants you to help him get a furlough."

"He seems to be a nice guy, and if he is as good a fighter as you say, I'll do what I can for him. Do you concur?"

"Yes, Senator. The team needs him."

*****

David knew the assignment he had just been given would take him away unexpectedly for undetermined periods of time. He also knew his parenting responsibilities would have to be put on the back burner for a while. Valerie had to be alerted, and above his normal contribution to his children's welfare, supplemental money should be provided in the amounts he would normally spend if he were with them on the weekends. Also, it would only be reasonable to consider the disruption his absence would cause in her life. She had been free to settle into her relationship with Tony Batone, and the time they had together when David was parenting would be considerably reduced if he was not there to take the kids. When making these considerations, he felt that the bonds he shared with Valerie, because of the children, were not dissolvable. What she did affected his life and vice versa. Friendship with Valerie was unlikely. Nonetheless, she would always be a part of his family because his children were her family, and he would do nothing to poison or distort those relationships. Valerie was reading from the same playbook and embraced David's reasoning.

*****

The doorbell rang, and Ken, knowing who it was, moved to open it. David stood there, framed by the door, smiling as if he had just won the lottery. Coming through the apartment entrance as if he were walking on stage, he was clearly in a good mood.

"Look at you," said Ken. "Smiling like the Cheshire cat. Is there a reason for all this bliss?"

"There's no particular reason," David said. "I just woke up on the right side of the bed. Life has been good to me, and today I get to spend time with you. What more could a person ask?"

"David, are you sure you're not in a drug-induced state?"

"High on life, man. Pour me something cold to drink and then tell me what you're listening to."

Ken walked into his well-appointed kitchen and poured David a cold glass of iced tea and began to answer David's question. He had been listening to Oliver Nelson's *The Blues and the Abstract Truth*. He knew David had probably not heard of it. So as had happened many times in the past, a listening session began.

"You're gonna love this album, David. All I'll say is the musical ideas determine the form and shape of each composition, and the structure is the blues. It's like you. A mixture. Classical, blues, down to earth, and almost irresistible. Let's start with the first cut, *Stolen Moments*. Pay close attention to Freddie Hubbard, Bill Evans, and Eric Dolphy. I think your nervous system has been genetically tuned to this sound. Tell me what you think."

David listened. The smile he owned when he walked into Ken's apartment never left him, and when the piece was over, he took out a pen and wrote down "The Blues and the Abstract Truth." The next day, he purchased the album and memorized every piece.

"We have some initial planning to do," said Ken.

"The way I figure it, each of us has a different job to do. You have to discover who is selling the arms. If we know that, we'll be close to who is hijacking the shipments," said David. "You can continue doing what you've been doing, while playing in the high roller clubs across Europe where money is being spent and deals are being made. There are a hundred snitches in each of those places that our assets can ply information from. I have to discover where along the delivery chain the info about the shipments is leaked and who is leaking it. If we can connect the hijacker with the buyer, the operation can be wiped out in one sweep."

"Yes," said Ken. "But I think we need to set a trap. How about this? After you learn who we can trust along the delivery chain, change how the links are made but only tell one person. We'll start from the beginning and only tell one person. If we get a hijacking, we'll know from where the leak is coming. The process has to be very systematic, but we'll have to trust some of our own people."

"We might have to give up a couple of gun shipments so the mole and the buyer will continue to trust the information without suspicion of an investigation. But while we are doing this, we'll refrain from sending money with the shipment," added David.

"You've got a month before the tournaments start. I think you should go to Africa and talk to the people who run the shipment links," Ken said.

"Good idea, Ken."

16

Jamil Hartley

David and Ken reported their meeting with the senator to Deputy Director Kent Williams, where they received a planned operational report. Deputy Director Williams told them the commandant of the Dover Airforce base would (on request) send ten crates of M27 infantry automatic rifles to Ben Guerir Air Base in Morocco located just north of Marrakech. In the '50s and early '60s, the base was an active US Air Force base leased from the Moroccan government and served as a back door into Europe and Africa. Until recently, it was also used as a refueling base for SAC and other long-range military flights. The base became a designated transatlantic refueling site, and although the US lease was expired, the excellent diplomatic relations between the two countries allows the US to periodically use two runways when needed. Here, the weapons would be offloaded and immediately reloaded on another transport.

"That's an accurate summary," said Williams, who had anticipated David's needs and sent for reliable help.

Much to David's surprise, the multi-armed, deep-reaching influence of the Company connected David with the person who would serve his purposes best. A day later, a handsome, well-dressed Nigerian knocked on David's temporary office door at Langley, introduced himself as Jamil Hartley, and sat down, showing no sense of discomfort.

"May I help you with something?" asked David.

"I think I can help you with something." The visitor smiled.

"Who are you?" asked David again.

"My name is Jamil Hartley. I'm told you might need some help in Africa. If it's true, I'm here to help."

"Do you have a resumé, Mr. Hartley?"

"It's not printed. I'll tell you my credentials. I prefer to be called Jamil, even by a neophyte like yourself," said Hartley.

David didn't bristle but maintained a steady gaze at his visitor. It became immediately clear to Jamil Hartley that David was not shaken or thrown by his brashness, so playing it straight might be wise.

"So tell me about yourself and how you might be helpful to me."

"When I came of age, I wanted to study aeronautical engineering, but I didn't have the money to study abroad. So I played football. What you call soccer. I was good and played on a professional level. I made enough money to pay my way to Carnegie Mellon University, where I graduated with a degree in aeronautics. At the time, the US was training a Nigerian Air Force. I qualified and was trained by Americans. We were trained to fly anything. I liked it, and the trainers liked me. After four years in the Nigerian Air Force, the Company came calling, and I've been working for them ever since. When they have a job in Africa where my services are needed, they call me first. I have twenty employees—five pilots, five mechanics, and ten ground personnel. Records are kept on an as-needed basis. I have a mid-size cargo plane, a twenty-passenger turboprop, and two bush planes each armed with two .50 caliber guns. We call ourselves African Bush Air. I have two kinds of clients—legitimate ones and the Company. When the Company calls, I respond. They pay me well. I live well. We've never had a mishap."

"The fact that you are in this building…" Just as David was finishing his sentence, the deputy director popped his head in the door and said, "Jamil is one of us. Treat him well."

"So what can I do for you, David Walton?"

The character who sat before him was interesting and quite unusual. Not a person you would meet every day. Smart and educated with a broad and quick smile, an irresistible personality, and seeming allegiance to the Company that had lasted for years.

"Let me give you some background, Jamil."

"In the last eighteen months, two shipments delivered by your company never reached their destination. Eventually, the merchandise appeared on the open market. We have a mole somewhere in the delivery chain. You might be able to assist."

"In what way?" said Jamil.

"I understand that you picked up the previous shipments from Ben Guerir Air Base in Morocco. I would guess that your personnel at the base loaded your transport. Is that what happened?"

"I think that's right. But if you are concerned about the trustworthiness of the Moroccans, in the future, I can ensure that only my men will unload and load the merchandise."

"Are you one hundred percent sure of your men?" asked David.

"I think so, but in the future, I will handpick the loading crew so that you can be sure of their loyalty and I will personally supervise the process."

"It is my understanding that you then deliver the cargo to Abéché, Chad, where it is unloaded, put on trucks, and driven a considerable distance to the rebels, who never get it."

"My contact in Abéché is an old friend who I don't trust one hundred percent. His name is Akua Klufa, an ex-heavyweight boxer who had some success but made his money doing odd jobs for rich Europeans. He loves to spend time where money flows like water and where his prospective employers can easily put their hands on him. He is a person who demands respect and does not blink when blood runs in the streets. Like me, Akua Klufa carries cargo but in trucks," continued Jamil.

"Can we find out if Akua Klufa has conspired in redirecting our cargo?" asked David.

"I like the way you talk, David Walton. You are the type who can keep a secret without telling a lie." He then continued, "Akua often depends on my four flying .50 calibers to protect his interests. With the threat of losing my support, I think he will tell me anything. I can know the answer very soon."

*****

Knowing David would be an alternate on the US aikido team, Ken sat with the designated person at the Company who could get him and his rhythm section booked at popular clubs in the cities where the tournaments would be taking place. Hotels and clubs attached to casinos would probably serve their purposes best. With the final tournament schedule before them, management in each city booked the Fabulous Ken Carle Trio. Posters were sent to each club in the cities where his trio would play. The itinerary would include Malaga, Monaco, Marseille, Naples, Sarajevo, Istanbul, and Alexandria. Ken loved the highbrow clientele in each of these gold-plated venues, and the variety of people he fraternized with made it easy to do Company business. Trying to find out who was selling American weapons to the highest bidder and communicate that information to David was the first item on his agenda.

Ken's first gig was a week in Malaga, Spain, with the promise that if he was a hit, his stay might be extended for a few days. So that he might have time to meet his assets, he arrived in Spain a week early. An arrogant Englishman and a pharmaceutical executive from the United States would be his social support. Each one knew Ken Carle was engaged to do what they did: listen and report. Their job was to take Ken into the places where a mere piano player could not go. Two others posed as merchants in scrap metal but were armed and dangerous Company men. Each one of them was supported by his own group of well-trained men. Ken spent time making sure everything was in place for his pursuit of the information he needed.

"Have you had much time to explore the city, Mr. Carle?"

"I was hoping you and your friends have explored enough to know who to talk with to get the information we need. This city is one of the oldest port towns in Europe. It has seen serious intrigue since it was established by the Phoenicians in the fifth century BC. Tap into these well-worn lines of criminality and find out who is selling American arms. As you know, I'm staying at the Grand Miramar Hotel. You should keep an eye on me during the day while I'm taking in the sights. Don't let me out of your sight. You might have something to tell me," said Ken, talking to one of his assets.

"We'll know where you are at all times. We will keep you safe and informed."

Two days before Ken started his much-advertised week at the Grand Miramar, he wandered the neighborhoods of Malaga and took in the sights. What remained of the ancient Moorish strongholds of Alazaba and Gibralfaro Castles stimulated his imagination about the century's long Moorish control of Andalusian Spain and its impact on Spanish language, art, and architecture, and how that influence ultimately invaded Spanish colonial provinces. Walking past the birthplace of Pablo Picasso and drinking coffee at a sidewalk tapas café, he saw many signs advertising the aikido tournament pinned to poles on the street. As he wandered the streets, he felt safe knowing he was being watched and protected by company men.

The Grand Miramar Hotel was a study in opulence. It was not the only five-star hotel in Malaga, but it was the place where the yacht-owning and international jet-setters congregated when they were on the Costa del Sol. Consequently, other well-heeled and deep-pocketed players from all over the world came to be seen and accepted into the rarefied atmosphere. The first evening he was scheduled to play, Ken walked across the lobby toward the piano room wearing a tuxedo and carrying himself with an air of sophistication. There could be no question that he belonged among the beautiful people. He was noticed, and that was no small feat.

By 7:45 p.m., many had finished dining and the music lounge was filling with those who wanted a drink or to engage in a little terpsichore. When Ken entered the room, his rhythm section had not yet arrived, and he was able to scan the lounge without attention being drawn to him or the music. It was a normal Friday night party crowd. The only thing that made it different was the many languages being spoken and the formal attire being worn. Otherwise, it was the Rainbow Room or the Algonquin in New York. A youngish woman full of energy and wants, enjoying the largesse of men who carried limitless credit cards, behaved as if she, too, had been graced by wealth. Ken guessed the more sophisticated piano stylings would be perfect for the first part of the evening.

*****

Good to his word, Jamil Hartley, through various persuasive means, ascertained that Akua Klufa was not the mole.

The information that trucks carrying extremely valuable cargo from Abéché, Chad, to the Sudanese border had to come from somewhere else. Akua, however, did provide a hint that might prove fruitful, and David was determined not to leave any stones unturned. What Akua said was that after the second delivery, one of his drivers said that he could no longer work for him and that he was going into business for himself. This was odd because it was well known that the driver was financially strained; he had more than one wife and many children. A man with that kind of burden does not quit his job to do risky business. Akua said the man was uncharacteristically jittery and anxious to collect his pay and leave. But upon later reflection, he thought there might be more going on. Nevertheless, time passed and the incident had been forgotten until now.

"Do you think Akua knows where this ex-driver lives?" asked David.

"Offhand, I don't. But finding him should not be that hard, especially if there is money offered for information. I will contact Akua, and together we will find him," said Jamil.

"When you find this man, Jamil, I would like to have a private chat with him."

"These are hard men, David. To get the truth will take more than a chat. Akua and I will find him and put him in a situation that you in the West would consider unthinkable. If there is something to be told, it will be heard."

"The sooner this happens, the better," said David.

"Give me two days," said Jamil. "You won't have to wait long."

David decided to walk the quarter mile back to the hotel. Trying to follow in the wake of automobiles, he walked through a sea of people moving in every conceivable direction, speaking unfamiliar languages. Every aspect and strata of humanity were on display. The bush people and farmers mixed with the urbanites, while the blinking lights of modernity could be caught illuminating the bleaker and squalid sides of the human struggle. While he was repulsed by the in-your-face poverty, he was given hope by the smart and thoroughly modern entrepreneurial efforts surrounding him in every direction. This was a melting pot of people that looked like him and where he did not think of himself as a black man with all that it implied in the American psyche. Instead, he was encouraged and hopeful for the future of a part of the world Europe had raped and enslaved for hundreds of years. When he reached the hotel, he was greeted by a man who wore a neat collared shirt sporting Jamil's corporate emblem, and as he turned to look upon the seeming chaotic disorder he had just walked through, two more of Jamil's men became evident. They had been with him every step of the way. That night, he slept well, knowing he was not alone.

Two days later, after he performed his morning rituals, David found Jamil waiting for him in the hotel lobby.

"I've not eaten," said Jamil. "We are going to have a full day. We should eat an ample meal for breakfast."

"I assume you have something to tell me?" asked David.

"I do, but let's enjoy a good meal first."

Both men scanned the limited menu and ordered eggs, steak, and a local vegetable David had never heard of. After a small glass of mango juice and a cup of coffee, they were each ready to talk about the day to come.

"Akua and I worked together and, with readily available talk, were able to triangulate his general whereabouts to find him. His name is Gustof Ofusue. Akua says he and his men called him Gus. He set up a small coffee shop and bakery and is doing quite well."

"I want to talk to him," said David.

"You will get a chance to talk to him about work and family matters."

"What do you mean by work and family matters?" asked David.

"You will find out soon enough. We have taken Gus and a few of his family members on a trip into the desert about an hour and a half from here. If he has anything to say, the peace and quiet of the countryside will loosen his tongue."

"How soon can we get started?"

"A soon as you say go."

The two men traveled far into the bush and then along empty desert roads of hardpacked sand and stone for a considerable distance. David had not seen terrain like this and knew that its remoteness would preclude knowledge of their presence. Although he would not speak the words, he was concerned that methods of information extraction might be highly questionable. Soon he could see an encampment on the horizon. As they approached, Akua and a few of his men stood in front of a large tent and waved. When Jamil and David exited the car and approached, the greeting was almost festive, as if they were meeting on the street after not seeing each other for some time.

"Would you like to get started?" asked Akua. "I reckon that since this sin might have happened on my time, I should be the one leading the interrogation. Would you both agree?"

"I have no objections," said Jamil. "Do you, David?"

"No."

"Then follow me," said Akua.

The three men climbed into the back of a covered, air-conditioned truck. *I'm in one of the most remote places in the world in the back of an air-conditioned cargo space*, thought David. But there in the middle of the space was a terrified man tied to a chair under the watchful eye of a gunman.

"Gus, I have some questions to ask you. If you answer honestly, you will not suffer. If you lie or try to lie, you and your entire family will die. You do know that we have your family in the tent outside waiting for a nice lunch. I would like to see you all go home and have a good life. So let's get started. You have been talking to someone about your job as a driver for my company."

"Please, Akua, the only person I have ever talked to is my partner."

"What partner, Gus?"

"My partner in the coffee shop and bakery."

"Does he work with you?"

"No. He gave me half the money to open the business."

"Why did he give you money?"

"He thought it was a good idea. He also would like to invest in the trucking business."

"What is this investor's name, and where does he live, Gus?"

"His name is Jakup Abbas. He comes twice a month from Sudan."

"What does he like to talk about?"

"He likes to talk about the trucking business."

It was beginning to be clear that Gustof Ofusue was not a willing or knowledgeable participant in the hijacking of Akua's trucks and the theft of the American arms and money. Jamil, David, and Akua were convinced that Jakup Abbas, with the ruse of starting a trucking company, had plied enough information from the unwary Ofusue, who was not involved in the plot itself. They would have to interrogate Jakup Abbas. Gustof Ofusue was terrified, and Akua instructed him never to discuss the incident with anyone on the penalty of his life and his family's life. He was then untied and allowed to join his family, and lunch was served, after which the entire caravan returned to Abéché. David thought the way the episode was handled showed a sensitivity far beyond what he expected. The ruthlessness and barbarity that might have emerged were replaced by careful questioning and truth from Gus under threat of having his seed wiped from the face of the earth. David paid careful attention.

What Akua decided was that in the future, he would not apprise his drivers of any details regarding jobs until the scheduled day. Doing that would preclude any possibility that information about the what, when, and where of the driver's employment could be known. Jamil found out that Jakup Abbas would be coming to visit Gus in two days, and when he did, Jamil and David would be waiting. Gus was to identify him when he came to check on his investment in the bakery and allow Akua to escort him away so he could be questioned. Unless Gus was lying or the timing of his visit changed, it was unlikely that Jakup Abbas would ever make it back to Sudan. The plan was to treat Jakup Abbas the same way Gus was treated. CIA assets in Sudan ascertained the names of Abbas's family and where they lived, making the fear of losing them an incentive for telling the truth. After which, he would disappear forever.

David knew time was running out if he was going to make the aikido tournament in Malaga. So far, he had learned very little, and his only lead still had to be interviewed. Ken had not yet communicated with David. He assumed neither he nor his assets in Malaga had discovered information that would lead to who the hijackers were and where they got their information. He could not forget that his cover was as a member of the US aikido team and as a member of the team, he had to be present during the tournament. If he wasn't, Senator Wilkins and Deputy Director Williams would not be pleased.

The next morning, as before, Jamil met David.

"You seem to enjoy breakfast in this hotel," said David.

"You should know that it's indeed the breakfast. It's the best in Abéché."

"I don't really believe that, Jamil. You're looking for me, an intrepid seeker of the truth, to be your sidekick. But enough of the bullshit. What do you have for me?" asked David.

"Through my team's excellent work and invaluable contacts," Jamil said with tongue in cheek, "we have located Jakup Abbas."

"Is this the truth, or are you trying to impress me?" asked David.

"Would I lie to you, David? You have to be impressed by the speed at which we in Africa can work."

"When do I get to see him? I'm running out of time. I have to be in Malaga in two days."

"My men have secured all the information they need about his family, and he is in the air now, on his way here. We can interview him tonight."

David thanked Jamil and made a point of making sure Akua knew his involvement in the whole episode would serve him well. Even without David's gratitude, Akua would get great satisfaction from knowing he was in part responsible for striking a blow against the man who tarnished his company's reputation. When the plane carrying Jakup Abbas touched down at a remote landing strip near Abéché, Akua ensured Gus was there to identify him as his partner in the bakery and as the man who had asked a lot of questions about Akua's trucking company and how it operated.

It was late afternoon when the truck carrying Jamil, David, Akua, and Gus slowly followed the red dirt road to meet the plane. The plane came in like a giant black bird, unsure of its ability to find a suitable landing. Then with a stabilizing transformation, it landed safely on the road, rolled toward the investigators, and stopped a hundred yards away. Gus was asked to stay in the truck with a pair of binoculars to identify Jakup Abbas, his partner in the bakery and the man who might be responsible for helping to hijack Akua's cargo trucks. Not wanting Abbas to connect Gus with his present circumstance as a hostage, Gus was instructed not to leave the truck at all. When Abbas was thrown from the plane, at the feet of three angry men with guns, Gus's only job was to wave a small cloth if they had the right man.

Once Abbas was identified, he was tied to a chair, and the interrogation began.

"We know who your family is," said David. "And we know where they live."

Akua then began to read the names and addresses of every member of his immediate family, if they were married, who they were married to, whether they had children or not, and the names of those children.

"One call will wipe your loved ones from existence. Everybody from your family line will cease to exist. There will be no past and no future, and you will not meet in heaven," said Jamil.

"What do you want from me?" asked Abbas. "Why have you taken me into the desert and bound me to a chair? I don't even know you. What have I done to you?"

"If you tell the truth, Jakup, your family will live and your line will continue. If you lie, they will all die. In the next ten minutes, the fate of your family hangs in the balance," said Jamil again. "Do you understand?"

And with that said, Jamil put his pistol between Jakup's legs and pulled the trigger. If he was not frightened before, he was terrified now.

"I have one round left in my gun. The round is tied to my phone. One question will determine your fate and your family's fate," said Akua. "Who paid you to ask questions about my trucking operation and who did you give the information to?"

Akua cocked his pistol and put it against Jakub's temple.

"I'll tell you. I'll tell you. Please don't shoot my family. He gave me money every time I had information. He's an Egyptian and his name is Sammy. I used my small truck to take him into Chad. I don't know what he was doing. When we returned, he asked me if I could be trusted. He gave me the assignment of finding out about Akua Klufa's trucks. I haven't seen him in a month."

"Where does he come from?" asked David.

"The last time I saw him, I picked him up from the airport in Geneina, Sudan. He was complaining about the dirt in Sudan and said he could not wait to get back to Monaco. He said he could live like a civilized person there."

"Are you telling the truth, Jakup?" asked Jamil.

"Yes, yes," he pleaded. "It's the truth. In the name of Allah, it's the truth."

"Is that all you know?"

Sweat and dirt ran down Jakup's face in rivulets that seemed not to stop, and he trembled in fear as he pleaded for his family. "All I wanted to do was feed my family. In Allah's good name, please have mercy on them."

"Your family will be safe, Jakup," said David. And with that, David walked back to the truck, followed by Akua. As the pilot and crew boarded the plane and began to taxi, the intense anguish that showed in Jakup's face seemed to relax. Perhaps it was hearing that his family would be safe. Maybe for the first time, he fully comprehended his life's struggles would now cease. Jamil approached Jakup from the rear, put his pistol to the back of his head, and brought his life to an explosive end.

17

Europe

Africa had given David a new lens through which to view the world. Its blackness embraced him and allowed rejection of some of the poison the West had injected into his worldview and that of many African Americans: that black people were alone in a sea of hostile whiteness whose sole ambition was to oppress them. He now understood like never before that he was not alone, that his physical attributes were not unusual, and that black civilizations have endured and will endure. But for all the progress the continent had made in emerging from beneath the brutal heel of colonialism, in many ways, it continued as a harsh, lawless place that allowed people like Jamil and Akua to operate with impunity. These two realities were embossed on his consciousness.

On the morning that followed the desert interrogation, David was on a flight to Malaga, Spain to meet his partner Ken and inform him about what had been discovered.

When David landed in Malaga, he checked in at the Marriott. Ken agreed to meet in a small café on Buenavista Plaza across from the Picasso Museum. After a partly cloudy morning, the afternoon was transformed into the kind of day that gave the Costa del Sol its name. The sun shone bright and clashed with a slightly cool breeze, demanding that the afternoon be spent out of doors. The plaza hummed with natives and tourists alike, causing an overflow of business in the cafes. Knowing the proprietor of the chosen café, Ken arrived first and waited for David inside a building whose age reached deep into the past. Its actual age was hidden by modern building techniques and furnishings influenced by early twentieth century style. The six-table café was perfect for a clandestine rendezvous.

When David arrived, Ken said, "Your timing is perfect, David." Then he waved to the waiter to bring another cup of coffee. "How was your trip to the motherland?"

"Enlightening on some levels. I think I'll go back and visit. There's something homelike about it. After all, it is the motherland."

"We can talk about the fun parts later. How was business?"

"Business was potentially good, but only time will tell. The ball's in your court now."

"What do you have for me?" asked Ken.

David leaned toward Ken and, just above a whisper, said, "Check out an Egyptian named Sammy who takes frequent flights to Sudan to a place called Geneina near Darfur and a hop, skip, and jump from where the hijackings took place in Chad. Sammy might live in Monaco, and if our information is good, likes the high life. If luck is with us, he should not be hard to find."

A waiter brought a second cup of American coffee and Ken drank a satisfying gulp. Then keeping David's obvious need for stealth, he leaned in and said, "We can have the wheels turning immediately. I'll communicate with you as soon as I can, but remember, you have a tournament to attend. Are you fighting?"

"Only if one of the three guys in my weight class can't. I checked today and everybody is in good shape and ready to go. You do realize that the coordination between our investigation and the tournaments is perfect given the intel we have so far. Our next stop is Monaco."

"Once we find out the identity of the hijacker and the arms merchant, we can set the trap and maybe identify the mole," answered Ken, still speaking low to maintain secrecy.

"Maybe I'll come to hear you play tonight. I need that kind of evening. Is that okay?"

"Of course, it is. But wear your US aikido sports jacket and come as a tourist."

*****

Four days later, the two investigators again met at the small café on Buenavista Plaza across from the Picasso Museum. This time, Ken told David the assets in Monaco required only one night to find what they needed to know. Tarek "Sammy" Jafari was a known fixer, who traveled the European money circuit doing jobs for those who needed discretion and plausible deniability. No job was too small, too dangerous, or too tasteless, immoral or illegal. Potential employers are only limited by their pocketbook. He can often be found at a bar or a poker table or fraternizing with the rich and powerful.

With the help of Interpol, it was also discovered that Sammy, traveling with an Egyptian passport and authorization from the South Sudan NGO Forum, made regular trips to southwest Sudan and the Darfur area supposedly to help get heavy equipment to the international rescue teams for building roads. Getting water and supplies to these areas draws numbers of NGOs that often worked at cross purposes, and large amounts of money were often lost to collusion and graft. Through bribery or threats, Sammy was often the recipient of wasted, skimmed, and illegal funds. Knowing who Sammy communicates with in Europe might lead to a known arms dealer.

The last night in Malaga, before the tournament moved to Monaco, the aikido team met and spent some time with the coach, after which they were given instructions as to when and where they should meet at the airport the next afternoon.

"Our week here in Malaga has been a good one. Each one of us has fought well, and without winning every match, we have been able to size up the competition we'll face the rest of the trip and we have time to adjust our strategy for the strong opponents. You have shown yourselves to be a competitive team. Now this will be the last night in Spain, so don't stay out too late," said Coach Brown.

Wagner Gerald stood in front of David while the coach was talking and while David chatted with his teammates. He tapped Wagner on the shoulder in a friendly manner. "Wagner, I'm sorry I missed your match, but I heard you won it with some very slick moves. Good for you. Are you going to stay for the entire trip?"

"I don't think so. The senator said he will probably want me back periodically, but I don't really know when that will be. So I guess I don't know. What are you doing tonight?" asked Wagner.

"I've made tentative plans. Why? You want to hang out?" asked David.

"Yeah! That would be fun," answered Wagner. "I know this great place called the ZZ Pub. It's at the intersection of Calle Tejon and Rodriguez streets. They play everything from rock to jazz on any given night. I'm meeting some friends there. It ought to be fun."

"If I can, I'll join you. What time will you be there?"

"We show up early, so if the evening looks like it's going to be a bust, we can leave and go someplace else. How about seven o'clock?"

*****

David returned to his hotel room a little tired and needing a nap before he spent the night carousing with Wagner. Remembering that he'd promised to spend some time with Ken this last night in Malaga, he donned his aikido team jacket, and at six thirty, walked out of the hotel to try to find the ZZ Pub. By seven fifteen, he was walking down an ancient cobbled street lined with a mixture of trendy boutiques and drinking establishments catering to everybody from grungy kids to deep-pocketed tourists. Not far ahead, he could see the sign announcing the ZZ Pub. When he walked in, his eyes had to adjust to the gloom before he could see at all. His sight slowly returned, and he found himself heading toward a group of four people sitting at a table near the end of the bar.

"David, is that you?" He heard Wagner ask loudly. As he approached, he could see that Wagner, like the other people in his party, was dressed in a casual but elegant style. Smiling with an authentic welcome, he said, "Come meet my friends, old and new. I'm so glad you could come." David stood smiling as Wagner introduced them one at a time.

"Everybody, this is my teammate David Walton, pound for pound one of the most dangerous hand-to-hand aikido masters I know. To my left, we have Sammy Jafari, an Egyptian NGO worker who travels back and forth to troubled areas in North Africa." When David heard the name Sammy Jafari, he almost lost his composure and exposed himself. "Next to Sammy is Hilda Sanchez, a popular radio commentator here in Malaga who believes that Spain should melt all the gold in the country's hundreds of churches and use it to pay its debts. Last but not the least is Gabe, who never knew his father and consequently refuses to use a last name. Gabe manufactures bicycles for the European market."

David pulled up a chair and joined his colleague. With the name Sammy Jafari ringing in his ears, sitting with the people he just met almost made him sick with the need to report back to Ken. It was nearly all he could do to join these people with a level of engagement and jocularity that would make his presence more than acceptable. When he finally calmed down, no hint of his affiliation with the CIA would ever be detected. Wagner Gerald handled the question of who he was—a teammate and casual friend he liked but of whom he had little knowledge.

"Is this your first trip to Malaga, David?"

"This is my first trip to Europe. But if the rest of it is anything like Malaga, I'm sure the rest of our trip will be memorable. There is just so much history, and the United States is so comparatively new."

"That is a fact," said Sammy. "But when your country is like mine, your entire worldview is shaped by history. One can't escape it."

Gabe raised a glass and sarcastically said, "Here's to Egypt, the most interesting country in the world." Then he added, "But what of its present?"

"Let's not get testy, boys. Each of our countries has shaped our worldview," said Hilda.

"But that's not the question," countered Gabe. "The question is about the history and how well that history has been preserved. That's what makes a place interesting."

"Are you sure?" Wagner added. "As a unified country, Spain's greatness came in conquest and the spoils of conquest. Hilda's whole argument is that those spoils, I mean all the gold taken from the Americas, which it sees as a treasured part of its history, needs to be sold off. If all that gold is confiscated so the economy can survive, will the church in Spain survive as we know it? Can it maintain itself as a tourist attraction without the stolen gold?"

"I, for one," said David, "will simply enjoy what I see and what I can know—how humans have best acquitted themselves in art, architecture, science, and literature. I don't know about science and only a little about Spanish literature, but art and architecture are memorable, and the Moorish influence is both surprising and interesting."

"David's approach is best," said Hilda. "Those are the things I love about Spain, not how much gold the churches can display in the worship of a wise two-thousand-year-old carpenter." And with that, she swiped the hair from around her neck so that it flowed gracefully down the front of her blouse and then looked at David with a sultry smile.

"How does a Spanish beauty like you get to have a name like Hilda?" asked Sammy when he noticed the look she gave to David.

"It's a question I've been asked many times. That and how I learned to speak English like an American. Well, my mother came from Amsterdam to fight with the resistance during the Spanish Civil War, and I went to boarding school in New England. So there it is."

"How about another drink? This one's on me." Gabe waved a hand to get the attention of the waiter, who served the next round.

"I'm afraid this will be my last," said David. "I have one more stop I promised to make before tomorrow's departure. So I raise my glass to newfound friends with the hope that we will one day be together again." Then to himself, he thought, *What a crock of shit.*

The rest of the party bid David goodbye, and under the table, David could feel Hilda's hand discreetly slipping him a card. And as he prepared to leave, two other friends came through the door and joined the table.

"I'll see you tomorrow, David," said Wagner.

"And when will I get to see you again?" Hilda said openly.

David kissed her hand and winked, saying, "I've got an idea. Why don't you walk with me and guide me to my destination?"

"I'd hate for you to get lost, David," she said, turning to the others for permission to leave. "David is a visitor to these shores, and he should have the welcoming attention of a native." Hilda and David walked out of the ZZ Pub and into the crowds of people whose vibrancy pulsated infectiously through the city. Finding David's arm, she locked herself in, and they negotiated their way along the granite tread stones. Once out of the crowd, they stopped to look into shop windows as they made their way.

"Would you like to stop and have a drink?" David asked.

"Unless you have a better idea, Hilda."

"As a matter of fact, I do have a better idea. I have a very expensive bottle of cognac I've had for a while. Our meeting might be the special occasion I've been saving it for." Hilda had an unspoken body language and facial expression that was very seductive, and David was not immune. "How about we taste it?" she said in a way that opened a host of possibilities.

David stopped walking and turned to look deep into her clear gray eyes, hoping to find an unequivocal yes. When he found it, he said, "I would love to share it with you." Hilda's eyes smiled alluringly, and looking into his, she said she would be pleased. The one shared wavelength was now clear, and they strolled into a more residential neighborhood just off a busy lane with a cute tapas bar on the corner. Clearly inhabited by those who could afford pastel-painted balconies and marble entranceways, Hilda unlocked the door and led David to the elevator and into her third-floor apartment.

David was stunned. In the midst of a city that celebrated its heritage was an apartment worthy of being celebrated in design magazines.

"Fabulous," said David. "I've never seen an apartment outside of a magazine that looked like this."

"My father was wealthy, my mother was a freedom fighter and decorator, and I make a good salary. So there you are. Welcome to my humble abode." She talked as she prepared herself to relax. She suggested that David do the same.

"In the cabinet next to the bar, on the second shelf, you will find an unopened bottle of Henri IV Dudognon Heritage Cognac. You, my dear, are the special occasion, and we will share it in celebration."

David removed his jacket and shoes and asked for the recorded music. Finding Hilda's collection, he couldn't read Spanish, but he could recognize the American and English album covers. *Clifford Brown with Strings*, which he recognized immediately, was a good choice for the occasion, and he put it on. When the first note of "Yesterdays" was blown, the evening moved in the direction they both anticipated. David poured two drinks of cognac and set them on the glass top table in front of the couch. Before long, Hilda joined David on her deep plush couch and initiated a toast. Sliding close with a seductive smile and raised glass, she said, "To a newfound friend. May you love your stay in Malaga and come back soon for more of what it has to offer." The phonograph played *Memories of You*, and its seductive trumpet sound spilled its sentimental character into the space inhabited by Hilda and David.

"I'll drink to that and to a welcome committee of one who simply cannot be refused," added David, who touched glasses with Hilda and sipped the cognac. With the taste of ambrosia on his lips and a Spanish nymph nested in close range, he reached with his free hand and gently guided her into his arms. As they rested the two glasses on the table, the sound they made was as if a starting bell had been rung. She smelled of roses, and the sensation was heightened as her ample breast and soft loins gently rested between his legs. She explored his lips and throat with her mouth, and her hand explored his body, feeling the strength of his manhood.

"You are much more than I could have imagined. Is there more?" whispered David, trying to add a little levity.

Hilda rested her foot on the floor and leveraged her body up from the prone position but never let go of David's hand. "Let's find out if there is more." She smiled as David was pulled off the couch and led to her bedroom. "Come on, I have a welcome present for you." Bending a little at the waist and using her index finger, she summoned him as they entered her bedroom. Then wrapping her arms around his neck, she kissed him, letting her full body feel his throbbing desire. Pulling away and looking into his eyes, she unbuttoned his shirt and felt his muscular body as his belt was unbuckled and his pants were carefully removed. Hilda dropped her robe off her shoulders, letting it find the floor. Foreplay had reached its zenith, and the pleasure of reaching the revealing moment had been exquisite. They both trembled with delight at the thought of more. Naked and lascivious, they embraced, drinking in desire. Then they kissed. A kiss that made them want more. *Clifford Brown with Strings* could no longer be heard. They could only hear themselves.

In the morning, David said goodbye with the promise to stay in touch and then returned to the Marriott to spend the rest of the day recovering.

*****

As day turned to evening, David could not wait to inform Ken about his encounter with Wagner Gerald and his friend Terek "Sammy" Jafari. When David entered the music room of the Grand Miramar, Ken was beginning to play the last song of his first set. Taking a seat in the shadows near the back of the room, David ordered a cup of coffee and listened to his friend play a swinging take of "Besame Mucho" while the jazz lovers in the audience clapped wildly. When he finished the tune to loud applause, Ken disappeared into the shadows and joined David.

"Nice arrangement."

"I thought I'd try something different on this our last night."

Looking at the tip jar and out of curiosity, David asked, "How much do you make in tips nightly?"

"If I made as much money in New York as I make in the five-star hotel circuit in Europe, I never would have left."

"Nice work, if you can get it, but I've got something better."

"Do you see that oversized champagne glass on the piano full of twenties and hundreds? How could anything be better than that?"

"This is better," David said.

"Okay. Impress me."

"You don't remember Wagner Gerald, a member of the aikido team who is on Senator Wilkins' staff. You went to the men's room. While you were gone, he talked to me in the ante-room the day we got our assignment from the senator. I think he's a trusted member of the staff."

"And?"

"Last night, I was invited to have drinks with him and a few of his friends. When I arrived, I was introduced as a member of the aikido team. One of the three other people at our table was Tarek "Sammy" Jafari, an Egyptian who supposedly works for

NGOs. It took all of my self-control to keep my mouth from falling open. I almost jumped out of my pants."

"Are you kidding? What a stroke of serendipity. I can hardly believe it. The possibility that our problem is Wagner Gerald is most interesting. Do you think the mole is that close to home?"

"I think it is," said David.

"I think it's almost time to set the trap."

"Before we do, we have to know which arms dealer Sammy is working for."

"So the links are becoming clear. Wagner, Sammy, Jakup Abbas, and then who? It's also time to look into the financial life of Wagner Gerald." Then just as his name was mentioned, Wagner Gerald walked into the room with Sammy.

"Do you see the two men who just walked in? Wagner is the white guy," said David.

"And I guess Sammy is the person with him," said Ken.

Ken motioned to the asset who protected him and asked that he get David out of the hotel without being seen. "I'll see you in Monaco." And David disappeared behind the curtains in the back of the room.

"We need to find some information immediately," David said to the field asset, Frank Coit.

"What do you need, David?"

"I need to know if Wagner Gerald and Tarek Jafari have had contact in the past. Perhaps as students. Also, check into Wagner Gerald's financials to see if anything is suspicious. We need that info now. Get back to me as soon as you can. If you can't find me, get it to Ken. Tomorrow we'll both be at the Hermitage. I hope you'll have something."

*****

In the morning, the aikido team took the four hour flight on Air France from Malaga to Nice and arrived at their hotel in Monaco in the late afternoon. Ken Carle was traveling at the same general time, and like the team, checked into the elegant Hermitage Hotel and Casino. Ken would start a week as the headliner in the tasteful Peacock Room and looked forward to playing in the famed venue that had been host to some of the more famous names in Europe and the United States. This included entertainers like Bobby Short, Maurice Chevalier, and Tony Bennett. After making contact, they agreed to have dinner in the hotel at seven o'clock. They met in the formal dining room, but ate at adjacent tables. Each impatient to pursue the investigation of the relationship between Wagner Gerald, his financials, and Sammy Jafari.

"I have not communicated with the Company yet, but it is important that we get the information we need as quickly as we can," said David.

"If the stuff we get is good," said Ken, "we'll have what we need to set the trap."

"But we need other questions answered first. I have questions for the senator, like, who in his office would have had access to the destroyed files regarding the shipments? If we get the answer we think we'll get, there might be other questions. Ken, when you get back to your room, use your dedicated phone to call the senator and ask him. Wagner Gerald is here, so he will have to get the information he needs about further shipments directly from the senator. We'll have to tell him when to share it with Wagner and how to share it with him," David explained.

"But we still don't know who's pulling the strings. Where is the payoff money coming from? Who is selling the weapons and to whom? When we get that info, we'll have it all," said Ken.

The two ate dinner, agreed to have a discreet drink later that evening, and then walked out of the dining room separately.

When Ken returned to his room, he called Washington. Though the senator was deep in sleep, he was true to his word and answered the call when he saw it was on the dedicated line from his anonymous team in Europe.

"Senator, Kenneth Carle on the line. I need some questions answered."

"Fire away, Ken." Not wanting to wake up his wife sleeping quietly next to him, he spoke in muffled tones.

"Who in your office had access to the X files and could know the dates of delivery?" Ken said somewhat cryptically. "If Wagner Gerald is one of them, compare any unusually large deposits in bank accounts to the dates of shipment or hijacking. If you find a correlation, let us know immediately. We might be on the verge of a breakthrough."

"I'll have the answer to your questions as soon as I can, Ken."

"We'll wait to hear from you. Sorry to disturb your sleep, Senator. Good night."

Later that evening, David and Ken sat at the bar with a stool between them. From the bar, each could see much of the room reflected in the expansive mirror that ran the length of the bar. In whispered tones, Ken told David of his conversation with the senator. Anyone seeing them from behind would not assume that the two were together. But when business was done, discussion turned to normal topics: music and the scheduled aikido matches. But before long, David felt a tap on his shoulder and turned around to find Wagner Gerald standing behind him with Sammy Jafari and an unknown man.

"I was hoping to see you, David," said Wagner. "You remember Sammy from Malaga."

"We were all sorry you had to go, David, especially Hilda. It was a fun evening," Sammy added. "I'd like you to meet a good friend, Alborz Tahare. We're going to get a table and have a drink. Would you like to join us?"

"I'd love to," answered David. "By the way, while sitting here at the bar, I met Kenneth Carle, a piano player who will be playing in the Peacock Room starting soon."

Alborz Tahare piped up, "I'm almost sure I've heard you play before." Then he turned to the others and said, "This guy is a fabulous musician." He turned back toward Ken and said, "I'd love it if you'd join us. Will you?"

"Thanks for the invitation, sure. I don't have to start work for another day."

"By the way, Hilda said she hoped you will use the card she gave you," said Sammy.

"I've considered it," said David, smiling. What Sammy said let David know Sammy was unaware he and Hilda spent the evening together, and that was good.

"In this part of the world, a casual liaison is not frowned upon," added Sammy, trying to encourage David.

At the other end of the bar, Ken caught the eye and head signal of the Company asset who had shadowed him since leaving Washington. He knew something was up.

"If you gentlemen get a table, I'll be with you after a pit stop," said Ken.

He followed his shadow to the men's room, while David joined the others at a table.

"You're about to drink with a man who has some power and another who does his bidding," said the Company man.

"Which is which?"

"Alborz Tahare is an arms dealer. Sammy Jafari works for him or anyone else who can pay him. He often does what nobody else will do. Be careful with these guys, they are not stupid. What Wagner Gerald is doing with them is anyone's guess," said the Company man.

"Leave a dossier under my sheets in my room. I've got to get back to my new friends," said Ken.

Ken washed his hands, squirted himself with a little cologne, walked out of the washroom, and found the table where David and the others had settled.

"So Wagner tells me you're on the American aikido team, David," said Alborz.

"I have to admit I'm only an alternate. If any of the team's first-stringers are not able to compete, the coach will call on me. It was Wagner's boss who made it possible for me to make this trip. And I would not be surprised if Wagner was responsible for helping him make the decision."

Wagner said nothing but smiled and feigned modesty, as if he made the trip happen but declined to take credit, even though he had nothing and everything to do with David being there.

"A competitor like you should not be an alternate, David," said Wagner.

"And Sammy, you live the good life. To spend time among interesting people in places like Malaga and Monaco is wonderful. The time I spent with Gabe and Hilda makes me want to stay. I've even entertained the possibility of trying to move here after my time with the Army is up."

"If you decide to do that David, look me up. I might be helpful in finding employment. A man with your skills will not have trouble finding a job. There is always a need for someone who is smart and can handle themselves," said Alborz Tahare.

As people began to come into the Peacock Room, Ken noticed a friend he'd last seen in Macau. It had been a long time, but a woman that beautiful and sexy, who can also play the harp prodigiously, is impossible not to remember. For the first time that night, he saw her harp on the stage and tracked her as she moved in their direction. As she did, Wen Lee saw Ken and rushed to embrace him.

"Kenneth, Kenneth, my darling!" She hugged him affectionately as they looked at each other excitedly. "I've not seen you since our week in Macau. You look great. How are you? I'm so glad you're here." Then she turned toward the stage and saw the manager telling her it was time to play. "Listen Ken, we do two things very well. One was make music. Let's do it now. Okay? We can talk about the other later," she said in an audible whisper that was not missed by others at the table. "I'll come over after the set and meet your friends."

Wen Lee took the stage and moved toward the microphone with a seductive gait that enraptured her audience. She introduced herself and then sat behind an instrument that was almost as beautiful as she was. A heavenly sound emerged from the plucked strings. Then she stopped.

"Ladies and gentlemen, I would like to introduce you to a man I've known for many years. Tonight we have in the audience a very special man and a fabulous pianist. Maybe we can get him to come up and play a song with me. Kenneth, stand and take a bow."

The audience clapped enthusiastically, cajoling Ken to agree to play. His tablemates smiled broadly and encouraged him with more clapping. Ken took to the stage, and after some quick deliberation, Kenneth and Wen Lee decided what to play.

"Maybe you recognize this one. We hope you like it," she said.

Ken played a languid bass line with rich multilayered harmony, punctuated by simple Thelonious Monk-like couplets at the ends of the melodic phrases. Wen Lee turned the harp and the melody it played into a dreamlike offering that sounded much like starlight. The music was irresistible, and the audience sat hypnotized by what they were hearing. Nobody stirred, and if one tried, the tumult of their movement was like blasphemy. The effect was unusual, especially for that time of the evening. When the last note sounded, the audience was embraced with a hush that lasted for a few seconds and then burst into an extended, energetic applause rarely heard in places like the Peacock Room.

"That was 'Stella by Starlight,' written by Victor Young, with beautiful piano played by Mr. Kenneth Carle. If my reading of the management's schedule is correct, Ken will be holding forth on the piano all next week."

Ken walked back to the table and was greeted enthusiastically.

"That might have been the most beautiful piece of music I have ever heard," said Wagner.

"I guess you never know who you're going to meet on a barstool," David added as he continued to play his role.

"If I ever find myself in heaven with an angel like Wen Lee, I'm going to insist that she be joined by you, Kenneth. I will also insist that 'Stella by Starlight' be heaven's theme song," declared Alborz Tahare.

Trying to be funny, Sammy said, "Do you really think people in heaven will listen to you?"

Maybe it was the wrong thing to say because both Ken and David saw Alborz give Sammy a chastising look, as if to say, *You've just stepped over the line, minion, and if it happens again, I'll slap you down.* It was clear Sammy was no pushover and could be as deadly as necessary. But he sat there without saying a word, strongly suggesting he was a subordinate. Given what they'd just witnessed, the two investigators were pushed in the direction of thinking Alborz Tahare might be the missing link, the moneyman, and maybe even the arms dealer. In haste, David finally decided to ask Alborz what he did for a living.

"Kenneth, you are a wonderful piano player, my teammate Wagner is a world-class aikido master, Sammy works for NGOs around the world, but I don't know what you do, Alborz."

"David, I'm an arms merchant," he said with a proud, confident air with the same matter-of-fact delivery that might be heard from a successful shopkeeper or builder of tree houses.

"An arms merchant?" David said with considerable surprise and a feigned naiveté. "Wow, I've never met an arms merchant. That's pretty exotic. How did you get to be one?"

Ken followed suit. "I've met people from all over the world and in almost every profession, but I've never met an arms merchant. Well, I guess I'll have to put that one in my book."

"It's a long story, gentlemen, so I'll give you the short version. I was born into wealth in Iran. While hanging out around Europe, I met a Turkish arms dealer who taught me the business and then died." He spoke his story, all the while keeping his eyes on Wen Lee and listening to her music.

"What a great story!" said David with an intonation suggesting that he was impressed and thankful for being among men who were doing such exciting things.

"Would you introduce me to the wonderful Wen Lee?" Alborz asked of Kenneth.

"I'd be glad to. But keep in mind she is a lady of substance and discriminating taste," Kenneth said in an attempt to dissuade any advances, but he also knew she could handle herself admirably in questionable situations.

"I'm going to give Hilda a call and ask her to come over. I'm sure she'll be glad to see you," Sammy said to David in a teasing way, as if he was encouraging a romance. David smiled and said nothing. He knew there was no time for a tryst. Under other circumstances, the thought of Hilda would have been energizing, but he also knew things would soon change in unpredictable ways.

As they listened to the music, quietly talking and enjoying the evening, a staff member from the Peacock Room whispered to Ken that he was wanted by the management. Ken excused himself and promised to return.

"They probably want to double his contract," Sammy said.

Almost immediately after, another man handed Alborz Tahare a note, and he left the table but returned in a few minutes. David knew something was wrong, and he was now alone among two or more very dangerous people. Now the whole plan ran through his mind. Had he been followed in Africa? Did anyone know of his relationship with Kenneth? If Wagner was the mole, did he suspect Kenneth and David were CIA working for the senator? So he calmly readied himself for battle and waited. But as he looked around the room, he could detect help was with him. The man at the next table with the beautiful woman was someone he'd seen at CIA headquarters. The waiter standing at the door leading to the casino was his shadow and protector assigned by the Company from the beginning. Nonetheless, his heart raced, and adrenaline surged to ready him for the impending altercation. He felt like he was at bat, waiting for the ball to be thrown and expecting a curve.

Kenneth soon returned wearing a dinner jacket. "After a few encouraging words from the booking manager of the Peacock Room, I thought I'd change into something a little more appropriate for the evening." Ken had gotten a full report about Wagner and Sammy from the senator that was left under the sheets in his room. What had become almost obvious was now confirmed.

"After the music you played with the harpist, how could he not encourage you?" said David, trying to reinitiate the conversation.

"We were right, David. The guy we saw coming into the bar was with the other woman. I just saw him." David knew instantly what Kenneth meant. Wagner was probably playing for the other team. Now the trap could be set.

*****

The next morning, Wagner Gerald got a call from Senator Wilkins.

In the storied Southern twang the senator was known for, he talked to Wagner Gerald as if he was a friend. "How is yo body holdin' up, boy? Ah read that ya'll won the first match. Keep up the good work. America needs a win. I also wanted to update you on what was happ'nin' here. You likely heard, but Harriette McKay left and took a job with *The Post*. She'll make a fine reporter. And oh yeah, we startin' the Africa project again. We think its okay now. We'll ship next week and we think it'll be there by the fifth of the month. The Republicans are still a pain in the ass, and my wife is still spending too much. We miss you, son. Call me in a week."

What Washington had unearthed before the previous night's dinner was that Wagner Gerald and Tarek Sammy Jafari were roommates and best friends in college. After college, they remained best friends, with frequent visits back and forth between Egypt and the US. It was also discovered that Wagner made some large bank deposits a week before each hijacking, totaling almost $600,000. Tarek Jafari had financed the entire enterprise. But now that the players were identified, the ruse could be initiated. Trucks carrying empty crates were driven to the designated coordinates in Chad. Since Wagner alone knew there were new shipments, he would be implicated, along with Sammy Jafari, who hired the band of thieves to intercept the shipments. The hijackers were caught in the process and thrown into prison in Chad without due process.

Wagner Gerald was picked up in Monaco by Company men. Within a day, he was interrogated and then disappeared in the custody of the FBI. Six months later, *The Washington Post* reported that a low-level staffer of Senator Wilkins had been investigated and charged with espionage. Tarek Sammy Jafari and Alborz Tahare disappeared. They were last seen by desert nomads stumbling around the Sudanese desert which was on the verge of war over disputed grazing land. They too seemed to have disappeared, and their bodies were later discovered. In a week, the shipments of arms to the Democratic Sudanese Front started again. David returned to Washington, and Kenneth continued to be the eyes and ears of US interests as he played his way across Europe, coincidentally in the venues where aikido tournaments were scheduled.

18

Opportunity

After solving the Wagner Gerald case, David remained with the Company for two more years. He was respected as a go-to agent and, more often than not, worked with his friend Ken Carle. He enjoyed the work and was seldom taken away from his children for uncomfortable periods. David had learned to like the work he did, but in truth, it was the only kind of work he had ever done. Working for the CIA offered attractive perks. Enough time and money to be a good father were high on the list. One of the other perks was one he thought little about but was often suggested by his colleagues: paid educational tuition. The government was willing to pay for credit-bearing courses at any school he wished to attend, and under some circumstances, even paid for room and board. David thought colleagues suggested this because others saw in him a certain lack of sophistication or cultural illiteracy. Right or wrong, his paranoia pushed him in the direction of school. And after some hesitation because of his limited formal education compared to virtually all of his colleagues, David enrolled as a night student at George Washington University. At first nervous about what to expect and with complete ignorance of what the experience would be, he approached the task with the same intensity and commitment he approached everything new. Not only was he startled by the amount of information he did not know, but he also absorbed that information with relish. He liked what he was learning in nineteenth-century history because it gave what he'd read of the Afro-American experience heft and context. He liked literature because it could communicate the best and worst of how humans behave within the contexts of their lives, whether artfully or not. He also loved the logic of science and its drive to reduce error and to carry humanity into the future. Though he was attracted to these things, it was the information itself that gave him a sense of power and understanding he had not known before. In short, David was seduced by Western liberal arts and the social and cultural evolution from which they sprang. For the first time, the idea of literacy took on a meaning beyond the ability to read and write. David wanted more. Along with the required courses, he began to take more advanced courses on the scientific side of psychology and on the philosophical questions that often sprang from psychological questions. Over the course of his undergraduate years, he found he was more interested in school than in working in an intelligence capacity for the CIA. After assisting struggling students in his classes, he also discovered what he wanted to do with his professional life. Finally, the boy who did not know what he wanted to do with his life was clear about where he was going.

After some discussion with his friend Kenneth Carle, David decided to negotiate a partial separation from the Company with the agreement that he could periodically be asked to add an extra set of eyes and ears to a problem. The Company would allow him to leave full-time employment but continue to pay his tuition in exchange for part-time employment. With only the GI bill, some savings, and a scholarship, David enrolled at George Washington University as a full-time student. His past experience did not prepare him for the adjustments he would be required to make. Older than most students, David missed the so-called freedom of the post-adolescent years—the time-consuming sexual fantasies fueled by raging hormones, the senseless consumption of alcohol, and the pervasive delusion that success would open its golden doors and the world would empty its largesse into his life. These were all issues he no longer had to deal with. He had been inoculated by the serious and time-consuming responsibility that only the military can provide, so he'd never appreciated the potential freedom afforded to an eighteen to twenty-four-year-old college student. David was armed with a limited and biased high school experience, the Army, the CIA, and a comparatively narrow life. He saw the students who swarmed around him as special. Most were nurtured in competitive academic high schools and were standouts in some extracurricular realm, and most had been given the opportunity to travel in at least one other culture or learned to speak another language. David had always been intrigued by the possibility of speaking French and with the schools foreign language requirement, he took full advantage of the possibilities. In addition to the students, the buildings themselves helped set the stage for a certain tradition of excellence that he took seriously. Many of the faculty were among the young lions in their respective academic disciplines, and most were noted beyond GWU as having the potential for making significant contributions. At first anxious and disconcerted, David soon settled down and began to appreciate the freedoms and explorations, both social and academic that play out during the college years. He waited by the offices of professors who he thought had something to say, and he discussed the implications of their work. He attached himself to students willing to engage in conversation about their interests or those who simply wanted to share their curiosity about this or that. He enjoyed the fruits of nubile sensuality but with the same quiet discretion and respect he had always shown his partners. For David, college was like an epicurean feast, and for three years, he savored every dish and filled himself with the good and the bad, the insightful and the ridiculous, the transformational and the inflexible. Then in his final term of undergraduate school and still hungry for more, he was accepted into a PhD Psychology program at Sherrington University with a full scholarship from the National Science Foundation. Much to his surprise, GWU awarded him the honorific designation of Departmental Scholar in Psychology.

His two boys came to his graduation, escorted by Valerie and her husband, Tony Batone. Ken Carle and his boss, Kent Williams, also came to congratulate David and wish him well. Though proud of his achievement, especially in the sight of his sons, the day was bittersweet. He would have given the world to have his father know that his son graduated from college and that his line, a chip off his block, finished near the top of his class. Pop would not have appreciated or even understood the work he did for the Army, nor could he have valued the importance of jobs like securing the safe shipment of arms to rebels sympathetic to democratic ideals. But graduating from college would have been the pinnacle. This one thing, more than anything else, would have filled his father with pride, and in turn, allowed David to unburden himself of what he thought his father would have wanted for him. Because David was who he was, he would carry the weight of his father's unfulfilled life and early death for the rest of his life and would never lose sight of where he came from and how much Pop meant to him. That poor, bedraggled, and defeated man with a deep abiding sorrow and an undying love for his long-deceased wife would always be his guiding light, his beacon in the worst of storms. This foundation would always be with him, even though his future was still unwritten.

19

Graduate School

Sherrington University and the small town surrounding it were tree-covered havens built over a few hundred years by the sons of the wealthy and the intellectual elite. With its Gothic buildings inspired by the models of Oxford and Cambridge, Sherrington aimed to achieve the same commitment to academic excellence and a comparable international reputation. Acceptance into one of its graduate programs was itself something to be proud of. The small number of applicants allowed to grace its hallowed halls knew much would be given, and consequently much would be expected. Of those accepted that year, David alone wore the colors of Africa on his face and the Jim Crow south in his heart. At this, more than any other time in life, he felt like "a fly in the buttermilk," conspicuous, exotic, and on display. Given the politics of the day, it was not just that he felt like an administrative experiment devised by some benevolent liberal, he had reason to feel like the object of suspicion. Correct or not, behind inquiring eyes, he thought he could read the hurtful question, "Why are you here?" He knew he was being measured and discussed. He also knew the betting odds were not in his favor. And in his defiance of that reality or of his own paranoia, his answer to himself was always the same, "I aspire to be a university professor." And for the first time, the work he did was not determined by the somewhat passive act of being chosen. This time, he would be the master of his own fate, able to follow the direction of his own mind and be the recipient of any acknowledgment that might accrue. It was clear to David that whatever else the elite Sherrington University was, it was giving him the opportunity to find and be himself. For that, he was thankful.

It might have been Valerie's promise that she would not allow their children to be far from David. It might have been the allure of Sherrington's quality public schools and academic atmosphere, but shortly after David arrived at the university, Valerie and her husband, along with the children, moved to the town. Now with the presence of his children, David could concentrate on his work and not have to bare the loss of Josh and Lynn while doing it. He and his children could share sports, do homework, talk about daily happenings, and spend lazy, aimless time wandering through life, guided in part by David's values and perceptions. Given the structure of the family, a more perfect arrangement could not have been devised. More than once he let Valerie know how thankful he was for her keeping her promise and how unusual it was. "If I was destined to have children, I could not have chosen a better person to share them with," he told her.

Sherrington's graduate program in psychology was unusual. The requirements did not include a plethora of courses that culminate in a prescribed number of credits qualifying you for a degree. In the psychology program, there were only three required courses. A year-long professional seminar covering the whole of experimental psychology and requiring extensive reading, a year-long statistics course extending through multivariate analysis, and a test requiring students to read the psychological literature in two languages other than their native language. The approach of the entire department was scientific/experimental. Every student worked in one or more laboratories with a faculty adviser or worked on their own general research problems with an advising faculty member in that study area. Except for the quantitative course and the language requirement, there was only a qualifying examination. Evaluations of graduate students were made in everyday conversations and problem-solving discussions about the work taking place in various laboratories or about specific experimentation. If there was interest in a particular kind of problem, whether theoretical or empirical, a student or group of students would search the literature, develop a reading list, and do the work to become informed. The unspoken expectation was that you would shape yourself to be like the faculty. After two years, students tested to qualify for the master's degree. Qualifying for the master's required passing examinations taken over the course of three days and covering a broad swathe of discipline-related subject matter. Also, students were required to develop a research protocol leading to publishable experimentation that had to be presented to the entire department and defended. At this point, the faculty made decisions as to who would be asked to pursue a PhD from Sherrington University. This was a critical time in the lives of students who had strained to satisfy the unspoken expectations of a revered faculty. Most students had been praised throughout their entire life. They had been held up as models of success and chosen as award recipients. But now they were being judged by an idiosyncratic standard that was never questioned. Three out of four students were given the master's degree and informed that another university might be a better fit. This often resulted in crying and the gnashing of teeth. Nervous twitches developed and insistence on reevaluation argued. Some, overwhelmed by shame and embarrassment, simply disappeared. Most often the decision not to support continuation had little to do with intelligence but much to do with a whole constellation of personal attributes that didn't align with faculty idiosyncrasies.

Fortunately for David, Sherrington tried to teach and required lessons he already learned. Without knowing it, the engineers at Heron Designs taught him how to be an integral part of a professional group while maintaining productive independence. The military taught him how to be disciplined and fastidious, and with the CIA, he learned the importance of a good strategy and research protocol. By nature, he was self-directed and independent with an analytic orientation. So as much as his physical attributes were salient in the beginning, what impressed the faculty even more was the ease at which David became a respected colleague in the halls of the psychology department. David as a recipient of the terminal degree became implicit.

In addition to the work that would allow him to blossom at Sherrington, David pursued a question that had nagged him for years: how did the medication Lopresid contribute to his father's death? Also, there was the nagging question as to whether his death was caused by the drug itself or confounded by the drug's tendency to instigate suicidal thoughts, causing his father to refuse medical treatment. Years had passed since it was taken off the market, and much more effective drugs for depression had entered the market. But before that happened, it was confirmed that the death and suicide rates in particular were three times that of patients not taking Lopresid. For David, the tragedy that left an open wound was that Tremont Pharmaceutical did not take the drug off the market until they had to. How long did they push Lopresid after they knew it was a killer? Reviewing the investigative articles written for public consumption, it became clear they were guilty of knowing and chose profit instead. He had been right about the drug and also about Tremont's motivations. Luckily, the drug was taken off the market after the class action suit had been filed. If nothing else, they might pay for their greed. The resolution was political and did not really satisfy his need for personal retribution. He blamed Tremont for his father's death and, for the rest of his career, participated in pharmaceutical watchdog efforts.

David was convinced that understanding human behavior and thought required an understanding of both an environmental analysis and an understanding of the nervous system. He studied the techniques of Pavlov and the associative conditioning literature derived from those techniques. He also studied Clark Hull and B. F. Skinner as well as the central and peripheral nervous system, paying particular attention to the motivational aspects of the limbic system and the hypothalamus in particular. It was impossible to investigate these things in humans, so he took a comparative evolutionary approach and studied them in animals. Unlike many who continually argued for a cognitive vs. behavioral analysis, from the beginning, David believed that biological predispositions helped guide thinking and behavior. So as most of the department's faculty were teaching only in the narrow area of their research, David was developing and learning how to prepare an advanced course that successfully integrated behavior, cognition, biology, and heredity. This effort alone brought him attention and well-wishers. In the last year of his residency at Sherrington University, David accepted invitations from other universities to speak about his efforts at achieving an interdisciplinary approach. These invitations led to post-degree job offers, one of which came from Flemington University, located only twenty miles from Sherrington and on its way to being respected by some of the better-known universities. Flemington University offered him a joint professorship on a tenure line in psychology and biology, an offer that was highly unusual and that he gladly accepted. In time, he would be an associate professor and then move on to a full professorship. Here is where David Walton would stay and spend the remainder of his career.

20

Ann

From a very young age, David and his father dreamed of seeing the exotic, romantic, and exciting parts of the world that came alive in their imaginations. While working for the government, he traveled a bit, but that travel was about work and not culturally informative or enjoyable. He was dropped in a foreign location to solve a problem, and even if he saw things, he could not understand them in context, so it meant little. Over time, friends and colleagues inundated him with tales of their foreign duty stations and travels and talked about the world as if they were card-carrying members of the places where they traveled. But because of some quirk of fate, David missed the charms of traveling and often daydreamed about when his chance would come. He knew it was just a daydream. He knew because he had to pay child support for his two boys, to whom he was totally dedicated. One day, the newspaper featured a story on the charms of Paris in the spring. The music, art, and history almost jumped off the page. He became immersed in a fantasy that lasted long enough for him to go deaf to the sounds around him and not hear the knock on his office door.

"Excuse me, Dr. Walton. If you have a minute, I'd like to speak with you and maybe get some advice on a couple of things." Rebounding out of his reverie and shaking himself into focus, he invited the woman at his door into his office.

"What can I do for you?" he asked.

As she walked through the door and took the four or five steps to his desk, Dr. Walton was able to evaluate her frame and thought it pleasing. The military and CIA training taught him to make and remember quick evaluations of people, and she was no exception. Being five feet five or six, the cut and quality of her clothes and the way she carried herself indicated she did not need resources.

"Well," she said in a tone that suggested she was there to get a solution to some problem and was willing to do what was necessary to get her way. It was clear she was ready to charm or fight her way to a solution that satisfied her aims.

"You probably don't remember me, but I took your Intro to Neuroscience class last semester. It was a large class, and I sat in the back at the top of the amphitheater and did not make myself known."

David engaged his prodigious memory and struggled to remember her in the class. Unfortunately, he could not.

She couldn't yet divulge the fact that throughout the term, she had developed an interest in him, not as a professor but as a man. She liked that he could not be rattled very easily. She was intrigued that he could be informal without losing sharpness and by the habits that made him appear street-smart, even though he was an academic. Most of all, she respected his close relationship with his children, who he wove into examples whenever he could. She found it endearing that he made his teenage children an integral part of his life because she also had teenage children she adored. *An interesting looking woman*, David thought.

"My name is Ann Hickman, and I'm a graduate student in philosophy trying to switch into neuroscience. I've been told you are the person who could help me negotiate the process so that I can get it done with the least amount of frustration."

"I think you might have come to the right place," he said. "I'm officially a graduate adviser. This is an unusual request so you'll have to give me some time. I don't know how long it will take, so what you can do is enroll in neuroscience courses while I find out what can be done. I think you should check in once a week and I'll let you know what's happening with your request. Was there something else you wanted to talk about?"

"There are probably many things I'd like to talk to you about," Ann said. "But for the moment, I would like to get this problem solved."

Walton's phone rang, and after a few knowing nods and grunts in response to the phone call, he said, "I'm sorry, Ms. Hickman, but I have to take this call. I don't know how long it will take to gather the information you want. You should check in periodically. But give me a little time. The bureaucracy sometimes moves at a snail's pace."

"Sounds good," answered Ann. With that, she turned and left.

Monday arrived and Dr. Walton started his regular routine. After teaching, he stopped to pick up his coffee and newspaper. As he walked through the building, he noticed a familiar face sitting in a mostly empty study room. It was Mrs. Hickman reading a text with an open notebook. Without hesitation, he stopped.

"Good morning, Mrs. Hickman. I'm surprised to see you this early." Looking up from her book and smiling, she said, "I'm the mother of two teenage children. Getting up early is a requirement, but if I had my choice, I prefer the evening. I feel more alive at night. But please, call me Ann."

"Since informality is what you prefer, call me David." Ann appeared to be around the same age as David and he really liked her smile and her style and wanted to stay and chat, but he had a meeting to go to. "It was good to see your morning smile, and if you'd like to drop by Friday, I'd love to see you." David turned and said goodbye. He walked to his office thinking about how effortlessly attractive she was. After David left, Ann sat with her book, thinking about what it would be like to be held in the arms of a man like David. It had been a long time since she felt the heat of attraction, and maybe it was stronger than she had ever felt. She wanted to make the next visit soon.

He did not know how attracted she was to him and that the attraction was growing. Both were new to the flirtation game but were not the type of people who would hesitate to take the next step. It was a dangerous game for each of them. For black men like David, it was much more. He knew that race and racism ran through the cultural fabric of America and could do damage. He could be fired for having a liaison with a student. She could throw her marriage into turmoil. Lives could be destroyed in such a way that it would take years to recoup, and when that kind of damage is done, getting back on your feet may never happen. Nonetheless, the attraction was powerful. Perhaps stronger than either of them had ever experienced. What I am doing, David said to himself. I hardly know the woman. Having such a detailed fantasy is crazy. She is interesting and definitely attractive, but I need to control myself.

For the next few weeks, each made an effort to be in the student center so they could see each other. Each day, they spent time talking about life, children, and school. Ann, in all her sophistication, was slightly silly and smart. David was witty and inventive. They got along famously, and the flirtation moved to another level. One Thursday, David looked for Ann but could not find her. He waited through two cups of coffee but still no Ann. Eventually, he gave up the search and went back to his office. Opening his door, he found a letter addressed to Dr. David Walton on the floor. It read:

Dear Dr. Walton,

> Circumstances beyond my control have made it impossible for us to meet before Monday. If things change, I will give you a call.

> Ann

David spent the rest of the day hoping for a call, but it never came. He waited past noon the next day, but the call never came. Disappointed, David went home to an empty apartment.

It was not until Monday morning they saw each other again. "I'm happy to see you, Ann. I hope everything is all right."

"Everything is fine. I had to do some business at my country club that other members could have done if they were the least bit thoughtful. At any rate, I resigned my committee assignment for the golf tournament and told them that with school, I no longer had the time. There was a little displeasure, but it's been resolved."

The weeks had gone by and as they saw each other more, there was something about Ann that seemed inhibited. He felt that something was being held back or unexplored. The occasional puckering of her lips or downward cast of her eyes. Changes in posture and breaks in the flow of her words suggested she was deciding to avoid specific topics or to obfuscate an area of her life she thought out of bounds. David thought it rude and perhaps aggressive to insinuate himself into every corner of Ann's personal life. All he could do at this point was gently guide the areas of her experience into the light of his own understanding. He was also fully aware that another man might not be looking for what he was looking for. Another man might want to bed her, and for all he knew, her interest might be exclusively prurient. Not knowing where his interest in Ann would take him, his best bet would be to go with his feelings, and page by page the nature of their relationship would be revealed. They met in his office, as always, he had to control himself.

"I think you know by now that I'm a good listener, and here I am, ready and willing," said David.

"Are you saying that you could take time now?"

"Yes," David answered emphatically.

"Okay then, I'll give you a snapshot of my life as I see it."

"I can't talk to my children. They're too young to understand. I can't talk to the women in my social circle because they're all a bunch of repressed defenders of their privilege. They see nothing but how wealth makes them look."

"What do you mean?" asked David.

Searching for a way to make it clear, she finally said, "My husband is a very successful man."

"What does he do?" asked David.

"He's the CEO of the Tremont Pharmaceutical Company, which I'm sure you may know is one of the largest pharmaceutical companies in the world. He travels constantly. I mean he's gone all the time. And when he's at home, he's not really home because there is always a meeting, a dinner, a gala, or a speaking engagement that he must attend. The only thing he gives the children and me is the financial wherewithal to do what we want and have what we want. That is why I decided to go back to college and get an advanced degree in something that was interesting and demanding. I needed something worth doing to take up my time. I need interaction and conversation with adult company. In short, I need some meaning in my life with experiences that take me out of the material world. My only real and meaningful adult company has been my best friend and housekeeper, Lorraine."

Upon hearing Ann's husband was the chief executive of Tremont, David's hackles went up. It was a visceral response instigated by a deep animus that had nothing to do with Ann. It was all he could do not to show his disdain for her husband and his company. He controlled himself, knowing his participation in pharmaceutical watchdog groups was his way to prevent future abuse and criminal behavior. David was suddenly aware of a subconscious desire to get back at Philip Hickman through his wife. In addition to her physical attractiveness, his hate for Tremont might also be a motivation to seduce Ann to satisfy some nebulous need for revenge. He pushed this thought away and resolved then that he would never let Ann know of his belief that Tremont was responsible for what happened to his father. To the best of his ability, he would strive not to link Ann to Tremont in any way. Composing himself, he focused on Ann's story of her relationship with Lorraine.

"How does that work? She's your best friend and house-keeper?" asked David in a voice that questioned the wisdom of such an arrangement.

"It's a story that I've told to few people. My husband doesn't know about everything. If I told him, he would not have allowed it. He grew up with servants who, to say the least, were not treated like friends. For him, household employees should be treated like servants. He likes being in command and likes to show his power and largesse. I didn't know it when we married, but his worldview is very much like those women at the country club. It's simply a male version. After my first child, I stayed with him out of self-preservation. Sometimes I look at him move through his social world, and it reminds me of a pageant."

"Many people would say you've landed in a pot of jam. They would say you've made it. You are one of the few who have the American dream. You're very lucky," said David.

"I would be lucky if I didn't have a soul. I would be lucky if I didn't see and understand how people suffer or if I didn't want to get my hands dirty trying to help or if I didn't want to expand my level of understanding about the world."

"These are all noble thoughts," said David. "But I'd love to hear more about your relationship with Lorraine."

"Are you sure?" asked Ann.

"I'm sure."

"When I was in college, my parents were killed in a car accident. I was devastated and felt a paralyzing sorrow. I needed professional help, but I didn't know it or how to ask for it. Trying to lift myself out of depression, I joined a women's shelter as a volunteer. I thought immersing myself in meaningful work would help heal my pain. Although I felt good about helping people in need, I needed help. One day, I encountered a woman sitting alone reading. When I approached, she said nothing and didn't look at me. I sat with her in silence.

"Of all the women I saw in the shelter, Lorraine alone had an interest in reading. She was not reading trash or the popular fiction of the day. She was reading literature. Theodore Dreiser, Henry James, and Mark Twain were among the people she read. I later discovered these were the names she remembered from her father's bookcase, so I would sit next to her and pick up the books she finished and read them as I sat with her. It took a few months, but she slowly began to talk. First, a simple yes or no, but over time, she began to talk with me about what we were reading. I never asked personal questions about how her life had led her to the shelter. I knew about some of the other women in the shelter. Drugs, lost jobs, mothers with children trying desperately to keep a family together and undiagnosed mental illness were just a few of the histories of shelter inhabitants' stories."

"Who Lorraine was finally began to reveal itself. She came from a middle-class family that, because of mistaken identity, had all been killed by local thugs looking for a stash of drugs. Her father was a successful lawyer who later became a well-known furniture and cabinet maker. Her mother was a painter who moonlighted as a political activist. Hiding under her father's workbench saved her life. At the age of twelve, she was thrown into one foster home after another. Rape and abuse followed her at every new placement, and Lorraine developed a pathological hatred of men and a deep distrust of women. By the end of my third year in college, Lorraine learned to trust me and attached herself to me. It was almost like a psychiatric transference. She would not let me out of her sight, and I liked her being there. Yes, her presence filled the hole left by my parents. I needed her. One of the things I liked about her was an artistic flair she'd show me but hid from others. Our conversations became increasingly intellectual, and believe it or not, she brought strength and clarity to my life. Although there was some talk we were too close, I knew I needed her. She said she would always protect me, and I wanted her to. My parents left me with a small trust fund, so I moved off campus and into a two-bedroom apartment in town. Lorraine took the second bedroom. I set her up well, and she took care of me. The deal was simple. I would give her a place to live, and she would prepare meals, keep the apartment clean, and be my friend. She would often go with me to class, sit through lectures, and help me appreciate the import of what we were studying. We would even shop together. If I have any taste or flair for fashion at all, it's Lorraine's doing. I came to depend on her as much as she depended on me. Over time, we each developed a strong attachment. If Lorraine did not know where I was, she became agitated. If I lost track of her, I worried. We were a team."

"How long did the mutual dependency last? And what did your husband think about your relationship with Lorraine?" asked David.

"Would the Queen's lady-in-waiting be dismissed by the King when they married? Of course not. My husband has a single focus. Nothing is more important to him than business. He loves his children, but he does not know how to relate to them. He knows nothing about sports or games of any kind. He is extremely serious, and close physical contact makes him nervous. I think he likes Lorraine more than he likes me because she is formal and serious when she interacts with him. She chooses his shirts, ties, and shoes. He wears a suit night and day and can impress anybody with his smart presentation and pocketbook. I find some of his gestures and expressions…let's say that I find them interesting. Every time Lorraine sees one, she rolls her eyes."

She continued, "When I met Philip, Lorraine and I were far enough along in our relationship that he was not a problem for her. In fact, he is the first man she allowed 'in' since being emancipated from the state's care. She liked Philip. By the time I married, it was almost a given that she was part of the package. As time passed, Lorraine defined the kind of relationship she would have in our lives. When the children came along, she called herself nanny and housekeeper. Even though she was well compensated for her work, Lorraine is like a sister to me, a second mother to my children, and a member of my family."

Although intrigued by what she had just shared, his only option was to trust that her relationship with Lorraine was, in fact, how Ann described it. Only time would tell its true nature.

*****

Vince Greenhouse was a professor in the Philosophy Department whose office was in the same building as Dr. Walton's. David had consulted him regarding what it would take to shift areas of concentration as a graduate student. He was a frequently published scholar and a respected colleague and often took administrative assignments when he was needed. It was also true Vince could not stay away from female students.

"I've seen you talking to a woman in the student center, David. I also saw her in the hallway near my office the other day. What a looker. I sure would like to buy her dinner."

"Are you always on the make, Vince?"

"Not always, but when I see something like that, my nature begins to rise and my instinctive tendency to stalk emerges. It's the proverbial mating call, my good man."

David did not want any suspicion or interference from Vince, who could be a formidable adversary, so he began to invent reasons why he should let this one go without trying.

"I asked one of my old spook friends about her Vince, and her husband might be a CIA operative masquerading as an international businessman. I think his cover is pharmaceuticals, and he's often in the media talking to the government. What he and the government are really talking about is anybody's guess. It's also been suggested by the same friend that this guy is dangerous, and worst of all, he's a jealous husband. If I were you, I'd walk away and go rekindle one of your previous conquests. I'd hate for you to disappear or be found stuffed in your filing cabinet or strangled by the bowline of that raggedy ass boat of yours or whatever those guys do when they're mad at someone. I can see the headlines now: professor dies under mysterious circumstances. If I were you, instead of tempting fate, I'd watch some porn and take a cold shower."

"When you talk like that, I know I'm about to cross 'the thin red line,'" said Vince.

He was fully aware of David's background and did not hesitate to take him seriously. He had seen David's training and physical abilities in action twice, so this kind of talk did not seem far-fetched.

One such incident occurred in the hallway just outside of Vince's office. After receiving an unwanted grade from Professor Vomsaal, another neuroscientist, a large and aggressive football player who was being denied graduation, came to argue the quality of his work. Already angry, his intensity increased when it became clear to him a mistake had not been made and his grade would not be changed. The student left, but expecting a volcanic response, Vomsaal locked his door from the inside. Returning to plead his case again and finding the door locked, the student exploded in anger and began banging on the door until it gave. His shouting and screaming at his adversary reached a fever pitch. The professor squealed for help. Others in the vicinity watched what was going on but were too frightened to try to stop it. David came out of nowhere, grabbed the student, and subdued him with very little effort. The assailant continued to try to attack and was twice thrown to his back, and instead felt the pain he intended for Professor Vomsaal. He stayed on his back until security arrived. It was quick. Others stared in disbelief at what had just happened. David walked back to his office and closed the door.

Unfortunately and much to David's chagrin, there was another situation that put his training on display. This time, the encounter was in a classroom full of students who were all in danger.

An early fall morning began with the sun, a slight breeze, and a sweater-wearing nip in the air. Vince, David, and Saul Kenton, who taught logic, congregated in David's office to have their morning coffee and discuss local departmental and campus-wide politics and scuttlebutt. The time they spent together in the morning helped seal their relationship and loosened up their performance skills in preparation to meet yet another class of students. This was their regular routine: coffee, talk, and finally a slow walk to their classroom building where each had scheduled their morning class so they might inhale the seasonal beauty of the campus. Tall seventy-year-old oaks and maples lined the walkways and stood sporadically on the lawns, giving the campus a grove-like feel. Interestingly, when the school had originally been built, no walkways were poured. Students and faculty simply took the shortest or most attractive route between the buildings and tramped the pathways of the campus. Once the pathways were established, only then were the sidewalks poured. This had the effect of saving existing trees and providing a template for future planting. So, each morning the instructors would admire the beauty and upkeep of the campus and reassure each other that being there was a gift worth keeping. The irony of their musings was that they were all tenured faculty and would not be leaving. The grass was green enough where they were. Students and faculty alike knew the three of them could disagree, but what was also known was that they stood together.

Twice a week, they would walk into their respective classrooms at eight o'clock in Edison Hall, and their lectures would begin. Professor Kelton used an integrated approach and would talk about philosophical ideas and schools of thought through an approach he had created. The textbook was supplemental. He would sit at his desk and talk. He would not tolerate lateness, sleeping, private conversations, or not paying attention. He would not tolerate disagreement without a reference and he considered a missed test or paper an indication of a student's character and would excoriate them in class. By midsemester, half the class would have dropped out, and the half that remained were treated to a first-rate education by a noted scholar.

One day, after class began, a slightly older student and veteran came to class late. Professor Kelton began to talk to him as if he were a delinquent child. It proved to be too much for the student, and he snatched Kelton out of his chair from behind his desk and started throwing him around the front of the classroom. A female student went screaming down the hall and knocking on doors for help. David opened his door, heard the commotion, and rushed to Kelton's room to assist. When he entered the room, the man had Kelton by the collar and was slapping his face like a bully would slap a woman. Without a word, David grabbed his hand in a special way and threw him across the room after telling the horrified students to leave and call campus police. Vince watched the man attack David unsuccessfully as David immobilized and slammed the man to the floor, bloody and defeated. The students were amazed, and Vince later said it was like watching a movie. Kelton was bruised a bit but otherwise unhurt. After that, David's campus reputation as someone you should not offend grew.

*****

Two or more weeks passed slowly, and David thought his next meeting with Ann was taking too long. He busied himself, but the thought of Ann never left his mind. He read student papers, answered mail, and opened letters. In one letter from the Academic Dean, he was alerted of his eligibility for a semester-long sabbatical, but for the sabbatical to be granted, a proposal had to be written, submitted, and evaluated in competition with others. The letter gave deadline dates and offered best wishes. He knew he would not apply, so he forgot it immediately. On Thursday, a few students came in for help, and grad students submitted progress reports; the day ended uneventfully.

When David reached home that night, Ann was still very much on his mind. He needed something that would alter his mindset, and as it often happens, his kids provided his much needed change of focus.

"What are you guys doing?" David asked.

"Dad, we need your opinion."

"Josh and I are trying to figure out which African country has the closest political and military ties with the US government."

"I don't know offhand," said David. "But if you give me a few minutes to hang up my coat and put my briefcase down, I'll be glad to join the investigation."

David knew this kind of question demanded much more information than could be discovered by two teenage boys on the Internet. He showed them how the problem should be approached, and with that instruction, they resumed the investigation and analyzed the available information.

"All arrows seem to point to Morocco," said David. "Do you guys agree?"

"I think I agree," Josh said.

"I'm not so sure," said Lynn, but after further consideration, he agreed it was likely Morocco, given how it was situated geographically, with no other country between it and the United States. It is also an Islamic country with strong ties to the Arabic world and the Middle East. In 1786, Morocco was an early ally after the American Revolution.

The investigation shifted to Morocco's history and culture. They discovered an interest in the souks, markets, and medinas of Morocco and in the realistic look they offer into what life might have been like in the first one thousand years AD. Every major city is blessed with both old and new sections. You can step out of the fifth century and into the twenty-first. These and other things excited them, and they spent the rest of the evening talking about how nice a trip to Morocco would be. The boys were hooked, and they went to bed ready to read *The Arabian Nights*. Even though the stories did not emerge from Morocco, the flavor of the stories was close enough. As

David slipped between the covers, he imagined Ann's face as Shahrazad and fell asleep with her and Morocco on his mind.

The next morning, David woke hoping he would spend some time with Ann. With his morning routine complete and the kids off to school, David whistled his way to work, and Friday being a day of very few classes, the campus was relatively empty. He waited through the morning hours doing small tasks and looking at the clock, waiting for his encounter with Ann. At noon, he heard footsteps in the hall; soon a coquettish head peered around his office door. She wore a tasteful frock in a fashion designed to turn heads. David composed himself.

All he could think to say was "Good afternoon, Ann. I hope you're feeling well. Did you come to show me your afternoon smile?"

Ann beamed and then pulled a chair past the side of his desk on the same plane as his chair. Crossing her legs, David could take in the full measure of her presence. "I'd like you to know that I've done my homework and can now tell you how you can switch your concentration to neuroscience," said David.

"You certainly have a way of getting right down to business, David."

"I like to take care of business first so time isn't wasted," as he pointed to a piece of paper in front of him containing a list. "Here is what you have to do, and these are the people you have to see. I've spoken to each one of them."

"I know it's been a while since we applied for a change in your course of study. A number of people had to consider your request. First the neuroscience department had to accept you. When that was done, the dean had to approve the change. Finally, the provost had to sign off on it." As he continued to explain the process, the afternoon sun streamed through the window, and shafts of light illuminated book bindings and cast an amber glow on the office.

"They will be expecting you. So that's that." David leaned forward in his chair, and the two began to chat with each other again. It was all so easy, and before long, their verbal play spilled over into playful touching. Ann stood and moved closer. "Is this too close?" she asked.

"I think the puzzle pieces fit," said David. With that, they were close enough to feel the rise and fall and warmth of the others breathing. Without any self-consciousness, they were in each other's arms and almost close enough for love. "I think you're right, David. The pieces do fit." Then slowly, gently, and lovingly, they kissed and smiled and then kissed again. It was not passionate kissing. Not an impatient or theatrical kiss certified by a movie director. It was a soft welcoming kiss that spoke only of their hearts' joy. Their meeting ended with a beginning. It was almost something unworthy of belief, but they both wanted it.

Before leaving, Ann, with one hand in David's and one noodling papers on his desk, noticed the letter offering a sabbatical leave. "Is this something you intend to do, David?"

"I've given it no thought, but it sure would be nice," said David. "I don't have a lot of time before I have to make a decision. Maybe I can talk about it with you. When can we see each other again?"

"By the way, David, I've noticed the diamond ring on your right hand and wondered about it. Does it have any meaning? Or is it just a ring?"

"The stone was given to me by my parents. It means everything to me."

"One day, you'll have to tell me, but now I have to leave. I will see you soon. Goodbye." David watched her body move as she walked away from his desk and into his imagination. As the last of her turned into the hall, he fingered his ring, knowing that she would be back.

21

The Undiscovered

When David landed the tenure track professorship at the university, he was also lucky to find a spacious two-bedroom apartment at the Executive House, a fifteen-story building designed for the successful business and professional class who did not want to live the Better Homes and Gardens lifestyle. Well-appointed and replete with amenities, the Executive House was much like a hotel. Clothes could be washed in the state-of-the-art laundry room or, for a monthly fee, left by the door and picked up, washed, ironed, and returned. Visitors had to be announced, and those who drove had their cars parked for them by attendants. The basement was outfitted with an up-to-date gym that required a membership and directly behind the building, a five-lane swimming pool with a lifeguard was the social meeting place for residents in the warmer months. Behind the pool, a two-story garage had on its roof enough space for two tennis courts and a basketball court, surrounded by lounge areas for relaxing. Each apartment had two parking spaces with additional spaces for visitors.

For teenage boys, the building provided enough activities to keep them occupied. Almost immediately, Josh and Lynn found boys their age living in the building with whom they could be friends. Because the life of a university professor is not a nine-to-five requirement, David was often at home, and the boys, especially in the summer months, could use the building's amenities with their friends or bring their friends home to eat, watch TV, play games, or read, which they did a few times a week. The Walton apartment became the place where the boys gathered. David became a surrogate father to many of the boys, and they, in turn, felt free and open around him.

Once, the boys bought an old sailboat and rebuilt it. David purchased a trailer for the boat and rented a slip at a nearby reservoir where they spent many hours of fun learning to sail. They hiked and fished and spent weekends in New York City. Greenwich Village, Central Park, and the museums played the background staging to the boys' life with David. Often the other boys of the Executive House were with them. They played chess, backgammon, and other games, but most importantly, they made lifelong friends.

One morning, before Ann's first visit to his apartment, Ken Carle dropped by to visit his old friend. It had been a few months since the last time, and David was glad to see him. As usual, they talked a bit about the Company and speculated about winners and losers in football. Though he was aware of Ken's father's health issues, he was not aware that he had lost his father.

"Why didn't you call me Ken so I might have given you some kind of support?"

"Things happened so fast, and my brother was so efficient at getting things done I hardly had time to prepare myself. You do know my father was responsible for my joining the CIA. When I could not make it playing music in New York, he made a phone call. He was such a good man and really well connected. I'll miss him."

"You okay?"

"Sure. I am not far from joining you as an ex-agent. Dad left me enough money to stop solving puzzles and start playing exclusively again. You know music has always been my first love. I really don't know when my retirement from government service will happen, but it's coming."

"Ken, look in the music closet and put something nice on. Or play something nice on the piano. What are you drinking?"

The two friends spent the morning talking and listening to music until Ken had to move on. He was meeting others in New York and did not want to be late. David never told him about Ann.

*****

David cleaned and straightened the apartment, put clean linens on his bed, and then waited for her to be announced by the concierge. Ann arrived at five o'clock. Her car was taken by an attendant and parked in the rear garage. There would not be a trace of her presence. She took the elevator to the sixth floor, found David's door, and knocked.

"Welcome to my humble home, Ann. Please come in." Ann beamed nervously as she crossed the threshold. Even though she wanted to be with David, she had never been alone in a man's apartment, and the voices of her parents and teachers swam in her head, screeching moral decline and potential danger.

"I'm so glad you came. I thought there was a chance you would get cold feet."

"You're not all wrong, David. I do have cold feet."

"Let's see if we can take the chill off."

David reached for her hand. Ann willingly extended her hand to reach his, and David walked her across the living room to a picture window that looked out over a suburban landscape with a background of a branch of the Appalachian Piedmont.

"Did you have any trouble finding me?"

"Not at all. Your instructions were clear and accurate."

"Would you like a drink? I make a great cosmopolitan."

"Yes, that would be great. You have a wonderful view, and the sunsets over the mountain have to be stupendous."

"The view is best in autumn. The colors seem to be exaggerated by the afternoon light reflected off the rise of the Piedmont."

Behind a roll top in his kitchen, he'd set up a bar for his alcohol. With a cosmopolitan in one hand and a neat single malt scotch in the other, David gave Ann her drink. She took a sip and smiled.

"Perfect. So you know how to make a drink."

David raised his drink, smiled, looked into Ann's limpid eyes, and offered a toast.

"To the lady who captured my attention."

"It's my turn," said Ann.

"To a well-rounded gentleman who pushed the right buttons without even knowing it."

They touched glasses and took a drink.

"What kind of music do you like?" asked David.

Ann looked toward the balcony wall and walked over to the piano.

"Do you play?" she asked.

"I've always wanted to. I even took lessons a couple of times, but mostly I play by ear and only a few songs. I can read fake books a little. But the answer to your question is no, I can't really play," said David. "Do you play?" he asked.

"I took lessons for a few years as a child. With some effort, I can still read a little, but I never do. I guess I need some inspiration and some good music. So why don't you sit down and play something?" asked Ann.

David sat at the piano and began to play "I Wish You Love." Ann sat down on the bench and leaned gently against David's shoulder and began to hum along with the sound of the piano.

"I've got a better idea," said David.

He got up and walked across the floor to the closet that housed his stereo and a considerable record collection. He started a reel-to-reel tape, and soft jazz-inflected recordings of the Great American Songbook filled the room. First was the sound of Ray Charles and Betty Carter singing "Cocktails for Two." As he left the closet, Ann met him halfway. They drew close and danced for the first time. Finding a comforting balance, they quickly relaxed into each other's arms.

"Ann, you're a perfect fit just where you are. Feeling your body against mine the way it is now, I could dance all night."

David could sense her pressing her body against his. He wanted to possess her. He also wanted to respect her. As he became aware of his own body heat, he looked at Ann and detected a slight glow that let him know that she was taking the ride with him. *Too soon*, he thought. When the song was over, he released her.

David walked into the kitchen to freshen his drink. Ann followed.

"Let me make your drink, David. A bartender at my club showed me a very simple trick that will transform good scotch into ambrosia."

She went around to the bar. "I also see that you like a good scotch. Great! Oh look, you have Cardhu. I'll use that."

"I'll just stand here and watch," said David.

Ann poured the scotch, cut a slice of lime, and dipped it into the scotch twice. She handed it to David and waited for a response. David sipped his drink, relished it, and gently pulled Ann closer. Ann leaned in, and David wrapped her in an embrace. Ann picked up her drink, walked to the living room, and sat on the couch. David followed her.

"I hope your feet are warming up," said David as he sat down.

"Yes, my feet have thawed, and I'm glad," she said.

"I do have a question."

"I can't imagine what that could be," said David.

Ann became sober, serious, and composed. Like the first time they met, it was clear to him that she was not a person who would stand for foolishness. "David, do you often bring women to your home and romance and seduce them? I must tell you that I don't want to be one in an endless stream of conquests. Being part of something like that would cheapen the glow and hurt me deeply. In many ways, you are a very attractive man. But if I'm offered cream, I don't want skim milk. I don't want to be a dupe in a con game. Tell me, David, are you real? Do you really want me? Or am I just one more conquest you can brag about? Tell me now. Because if I find that you only want to use me, I will not allow it, and you will find yourself with an immediate reputation as a womanizer and a cad."

David was stunned by her words and could hardly stay composed. He was pulled out of his romantic mind and into a space where consequences could be real. It was a space where fantasy was only trumped by truth. Ann wanted the truth. She did not want a reflection of her own imagination. She wanted to know David's real intentions.

"You have qualities that I find attractive," said David. "You stir my imagination and my hormones. I think about you all the time. What will come of my interest? I don't know. What I do know is that you have a similar interest because you are here with me. Am I just a plaything to you? Will you capture me and then throw me away? You see, I, too, have a heart that can be broken." He then paused and said, "Before anything else, I am first and foremost a father. Where we are now sitting is my home and the home of my children. Only close friends and family come here. Have I dated in the past? Yes. Am I dating now? No. Unless your being here is a date. Has my front door been a turnstile for women? No. Have I fallen in love with a woman in the past ten years? No. Have I fallen for you? Maybe. Would I try to deceive you? Never. Do I want to hold you in my arms every time I see you or think of you? Yes. Can I control that response? No. Do I want your friendship? More than you know. Can I predict the future of our friendship? No."

Sitting still for a moment, neither said a word. They sat looking at each other, considering what each had said, letting the real meaning of the words sink into a visceral understanding. The minute that passed seemed long before each of them wanted what the other wanted—each other.

"Before we go any further, there is something we need to talk about."

"Okay," said David.

After a clumsy start, she began to talk about the deep inadequacy she had felt since being married. She said it was her responsibility to satisfy her husband's needs and even though she has tried, he has no real interest in sleeping with her. She suggested her anatomy might be too small.

"Our time together would last no more than a minute, and he'd roll over and complain that something must be wrong with me. I think he may be right and I don't want to disappoint you and be rejected. That would be too much to bear. So if that's going to be a problem for you, tell me before this goes too far."

"I don't know what other people have said to you Ann, but I just want to hold you in my arms," said David, in no way believing what Ann had come to think of herself. She could turn him on simply by smiling at him.

David looked at Ann for a few moments without expression and then took her by the hand and led her to his bedroom. She did not resist. First, he dimmed the lights to soften the atmosphere and turned the stereo speakers to a little more than a whisper. The singing of Ray Charles and Betty Carter's "For All We Know We May Never Meet Again" spilled its sentimental essence into the room and provided a background for love. While listening to "So love me tonight, tomorrow may never come," he loosened her hair so it fell free. Their breathing quickened, and they slowly undressed, marveling at their nakedness and what they had each discovered. The time had come. The flirting, the fantasizing, and the distant sexual desire were now real. David hovered over his eager partner. First, kisses that traveled down toward her navel. His hands gently found her breasts and thighs. His eyes drank in the beauty of her nakedness, and he quivered with delight. Ann knew nothing of this. She knew nothing of the kind of love that legitimized lust. *This is truly heavenly*, she thought. Grabbing a handful of the sheets, she held on, repeating, "Please, please..." without awareness of her fervent prayer. David whispered for permission to continue and then teased her loins.

"See, I told you I was small," she said with a hint of shame.

David said nothing. Then it happened—a slow opening that accommodated and welcomed a warm and powerful man. Ann's consciousness exploded with such intensity that she sensed nothing but David making his way into her soul. Her hands found him and tried to pull him into every cell of her superheated body. She was vocal as they were caught in an emotional euphoria and ecstasy bordering on a mystical transcendence that shook her entire body. David loved her with such intensity that he cried, and she wiped his tears.

"David, I think I had an orgasm. I've never felt anything like that before. You were inside of me. I loved it and I want more."

"What did you say about small?"

Ann never let go of David and after a while began to wedge herself beneath him again. And again she followed the slow and gentle ascension of pure pleasure ending in an explosive event that ingested them both and transported Ann to an indescribable place of total sensory consumption. She clung to him as if he was her last hope for survival, and every sensory nerve in her body screamed with delight. They lay holding each other, not wanting to let go.

"My god," said Ann. "I'm forty years old and have never felt such intensity before. I just gave myself to you, body and soul. I've never in my life done that before. I've heard those words, but I never knew their true meaning. I think I know now," she whispered. "David, I'm yours, body and soul."

David said nothing. Ann's words unlocked a door housing a flood of emotion that he could not help spilling onto Ann. Neither of them really understood what was happening to him. He wept while smiling and, for a few hallowed minutes, felt what he had waited for his entire life—a love so complete and unconditional it could gather all his wishes and fantasies, his needs and desires—and focused them onto a person whose simple presence could satisfy him body and soul. He now had some understanding of what he had missed and what he was missing in his life. It was what his mother had given to his father as they lay beneath the walnut tree. It was the kind of unconditional love she would have given to him. The man had come face-to-face with his infancy. When the two realities collided, it left him completely fulfilled and exhausted.

"You have finally come to me, and I no longer have to wait. I am yours body and soul." He said it like a vow, almost like a sanctified prayer, consecrated by what they had just discovered in each other.

*****

After more kisses, some play, and the most exciting and memorable experience she had ever had, Ann returned home, exhausted and needing sleep. She wished she could have fallen asleep in David's arms, but that was not possible. The thirty-minute drive from David's seemed to last forever. David's home was a comfortable nest. Hers was a little more complex.

The six-bedroom house was positioned on fifteen acres of beautifully landscaped property partially hidden by mature trees and flowering shrubs, with a circular drive and a double-doored entrance bordered by eight-foot columns. A four-car garage in the rear was connected to the house at right angles by a closed portico. A vehicle for every need filled the garage and was cared for regularly by a local mechanic. A large barn, greenhouse, and potting shed helped set the functional and picturesque scene. Unless one worked in this part of the township, you wouldn't know it even existed.

As Ann put her key into the back door that opened onto the kitchen, Lorraine was sitting at the counter. The boys had gone to their rooms, done their homework, and readied for school the next day. The house was quiet, and Lorraine was on her third cup of coffee in anticipation of Ann's return.

"I hope your day went well," Ann said.

"I'm sure not as well as yours. Or am I mistaken?" said Lorraine. "You look exhausted."

"You're right, I am exhausted and I'm going right to bed. How about we talk in the morning after the boys have gone to school? I think we need total privacy," said Ann.

"I've been waiting for the punch line since you left for school," Lorraine said, playing into the storyline. "Now you want me to wait until morning? Ann, this is torture."

Lorraine gave Ann a pouty look of disappointment because she wanted to hear the details of her evening with the professor. She cleaned up around the kitchen, turned off the lights, and went to bed.

Ann was exhausted, but lying in bed still tingling from the evening's activities, she mused over every minute of what had transpired with her first real lover. It was no longer a vague girl-like aspiration born of ignorance. It was now real, and she legitimately felt like a woman of the world. She fell into deep sleep with a giddy smile.

Morning came as promised, and Ann woke to the sounds of songbirds and a bright morning sun that filtered through sheer white curtains. Lying in her solitude, she tracked the songs of the birds, which she had seldom done before. Then looking out of her window at the rolling hills that adjoined her property, she felt ripe and in love with her body. All she could think of was David.

Lorraine saw the boys off to school and then waited for Ann in the kitchen with a freshly brewed cup of coffee. Trying to anticipate the story, she smiled at the list of possibilities. Unlike Ann, who attracted men who only wanted to charm her, Lorraine only had memories of male brutality. A hard crust of fear and defensiveness surrounded her emotional vulnerability. Though she would never utter the thought, she often wondered what being loved by a man would be like. Before long, Ann strolled into the kitchen with a smile.

"Would you like a cup of coffee? I just made a fresh pot."

Lorraine poured the coffee while Ann thought about how to share her experience with David.

"So," said Lorraine, "start talking."

"Well," said Ann. And with that, she began to give her friend an almost moment-to-moment summary of her evening with David. Lorraine sat with an open mouth, wishing she could have been a fly on the wall. Being a fly on the wall was not all Lorraine thought about. As Ann told of her evening and the intensity and depth of her experience, Lorraine was not just captivated by what her friend shared. As the story unfolded, she found she was becoming aroused by Ann's experience. As far as she knew, this was the first time her body responded this way to the discussion of love tied to sexual expression. Her memories of physical and sexual abuse always emerged and became a steel wall between her body and the essential elements of relationships with men. She was almost frigid. That was not the case this time. This time she could feel a tingling in her loins and an almost undetectable quickening of her breath. She didn't even notice this until she found her hands damp, resting on her thighs.

"What did he say when you told him you were small?" she asked, unable to help herself. "What did you feel or know when you opened to accept him? What did you think when he entered you—how did he smell?" Ann did her best to relay the details.

"What was your reaction when you found out that your size was not abnormal?"

"Cleansed."

At that moment, Lorraine had a revelation. An epiphany. Something deeply woven into the complex web of her mind that was, in part, guiding her life's choices. It might have been an illusion. The sleight of hand that made her a victim of abuse began to be questioned. Not consciously, like a thought, but like the ephemera of a slow cool breeze that aids our comfort. Maybe the hateful venom injected into her by abusers was not hers to carry. Maybe the monsters were theirs to bear or tame.

And maybe the web of poison would begin to loosen its grip on her life. Maybe, like Ann, her need to defend herself against the ravages of abuse by hating men existed only in her psychology and was not necessary. Maybe, at last, there was a glimmer of hope.

Lorraine sat listening quietly, and that signaled Ann to ask if she was okay.

"I'm so happy for you, Ann. This will stay within the walls of our sisterhood. Nothing could have made me happier."

David and Ann planned and plotted when his kids were spending time with their mother. Ann took an afternoon class and told her family it was a night course. For her, it was never a problem because Lorraine was always there and her husband was never home. The two lovers spent Monday and Thursday evening together, an arrangement that worked in each of their schedules.

One evening, while dining in what they thought was a secluded rendezvous, a familiar face stood before their table. It was Professor Vince Greenhouse from the university with a "caught ya" shit-eating grin on his face. Without saying so, Vince clearly wanted to know why they were having dinner together. This was his chance to start trouble, especially given the competition for the limited number of sabbatical slots they had applied for. This could be a major problem, but David and Ann had anticipated this moment by always leaving a third-place setting and a third glass of wine on the table that they used. Vince was invited to sit down and join them.

"I thought I was the only one who knew about this place," said David. "The kids are with their mother, so I decided to have a nice dinner out by myself, and who do I run into but Mr. and Mrs. Hickman? Then you show up. Oh, where are my manners? Have you eaten, Vince? Have you met Mrs. Hickman?"

Vince showed signs of incredulity and sat down.

"I've seen you around campus, but I have not had the pleasure of meeting you. Where is Mr. Hickman?" asked Vince with the express purpose of trapping them. Without hesitation, Ann said, "My husband took a business call in his limo. I'll join him when I'm finished."

She soon finished her meal. "It was so nice meeting you. May I call you Vince? And good night to you, David. My husband is patient but not infinitely so." She put on her jacket, took her purse and left.

David and Vince rose and said good night to Ann. David finished the rest of his meal, and they had another drink together while chatting about campus politics. Seemingly, Vince was convinced that the three of them meeting in that restaurant was all happenstance and there was nothing to be suspicious about. At least, David hoped that was true.

*****

Sadly, David and Ann had to keep their relationship secret because Ann's circumstances were combustible. Philip was a powerful man who needed to maintain a certain stability and decorum. With the media being what it was, propriety was the watchword, especially in the midst of his company's overseas expansion. Ann was his trophy, and Philip was a very jealous man. This was especially true for David, whose blackness might have been an additional embarrassment for him. If Philip ever found out about David, he would do everything he could to take her children and leave her destitute.

"We have to keep our love a secret," said David. "With my existing financial burdens, my current salary could not support us."

"And I have never held a job. Finishing schools and college may sound nice in conversation, but the truth is I don't know how to do anything but love my children. And you, of course," Ann replied.

*****

The university's Board of Trustees had originally given the president eight sabbatical slots. As eligible applicants increased in number and faculty voices were raised in protest, the board approved four more to try to meet the demand. As fate would have it, there were some prospective faculty who, for a variety of reasons, chose not to complete the application process, leaving more slots than applicants.

"If we're lucky," David said to Ann, "I might be granted the sabbatical because there are more slots than faculty applying. It seems to me that the only way I won't have it granted would be a poorly conceived proposal."

"I saw how hard you worked on it. It seems to me that transposing French language educational strategies into a culture whose primary language is Moroccan Arabic is worth serious consideration."

"Let's hope your assessment is correct," David added. "We'll just keep our fingers crossed and hope for the best. The opportunity to travel to both Marrakech and Paris is far beyond anything I could have hoped for."

*****

Another two months passed and the politics surrounding the sabbatical committee subsided. It was partly due to the abundance of slots and partly because people like Vince could no longer see the necessity of increasing his chances by playing political games. It now looked as if only poorly conceived or poorly written proposals were going to be rejected. Finally, the committee made its recommendations.

Ann was concentrating on a neuroscience problem in a study carrel on the other side of campus. When she answered the phone and heard David's voice, she smiled affectionately.

"Ann, I wanted you to be the first person to hear the news," said David, his smile detectable through the telephone.

"I don't want to say it, David. I want you to tell me."

"I walked into my office, and my secretary Betsy knocked and handed me an envelope. She had a look on her face that was part anticipatory excitement and part regret, I couldn't read her. When I tore the envelope open, I read one line. It said 'Dear Professor Walton, the sabbatical committee has recommended to the president that you be granted a sabbatical for the spring semester.'"

"Ann, I thought I would jump out of my skin!"

"All Betsy did was give me a thumbs-up, smiled, and skipped out of the room."

"Do you know what this means for us?"

"Yes, I do. It means that for a little while, we won't have to hide. We can share our love openly. What a gift. You did it, David, and you did it for us. When can I see you? I want to see you now."

"We have a lot of planning to do, Ann. Are you ready?"

At that moment and before Ann could answer his need for planning, she received a call on her other line. Switching over, she recognized urgency in Lorraine's voice.

"I need you and I need you now!" Not knowing exactly what the call meant, Ann switched back to David, congratulated him again, and promised to call back as soon as she could. She packed up her things and drove home. Wanting to maintain a level of calm and with safety in mind, she drove through the trafficked streets of Flemington and onto the county roads that led to Lorraine.

When she arrived, her friend was nowhere to be found. Finally poking her head into a room with a bay window exposing the patio, Ann saw her sitting with a glass of wine near a fountain by the rose garden.

"I think I'm gonna have a nervous breakdown," said Lorraine.

Ann could see an uncommon nervousness in her face and what looked to be a need for help.

"What is it, Lorraine? Are you okay? Did something happen? Are the kids okay?"

"Everybody's fine except me, Ann. Pour yourself a glass of wine. I need to talk."

Ann changed into lounging clothes, poured herself wine, and sat across from Lorraine, ready for her to dish.

"What's up with you?"

"Not knowing how to think or talk about it, I really don't know how to start. So I'll start from the beginning."

She took a deep breath, looked Ann in the eyes, and started to tell of her experience.

"After I dropped the kids off at school this morning, I went to the club to get breakfast because I didn't want to cook. All the regulars were there. I chatted with the wait staff, and a couple of the girls in tennis duds stopped to say hello. By the way, Lisa Wright said she would call you. I then ordered something to eat. People came in and out of the breakfast room, and soon my food was served. A man I never saw before came in, sat at a table facing me, and ordered. I saw him looking in my direction, and he soon got up, walked to my table, and asked if I would mind if we had breakfast together because he disliked eating alone. I panicked and didn't know what to say."

"What did you do?" asked Ann.

"I was mortified, and then he apologized for rudely interfering with my solitude and began to walk away, but before he did, I stopped him and offered him a seat. The waiters brought his meal to my table, and as we ate, he began to talk. He asked my name and told me his. His name is Jonathan Westerfield, and he recently joined the club. Other than those he encountered navigating the membership process, I was the first person he met."

With Lorraine's history of experiences with men, Ann knew what she was being told was monumental in scope. Except for Philip and a few longtime friends at the club, Lorraine did not relate to or trust men at all. Talking like this to a man meant that she was making a leap of faith; it was not something that should be taken casually. In all the years they knew each other, she would not have wagered that this day would ever come.

"What else did he say?"

"He told me he trained to be a medical doctor, but he never really practiced real medicine. He said people all over the world were suffering and it was our duty as human beings to do what we could, if we could find the cause of their suffering and bring the right resources to bear. I asked where he had been in the world, and he said everywhere. 'Is that all you do?' I asked. He said when he found the time, he also loved to work with wood."

"Then what happened, Lorraine?"

"We finished eating, and then he said he would like to have breakfast with me again. He would like to talk with me again."

"I simply smiled, and he walked away. He likes to make things out of wood. Do you think he knows about my father?"

Ann had become so enthralled by what Lorraine was telling her that her glass of wine sat untouched. Injecting any action or thought into this moment would pollute the purity and transformational nature of its telling. This was a conversation she had waited years to have. The two of them had an unbreakable bond, and each one of them, in her way, was like a young girl discovering what it was like to be a woman. To get there, Ann had to overcome the restraints of accepted morality. Lorraine had to heal a fractured psychology.

"So what are you going to do?" asked Ann. "Will you have breakfast with him again?"

"Oh, Ann, I'm scared to death. What should I do?"

"Do you really want advice from me?"

"Yes!"

"Then do nothing. Have breakfast at the club periodically. What will be will be."

Rising out of her chair, Ann extended a hand, and Lorraine rose and took it. They gathered each other into an embrace and celebrated the breakthrough.

*****

When David reached home, he told Josh and Lynn he had been granted the sabbatical and all the fun they had studying Morocco would end with an actual visit. For a few minutes, they were jubilant and ran around in celebration and then called their mother to tell her the news. Then they turned on the computer and began to identify the places they wanted to see.

22

The Lie

"No," said Ann. "Here we are in this beautiful house and grounds, and where are you? Gone eighty-five percent of the time for the last few years. What do you expect me to do, Philip? Sit and look out of the window at the landscape?"

Ann could see the little telltale signs her husband showed when becoming impatient—the slight turning up of the left side of his mouth, an increased frequency of blinking, and how the pinky on his left hand twitched. When she saw these tells, she knew he was about to quit the conversation. When it came to family, she knew he was about to fold.

"You do understand that, like you, I also have aspirations for my life. Of course, we love the children and will do anything for them, but that is not what I'm talking about. You are the one who encouraged me to go to school. I love it. I hope you know that I'm not just learning facts and figures. I want to know about the world."

"Ann, you must know that building this business in Argentina will position me as the chief executive officer of the largest pharma company in the world."

"But I don't want to go to Argentina, Philip. I have absolutely no interest in that place, and by the way, neither do the children. They want to stay home and in school with their friends. They want stability in their few remaining childhood years."

"So what do you want?" asked Philip.

"I haven't talked about it much, but I really enjoyed the art history course I took last semester. I was so taken by that experience that…" Her voice trailed off into what Philip perceived as typical female emotionality for which he had no patience.

"So I ask you again, what do you want to do?" asked Philip. He showed even more agitation and put some distance between them as he changed clothes in preparation for an evening out with colleagues from South America.

"A few of the girls from school just returned from France and took a language course there while studying art at the Louvre. I want to do that. I never asked before because I was certain you would never give me that kind of latitude. You get to constantly globe trot, and I want to have a meaningful experience like that. It can even be arranged by the university," answered Ann.

Philip said nothing. The silence continued for a few minutes as he thought. They descended the circular staircase and entered the family room where the children and housekeeper were talking and laughing.

Eventually he spoke, still with some irritation in his voice that he himself could not detect.

"So you want to go to Paris and study French and learn about European art. How long does this kind of experience usually last, Ann?"

"From what I understand, it can last up to a year or as little as a single semester."

"And what about the kids?" asked Philip.

"Lorraine is here. She cooks and cleans, so nothing will change for the kids, and most importantly, she is like their second mother. They respect her unconditionally. The school and the club accept her as a guardian as well. They would miss me if I was gone for a while, but their routine would not change at all."

"So you're talking about a few weeks, Ann?"

"I don't know what I'm talking about, but I'll find out and provide you with some information."

The very next day at school, Ann visited the relevant offices and found the information she needed. At dinner that night, she shared the information with the family. After reviewing all the options, she said, "Under no circumstances could I take an entire semester. I would be away much too long. The only one that makes sense is the shortest experience. Maybe one day we can all take a longer one. That is what most people get to do when they graduate from high school, isn't it, kids?"

The thought of traveling to Europe tantalized them all, and after some discussion, even Lorraine wanted to go. Philip warmed to the idea as Ann regaled the family with the possibility.

"I could go and study the French language and European art during the months of May and June and be back when the kids get out of school. Could you handle things without me, Lorraine?"

"I handle these kids most of the time anyhow, but if I am to do *all* the work, you've got to give me a raise, Philip," said Lorraine with her hands on her hips, trying to be funny.

"During that time, you'll be in Argentina, Philip," said Ann, "and we can all keep in touch by phone. So what do you say about all this?"

"If the family doesn't mind, then I guess I don't mind," he said. "Will the school make all of the arrangements?"

"Yes," answered Ann. "I do have one requirement. I need to have my own space. Living with a group of female college students is too much to ask. I'm not going to hang out with them and I don't want to be a chaperone. I would like to get my own apartment, Philip!"

Philip figured that he'd gone this far, so he might as well go all the way. With so much business on his mind, he really didn't need the addition of family aggravation.

"I'm beginning to think this kind of experience might be good for you, Ann. What do the rest of you think?" asked Philip.

"Go for it, Mom."

"Yeah, Mom, go for it!"

"Lorraine, you sure you can manage things for a while if she goes?"

"I've been handling things since the kids were born. I'm not going to have any trouble if you're gone."

"Well, I guess it's set. Ann's going to Paris to study art," said Philip. His agreement also included an unsaid commitment to keep her safe while she was away. Wherever she went, she would not be alone. He was too important and high-profile to let her skip through the world and put his position in jeopardy. She would be taken care of.

23

Morocco

David and his two sons stepped off the Moroccan Air flight from London with great anticipation. Built by their imaginations and fueled by the travel books and Internet searches they studied over the past few months, they felt they were about to step into a dreamscape. Unfortunately, what they faced was a modern airport with abundant security personnel standing at strained attention with Uzis strapped to their shoulders as they surveyed the comings and goings of travelers. The sight and the feeling it instigated made it clear they were no longer in the United States of America, and the assumption of safety could not be made automatically, which somewhat frightened them.

Josh and Lynn looked at each other in astonishment. Josh said, "Dad, did you see those guards?"

"Yes, I did," answered David. "I guess with all the trouble in the world, the government thinks this kind of display is necessary."

"I've never seen a real Uzi before," said Lynn. "These guys look tough."

"Dad, did you have one of those when you worked as an analyst in Washington?" asked Josh.

"No, I didn't." David laughed and thought it might be time to contain his son's public wonder about his past.

David stopped walking, looked sternly at his sons, and said, "Listen, boys, I want you never to mention I worked for the government while we're in Morocco. Do you understand why?"

Both boys looked at their father. Lynn said, "Yeah Dad, we do." Josh gave an affirmative nod.

As the three Americans walked out of the airport and onto the street, the world felt different. Women with head scarves and burkas and men wearing what looked to the Waltons like nightgowns with hoods flowed back and forth along the walkways, hawking pastries and tourist doodads. Business people and families with two or three small children rushing back and forth, trying to manage luggage and make flights, contrasted with the hustlers and beggars who leaned against the outside wall of the building. The curb was lined with cars and drivers who held up cards with the names of contracted pickups, while taxis competed for fares. Yelling and honking and hawking filled the air and enhanced the confusion. Through this swarm of activity, David saw a card with the name Walton written clearly in English, so the family moved toward that car and out of what felt to them like utter chaos. As the car sped through the broad boulevards and thoroughfares lined with palm and orange trees, the red city began to unfold. Massive eleventh-century gates and imposing twelve-foot rust red walls surrounded the old city and hid what the Walton kids soon learned to call by name, the Medina. By the time they reached their accommodations, they were hooked and wanted nothing more than to explore this place that had already captivated them. The hotel was situated on the Djemma el-Fna, the massive main square that came alive each night with festive displays of Moroccan musical culture, exotic foods, snake charmers, traditional drumming, and water sellers dressed in twelfth-century costumes and dispensing water out of goatskin bags. Figs, dates, prunes, and other fruits were piled high on carts with canopies. Fruit carts were an integral part of the square and did vigorous business. Surrounding the square and in some places outside the square was a labyrinthine rabbit warren of endless large and small shops and stalls with tin roofs and men selling just about anything one could imagine.

By the time they settled into their hotel, the sun-warmed day in northwest Africa began to end, and the evening midwinter weather invaded the warmth and cooled the night air.

"Dad, can we go out tonight?" asked Lynn.

"I think it would be best if we stayed in tonight. We've had quite a long and exhausting day. I think our time tonight would be best spent organizing ourselves for our stay here and deciding what a tentative itinerary could be. Also, I have to call my contact at the university and touch base," answered David.

"I think I want to have something to eat here and spend some time in the hotel talking to that guy at the desk about stuff," added Josh.

The next weeks were spent exploring. They wandered the souks and bargained with shop owners to get the real prices for the things they thought interesting or memorable. They strolled through the often-crowded streets and narrow alleys, meeting street kids who spoke three languages. Talking to people about America was their favorite pastime. Time was spent in and around the Medina. Camel rides in the dark and visits to centuries-old palaces and gardens consumed their days. The boys even made friends with local kids who took them into the souks, taught them how to speak some Arabic words, and showed them how to negotiate prices for goods. While walking through the souk, Lynn and Josh saw a silversmith working the metal by hand. Remembering their mother's desire for a silver coffee service with a tray, they stopped and asked about the price of such a purchase. After negotiating the bottom-line price, it was still too expensive. They then took another tactic. Negotiating a price for each piece at a time, they were able to buy a coffee and tea service for almost half the price of the original coffee service alone. They walked back to the hotel triumphant. Proud of what they had accomplished, David congratulated their effort. Every afternoon at about one o'clock, they would join new friends around the Djemma el-Fna for a glass of mint tea and snacks of some kind. In the evening, they would return to the square.

They spent the time exploring the Atlas Mountains, where handmade rugs, kilims, and intricately carved woodwork could be bought for more than reasonable prices from artisans living a life like that of their ancestors. That exploration included a five-day mineral and fossil collecting tour. Most of the trip was in the mountains and gorges of the Anti-Atlas. They met fossil diggers and mineral miners and in the process collected excellent specimens.

Toward the end of their stay, the Waltons traveled to the southern city of Agadir, where the mild winter climate averages sixty-nine degrees and great beaches made it a major "winter sun" destination for European travelers and people from the Sahara. The highlight for David was the fifteenth-century marina with its Moorish architecture and shops that made an indelible impression on him. They all vowed that someday they would return.

The last days back in Marrakech were spent in the Medina saying goodbye to their newfound friends, having a glass of mint tea, and enjoying a final embrace from the Djemma el-Fna. Josh and Lynn Walton used the evening to prepare to return home and, although weeks late for the start of school, were more than grateful for the experience. In addition to helping the boys, David prepared for the work he had to do for his sabbatical project.

*****

After the boys' departure, David worked for most of March and April with his colleagues in Morocco, got what he needed, and prepared for his next stop: Paris.

*****

David had already done most of the work on his Paris project and had only to wait for Ann to come. He was ensconced in a fourth-floor apartment near the University of Paris. Ann took an apartment a block away. Each of them could hardly wait to spend the next two months fulfilling the romantic dreams they both so diligently planned.

The flight to Paris was long, and Ann talked to a few people, including an attractive middle-aged man with a thick red mustache who she liked and to whom she talked of her intentions to study art. He too would be spending time as a tourist in Paris. At the airport, David waited impatiently at the arrival gate, and upon disembarking, Ann threw herself into his arms. After a long embrace that ended in a joyous hello and a passionate kiss in the middle of the crowded airport concourse, they hurried to be alone, each with dreams fashioned by starry-eyed visions of Paris in the spring. The rest of the evening was spent making love and talking until the need for sleep led them to wake to a glorious new day and the beginning of their plans. Fulfillment of David's longtime fantasy of travel and Ann's need to be loved lay before them. They had each freely willed it and overcome the fatalistic thrust of habit and inevitability. For the first time in many years, they felt free; they were the regulatory agents of their own tomorrows.

"How are we gonna start our adventure, David?" Ann asked as she looked with excited anticipation through the diamond-patterned leaded windows at the city with rows of gray zinc roofs and mysterious spires and domes.

"We first have to call home and let our families know we are here and doing well. Then you must connect to your classes and let your family know you are busy and will contact them on a regular basis. That should keep them from wondering," answered David.

"How will we start our adventure?" Ann asked again with impatient hopefulness.

"Well," said David. "Since coming, I've read two Paris travel books. I've even done some exploring and have decided to impress you with my knowledge and seduce you with Paris."

Playfully interrupting, Ann put on her best come-hither pose and said, "You're seducing me does not require Paris, David."

"I don't need Paris to want to seduce you, my love, but it will add a little adventure to garnish the experience."

"I think the romance of Paris is wandering down its ancient streets, which are piled with layers of history and yet still swing to the rhythm of a lived-in cosmopolitan metropolis," said David. "I'd like to make some suggestions."

Before he could finish, Ann said, "I'd like to get back to the seduction," and before he could speak, they were wrapped in single-focused passion and Paris stopped existing. For a time, nothing existed but the all-consuming intensity of their love. It would take a nearby church bell to awaken them to the reality of time and space. When David glanced at his wrist watch on the table, the morning was all but gone. The afternoon of the first day was spent having a long leisurely lunch at Le Petit

Littre's sidewalk café in *Saint-Germain-des-Prés*. The weather was warm, and the feel of the musical Parisian atmosphere was all they could have asked for.

As the days passed, Ann attended her French language classes twice a week and looked forward to afternoon art classes at the Louvre. Classes were often followed by dinner at a mid-priced restaurant recommended by a friend. They discovered the best time to see the city was in the early morning mists and often crossed over the river behind Notre Dame and watched the barges from the cobbled quaysides of the Seine, or they would sometimes pop in for coffee and croissants at a café under the arcades overlooking the Louvre pyramid.

"Hello," said Ann to the man with the red mustache at the next table. "Aren't you the gentleman I met on the plane?"

"Aren't you the lady who sat in my row on the plane?" he said to be funny. They both laughed at the smallness of the city and the world and then said goodbye.

When convenient, David and Ann would walk through the gardens of the Royal Palace, a small romantic park in the city with colonnaded galleries hidden from the outside world. They kissed in discreet doorways that led to interesting discoveries like Roman amphitheaters or where fashion boutiques occupy mansions that once held literary salons or where restaurants serve their wares inside ancient monasteries. Ann insisted on some venues. The Musée d'Orsay on the left bank, Montmartre on the right bank, the Paris Opera, Luxembourg Garden, and the Palace of Versailles, where Ann lost her new sunglasses and where she thought she saw the man from the plane with the red mustache again.

Once, Ann thought she saw the man with the red mustache outside of her apartment building looking toward her window. Another time on the street, as she turned to see a passing fashionable dress, she thought she saw him again. Strangely, when she thought she saw him, she was almost always alone. Experiencing a touch of paranoia, she mentioned the sightings to David. He was not alarmed and did what he could to eliminate her concern. He knew intuitively the chance of them being followed at the behest of Ann's husband was highly probable. He also knew that the only way to deal with the possibility was to catch the spy.

One morning, they left the house together, planning to meet at one of their favorite cafés. Turning left at the corner and waving goodbye, David circled to the back door of the building and looked through the building's front window. As he did, a man with a thick red mustache passed the window walking in Ann's direction. In a few quiet steps, David caught the man, pushed him into a doorway, banged his head against the wall, and shoved something into his back that felt to the man like a gun.

"Please don't hurt me," said the man. "Take my money and my credit cards, but please don't hurt me."

David recognized the voice immediately. The pitch, timbre, and phrasing he knew and recognized as a friend.

"Ken, Ken Carle?"

"At your service, Dr. Walton," the man said with familiarity and in recognition of David's achievements. "I wondered how long it would take you to catch me."

"What the fuck are you doing? Who are you working for?"

"Take the gun out of my back and I'll tell you. Did you have to bang my fucking head?"

David removed the Coke bottle from Ken Carle's back and allowed him to relax. A little blood and a big headache are the least that might have happened. Ken understood that. They had been friends when they both worked for the Company, and the friendship continued. When working together, they were responsible for a couple of consequential jobs that helped the USA avoid a war footing. When David left, Ken thought about following but instead stayed and continued to get assignments around the world as a musician and CIA operative. Observational status and reporting were his reward for his good work. Soon they both relaxed and leaned against a parked car to talk.

"So who are you working for, Ken?"

"You must know, David."

"I'd like to hear it from you. For old time's sake, I expect a complete report," said David in an authoritative voice with tongue in cheek.

"You know Tremont Pharma is still setting up shop in a few places around the globe. They've been in bed with the NSA for a long time, and we promised to protect the families of a couple of their executives. Philip Hickman is one of them. You know, the husband of the woman you're sleeping with."

"Does he know?"

"I haven't told a soul. When I got to Paris and discovered I would be protecting her from you, my whole attitude about this job changed. It was not my job to judge the nature of her academic lessons or who she was walking to school with. My job was to keep her safe from harm. I know that you can probably do that more effectively than me, but I do have to be present to protect."

"Might I assume that your reports will not include me?"

"You might assume that."

"Tell me, what's the skinny on her husband?"

"You don't know?"

"Know what?"

"The fact is his international work is good for his family and good for the country. The family knows nothing of his private life away from home. You would never suspect, but it's been confirmed—the guy is definitely gay. He sleeps with some of the most powerful men in the world. The intel he collects is invaluable."

"You know that he is partially responsible for the death of my father."

"How so?" asked Ken.

"By selling a drug that he knew was poisonous. The drug left me an orphan. That was a long time ago. By the way," asked David, "what's with the red mustache?"

"Do you like it?"

"It takes some getting used to."

While Ken held his aching head, they talked about their work together and mutual friends. David was told of Ken's intention to leave the Company, and the two promised to get together as soon as they could. The fact that they could not be seen together shortened their time and hastened their goodbye.

"It's been good seeing you, Ken. We have some catching up to do. When this is over, look me up at the university. I'll buy you a beer."

"I'll tell Ann the man with the red mustache is no more than an interesting happenstance. Maybe you should bump into her again and refer to me as her husband so she does not suspect you have been sent by Philip Hickman."

"That's a reasonable idea."

Ken said goodbye and walked away, holding his head.

24

Homeward Bound

The next few weeks were beyond expectation. Every day was a new adventure and an opportunity to fill themselves with the glories of Paris and with an ever-present love that lifted them with happiness neither had ever known. Sometimes Ann's place was more convenient, and other times it was David's, but they never found the need to be alone. They liked each other's humor and knew how to play together. They disagreed and argued about art, language, and fashion, and David spent time explaining aspects of brain structure and function that Ann was curious about. The last week before departure, the disagreements moved into a different realm.

"I need to be happy. I mean the kind of happiness I feel right now with you," said Ann. "When I think about the past nineteen months, what I've felt is all new to me. We respect each other, our moment-to-moment perception of the world is very similar. You can tell by the way we interact. The nature of my intellectual curiosity is similar to yours. In our interaction, there is balance of play and earnestness that's appropriate for two adults. I love you, David, and I'm happy with our love. And I'm really happy with our more intimate moments."

David responded, "That's a mouthful, sweetheart. And just for the record, I love you too. I've been waiting for you my entire life, and you've finally come. I've never needed to be happy, but I can truly say that I need you. What I mean is that I need you in my life. The happiness I feel could only come through you. I don't think that I could ever let you go." David unconsciously touched his ring with his left hand. He felt relieved. After spending most of his life in the shade, Ann's presence showed him the light.

"But there is another viable reality," said David.

"How could there possibly be anything else?" asked Ann.

"Health, ease of life, and love are what everyone wants. We struggle to have these things and we might not get them, but we all strive to have them. Ours is not an uncommon position, but happiness involves being focused on the present. What's happening now. But many people think that meaningfulness is more important. It involves thinking more about the past, present, and future and the relationships between them. Happiness is fleeting, while meaningfulness will likely last longer," argued David.

"Come on, David. Happiness is what everyone wants."

"I don't disagree, but happiness comes largely from what other people give to you. When what you need and get from others is gone, happiness tends to leave. Meaningfulness, on the other hand, is derived from giving to other people." At that point, David stopped his musing and remembered the goodbye party Ann's art instructors were having for her class.

"We've got a party to go to, Ann," said David. They rushed through the door and walked quickly down Boulevard Saint-German. Neither forgot the conversation, and both continued to think about the implications, though they never spoke of it again. A few nights later, while having an early dinner at a sidewalk café near their apartments, Ann saw the man with the red moustache approaching on the street.

"Hello," she said. "There you are again." The man stopped and took off his hat to be polite.

"You are certainly a ubiquitous presence. I have come to look forward to seeing you in my travels around Paris. I guess we Americans have very similar agendas," said the man.

David looked on with the eyes of a casual observer, never once betraying his knowledge of the man who stood before him.

"David, this is the gentleman I met on the plane and have been seeing and telling you about."

"So I finally get to meet the mysterious man with the red moustache," said David.

As he had previously, Ken affected a mild German accent and said, "You, sir, must be the lady's gentleman friend. It's nice to finally get to meet you. My name is Wilhelm Kohl. I come to Europe on business often but never to Paris. I am sure we will meet again. But right now, I am late and must depart. We must all have a Schnapps together, no? Until then." David struggled to hold back a laugh.

Mr. Wilhelm Kohl quickly tottered off, leaving Ann mystified and David with a humorous knot in his stomach. "Are you as baffled as I am?" she asked with a tickle in her throat and a broad smile on her face. "You just never know, do you?" she said, trying to hold back a full-throated laugh. But together, they laughed until their facial muscles cramped—he at the hilarity of the ruse and she at the existence of unlikely personalities that tickle your sensibilities.

*****

Heavy rain made leaving Paris dank, dreary, and laden with a blanketing regret. David was quiet, and Ann peered through the rain-washed window with her head turned toward a city she could barely see from her side of the taxi. Paris had been at the height of its splendor, and the rain robbed them of a last view of the city that helped consummate their love. David reached for Ann's hand and held it tight. As they approached the airport, she laid her head on his shoulder. He was stricken by a deep regret that their brief interlude in Paris was over and might never happen again. Ann also felt the tug of her children and her friend Lorraine. Was she willing to take the leap, publicly confess her love for David, and chance losing her children, Lorraine, and a life of comfort? Thrown into the most intense conflict of her life, Ann's inability to resolve her vacillating indecision left her exhausted, stressed, and needing David's love.

When the plane landed, they waited for baggage together. For Ann, there was an abiding sadness that came with the necessity of home. The freedom of loving openly was now gone, and she would have to replace it with dishonesty and stealth. The stiffness caused from sitting long hours in tight airline seats, mixed with the deep regret of having to leave Paris and face a marriage that gave her no real emotional satisfaction, left her weak and in need of David's strength. But she could not have it. She could not reach for him or lean on him or cry for him. Now she would be alone with secrets she could not share.

David was also quiet, in part because the flight was tiring and in part because he intuitively understood what Ann might be experiencing and did not want to make it any more difficult for her. He, however, knew that life was about to change and he was ready to take on the pain and incomparable emotional effort required when families are torn apart and reconstituted. He also knew they would have to be very smart and strategic in their planning, and it had to start now.

"Because your husband will meet you at the airport, I won't walk with you as we go into the arrival area. It's too soon to declare our love. Doing it now would cause an unwanted reaction, and Philip would strike out at both of us. We must do it in a way that causes minimal negative fallout. However, if he sees me carrying your bags, his social history and politics will cause him to perceive a servant. He will not see a man with a plan. The whole thing needs to happen in a way that does not harm our families. We still need to be furtive until the time is right."

So with Ann walking slightly ahead, they ascended the gangway where the friends and family of the passengers were waiting. Upon seeing her husband, she waved and approached. David followed with the luggage. She kissed her husband on the cheek, and David dropped the luggage at his feet. Ann thanked David like one would thank a skycap, and Mr. Hickman tipped him twenty dollars. The ruse was successful. David walked to a waiting cab and went home.

25

Freedom

All summer, David made many attempts to contact Ann. He called her directly from home. He called from his office phone and through his secretary, and even had the "Travel Abroad Program" at the university attempt contact, all with no success. At one point, he even drove to her address to inquire about her. A groundskeeper told him the family was not expected back home anytime soon. That was all he knew. David even called the school Ann's children attended, to no avail. Desperate to find her, he even called country clubs to inquire about her membership. Despite his innate ability to control himself, David was out of his depth and beyond the limits of his ability to be restrained. He was frantic and frustrated by not having her. His friend Ken Carle had left the CIA after his assignment to protect Ann and no longer had access to information. Josh and Lynn could feel something was wrong, but what? They didn't know.

I will not believe it meant nothing to her. I know it was much more than a lark. What she felt for me was real. I didn't ask her to run away with me. I didn't ask her to leave her husband. We could have continued as we were. She didn't have to change a thing. Why would she leave me? Did I kiss her too much? Or too little? Did her husband force her to go away? These thoughts and others of equal urgency filled his thinking and persisted.

A hundred questions and possible answers clogged his mind and twisted his ability to cope. He had become obsessed and compulsive in his attempts to find her. As the summer wore on, the frequency with which he searched decreased until the attempts almost stopped. Slowly, the obsessive/compulsive trap he allowed himself to get caught in reduced in intensity. Slowly, he returned to something close to his old self, but the hole in his heart would not heal.

David had calculated his future with Ann, but his calculations were not correct. What he wanted was Ann in his life any way he could have her. He loved her, and that was all that mattered. He'd found hope for the future and had been neither fearful nor inhibited. Summer had come, and to him, he knew they would be together. What he did not fully consider was the pain and heartache a union with Ann would cause her family. He hadn't realistically calculated what the financial burden of blending with Ann would do to his already stretched finances. Plus two sets of kids who may or may not get along. What would happen to Lorraine? He'd never considered such questions; he trusted the intensity of his love was all that was needed. Love would conquer all. This trip had opened the seemingly impenetrable door to romantic travel, and Ann had made it possible. As experienced as he was in the things he knew, David had been trapped in his own delusions because he could not see what was meaningful in her life. He could not appreciate the past, present, and future in Ann's life and the calculations she needed to make.

*****

As the season ended and the fall semester began, school started and David found himself teaching an Intro. to Philosophy class again. Looking over the class, he asked the perennial question about free will and determinism. This time, his comments differed a little from his past deterministic arguments.

"Yes, previous choice and habit do control your behavior," he said. "However, you as a human being are gifted with the ability to redirect that trajectory and move in a completely different direction. It is a simple matter of will. Will you exercise independence of thought and find your freedom or not? What you do will answer the question for you. Sometimes when you want something badly enough, you can make it happen in direct opposition to previous choices and the history of your experience," said Professor Walton. As the class ended, two articles were given as required reading to be discussed the next week. Each considered the relative value of happiness and meaningfulness. He had never talked about the difference before but thought it would be a good practical exercise. Something that could have impact on his students lives.

*****

Years passed, and David retired from the university. He never married but spent a good deal of his time traveling and participating in the lives of his five grandchildren.

"Grandpa, Grandpa! A man named Uncle Ken is on the phone." David lifted himself out of his chair in the yard and quickly entered the house and answered the phone.

"Hello Ken, what a pleasant surprise. It's been almost three years since we've talked."

"I know, David, but I've been asked to do a series of lectures organized by the music faculty at the university. Boy, they've developed an interesting jazz program in the last few years. I think they liked my book about Bootsy Johnson and how he influenced my career. You know, I'll talk a little about the history of jazz and play a little. It sounds like fun. Of course, they will put me up at a hotel. If you've got room, I'd rather stay with you."

"I would be happy to have you, Ken. Whatever the kids have planned, we'll plan around it. That's great. Come as soon as you can and stay as long as you wish. You and I need some 'us' time and the boys would love to see you."

"It's settled then. I'll call the university and let them know I've made my own accommodations. I'm sure they will like that. I'll see you two weeks from Sunday."

"Great, see you then."

David put the phone down ever so gently and lingered in the infinite time a few seconds can become. An unlikely friend, Ken was one of the people who helped form the fabric of his life. Their adventures were all unforgettable and, though sometimes dangerous, added spice and gave him a sense of pride. The friendship between them had given continuity to most of his life. For that he was thankful.

Every morning he would say a prayer for the people he loved, and like Ken, Ann Hickman was always included.

One summer afternoon, while playing backgammon in the yard with his grandson, the mail carrier approached.

"I have an international letter here, Mr. Walton, that you need to sign for."

David reached for the letter addressed to Dr. David Walton. There was no return address. No one had referred to him as Professor or Doctor since his teaching career ended. Upon opening the folded letter, he saw one handwritten line.

You have been and will always be with me. I will never forget.

There was no signature, but he knew. He had waited through the years for her. The hidden hope and anticipation that she would come finally came to an end. When it did, the truth of his life flowed through him, and he at last realized that he, in some ways, had become his father, paralyzed by the intensity of love he had for his woman. He was holding on hopelessly to a dream and a fantasy that could never materialize. Overcome, David sat down in the grass, unconsciously fingering the stone in the ring on his right hand. Unconsciously, he had hoped to find his mother in the intensity of love he projected into his illusions. But his mommy never came and now the wait for Ann was over. Looking toward the heavens, David cried for all that was and all that could have been, but most of all, he cried for Ann Hickman and hoped she had found happiness.

And at last, he was free.

END

About the Author

After being honorably discharged from the Navy, Daine earned a bachelor's degree in Psychology from Delaware State University and a master's and doctorate degree in Experimental Psychology from Princeton University. He served as chairperson and professor in a number of universities while engaging in basic behavioral research and teaching. After forty-five years, he and his wife, Ruthann, have retired and live in Maryland.

CPSIA information can be obtained
at www.ICGtesting.com
Printed in the USA
BVHW031023040820
585342BV00005B/45